BUFFER ZONE

FUTURE WARS, BOOK 1

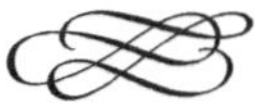

CONNIE SUTTLE

To Walter, Joe, Larry, Lee, Dianne, Sarah and Mark.
Thank you.

And for the teachers of Oklahoma—you deserve better.

ACKNOWLEDGMENTS

As always, this book is the result of collaboration. If it weren't for the support of my editor, my cover artist and my beta readers, it would be less than it is. All mistakes, as usual, are mine and no other's.

About the Author:
Connie Suttle lives in Oklahoma with her husband and a conglomerate of cats. They have finally banded together to make their demands, which has proven disconcerting to all humans involved.

You may find Connie in the following ways:
Facebook: Connie Suttle Author
Twitter: @subtledemon
Website and Blog: subtledemon.com

Blood Destiny Series:
Blood Wager

Blood Passage

Blood Sense

Blood Domination

Blood Royal

Blood Queen

Blood Rebellion

Blood War

Blood Redemption

Blood Reunion

Blood Recall

Blood Alliance

Legend of the Ir'Indicti Series:
Bumble

Shadowed

Target

Vendetta

Destroyer

High Demon Series:
Demon Lost

Demon Revealed

Demon's King

Demon's Quest

Demon's Revenge

Demon's Dream

God Wars Series:

Blood Double

Blood Trouble

Blood Revolution

Blood Love

Blood Finale

Saa Thalarr Series:

Hope and Vengeance

Wyvern and Company

Observe and Protect*

First Ordinance Series:

Finder

Keeper

BlackWing

SpellBreaker

WhiteWing

R-D Series:

Cloud Dust

Cloud Invasion

Cloud Rebel

Latter Day Demons Series:

Hot Demon in the City

A Demon's Work is Never Done

A Demon's Due

Seattle Elementals Series:

Your Money's Worth

Worth Your While*

BlackWing Pirates Series

MindSighted

MindMage

MindRogue

MindMaster*

Black Rose Sorceress Series

The Rose Mark

Rose and Thorn

Black Rose Queen

Queen of Thorns and Roses

CHAPTER 1

Krelk Homeworld
Je'Dik Dis'Rai

"You have the list, my child. Each world has been carefully plotted and timed for takeover, while the Alliance armies are engaged elsewhere."

I studied my father. He'd given me so much already; technology we wouldn't have for another three centuries, transportation and factories needed to produce such technology, and weapons such as this world had never dreamt of.

I'd inherited his intelligence, too, and I felt that gap between myself and other Krelk; they were slow to understand much, and I had little patience.

"Where are you going, Father?" I asked.

"I have your brothers to attend to," he lifted an eyebrow, letting me know I was asking too many questions.

"Of course, Father. Will I meet them, one day?"

"I believe you will, if you follow my instructions exactly. Now, there is one last thing before I go."

"What is that?"

"A warning. You will not be unopposed when you initiate my

plans. I believe you will defeat our enemy however, if you remember this; never, under any circumstances, let them look upon your real eyes. You have the means to disguise them—use it."

Curiosity swamped my mind, but Father had already sent a silent warning about too many questions. "It will be as you say," I dipped my head to him.

"Never forget that you are a demi-god, my child. You hold everything you need in your hands and in your mind. Make me and your brothers proud."

"It will be so."

Mississippi River, Midnight
Clare
Hunters!

They weren't supposed to be here, but then everybody knew the Krelk were the worst liars ever. Dropping below the water line, I swam toward the entrance to my den as fast as I could.

Then, shrinking farther into my tiny cave on the western bank of the Mississippi, I struggled to control my trembling. No, I wasn't large enough to be sent to the cage fights. I'd be forced to stay in my current shape and led around on a string, subject to some Krelk offspring's dangerous whims.

A full moon hung over the Mississippi's dark waters, meaning this was the time for hunters to arrive and take whatever they could capture. A device would be clamped to the backs of our necks and we'd never be able to shift back to human again. It was how they justified their enslavement of us; that we were only animals instead of sentient humans.

The Krelk had killed more than two-thirds of the human population, too, but they made the excuse that they'd thought them animal as well, until their High Council, wherever that was, decided otherwise.

When I heard the first yelp, even underground, I couldn't breathe.

Was that a shifter? Few shifters could take on a Krelk and their weapons and either survive or avoid being stunned. That's how we were captured—frozen and only barely able to breathe while we were caged, tagged and hauled away from the buffer zone.

Another yelp—followed quickly by a third.

This was no shifter—the Krelk were the ones screaming. Terrified but still curious, I dipped into the watery entrance and slowly made my way out of my cave to peek at the river bank above my head.

A dead Krelk dropped into the water nearby, making me jump and squeak in terror.

"An otter?" Someone leaned down to look at me.

Not a Krelk—I knew their scent. This—I'd never scented someone like this before. I scrabbled backward, afraid of this newcomer, too, even if he did appear humanoid.

"Don't be afraid—I killed all of them."

I backed all the way into the water and scrambled to swim to my cave before he could grab me. Once there, I refused to come out.

"I understand," he said, loud enough that I could still hear him. "Be safe. I'll patrol farther down, tonight."

I listened, my heart beating so rapidly I feared it would burst while his footsteps, light as they were, faded as he walked southward.

He'd killed six Krelk, and I'd never heard one of their weapons fire.

Who could do that?

"I heard John found a couple of headless Krelk floating toward Arkansas this morning," Sanjay told me as we prepared to open the hardware store. Sanjay was werewolf and neither of us had much sleep the night before.

I thought about telling him what I'd seen during the full moon, but decided to keep it to myself. It sounded too much like a hallucination, actually. Still, I clung to the hope that someone who could kill Krelk so easily actually existed.

Besides, I couldn't describe the man to anyone—it was dark and his face was in shadow. I only knew his scent, and it was so foreign to me I had no way to explain it.

"We sold out of pipe wrenches yesterday," Sanjay sighed as we turned the open sign toward the glass.

"You think it's true, then, that the Blackhearts are coming this way?"

"Could be just rumor, like the last time." Sanjay shrugged and moved toward the register.

"How many pipe wrenches did we sell yesterday?" Aaron, owner of Aaron's Hardware Emporium of Fairlawn Point, Missouri, walked in, causing the bell over the door to jingle. I winced at the noise and hoped there was still coffee in the breakroom.

"All of them," Sanjay told Aaron. "We're out."

"I hope we can get more out of Minnesota. It's difficult enough as it is, getting iron to the manufacturer. Right now, the Krelk are trading iron for crops to feed their slaves, but we all know where that can lead."

Every decent person in the buffer zone worried that one day, the Krelk would demand a trade in shifters for metal and other necessities. They couldn't get their breeding programs to work, and they were stumped.

Nobody told them that removing the tag on their slaves' necks and leaving them humanoid would do the trick. Besides, having humanoid slaves was outlawed by their own council.

That left the rest of us at the tender mercies of their hunters and those among us who'd sell their own families for comforts offered by the Krelk.

The Blackhearts, a vampire gang, would be the first to make deals with the devils, I figured. They'd kill anybody who argued with them, and even the ones who didn't argue. They kept a stable of human slaves themselves, to feed upon. Other vampires opposed them at times—if they wanted to commit suicide.

My mind wandered back to the man the night before, who'd killed six Krelk hunters. Could he kill rogue vampires, too, if they showed up in the St. Louis area?

Next to the Krelk, the Blackhearts were the most feared in the buffer zone. If they rolled into your town, death and trouble followed. Until recently, they'd been satisfied staying far south of Fairlawn Point.

Something had changed, however, and now they were headed north.

"I saw John on the way in," Aaron said while Sanjay went looking for order forms for more pipe wrenches. Internet was a thing of the past for us—the Krelk had their own system built since taking over, and we weren't invited to join.

We relied on a mostly-reliable postal service instead, and that meant Aaron would send two orders, just to make sure one arrived intact at the manufacturing plant in Minnesota.

"What did Sheriff John say?" I asked.

"Trouble coming this way, I think. Probably why we sold out of pipe wrenches yesterday. We have customers coming down from St. Louis, even, because they're out, too. I haven't checked with the jeweler, but I'd bet there's a lot of silver melting going on."

Coating weapons with silver was the best known defense against the Blackhearts, and the heavier the weapon, the better. Get silver embedded in their brains and it usually did the trick—it slowed them well enough that you could get a death blow in, if you acted quickly enough before they killed you.

In the buffer zone, silver was more valuable than gold—by a long shot. I thought about telling Aaron of the man from the night before—or going to the sheriff myself and telling him, but I pulled that idea back quickly.

Maybe I'd dreamed the whole thing—or was so scared I'd imagined it. Either way, maybe it was a good thing if that information didn't get out for a while—for the man's sake if he did exist. We didn't need Krelk law enforcement combing the buffer zone for a murderer who could take down six of their kind.

"Got any pipe wrenches?" A customer walked in, brushing a few raindrops off his jacket. Spring in the area meant rain as often as not, and the potential for flooding, too.

"Sold all we had yesterday. I'm ordering more, but that could take two weeks or more," Aaron replied. "We have hammers of all kinds, from sledge on down."

"I'll take a look."

"We have some chipping hammers and machinist hammers you may be interested in," I led the customer toward the proper shelves in the back of the store. "Both have nice, strong points, good for making holes."

"Now, that I can handle," the customer hefted the chipping hammer in his hand. "I'll take it."

"I'll ring you up. Anything else for you today?"

"No, I think this will work for now."

He was all human—I could tell by his scent. "Need a bag?" I asked after taking his coins.

"Will I get arrested for carrying this around?"

"I doubt it."

"Good. Thanks for the recommendation." He nodded at me, then headed for the door. The door tinkled again as he went out, while allowing another customer inside. We were going to sell out of hammers, I could feel it.

"You may as well just stay in the hammers section. I'll send Sanjay to the shovels," Aaron handed me a cup of coffee as the new customer sauntered around, checking out the displays around the door.

I heard the door open three more times before I reached the shelves where the hammers hung.

"This is the longest day ever," Sanjay yawned. It was five-fifty, ten minutes before closing for the day.

"Sold out of hammers and shovels," Sanjay told the man who walked through the door.

"I need waders," the man said, lifting a dark eyebrow at Sanjay. "Have those?"

"Sure do. Want hip waders, chest high, boot-foot?"

"Show me everything you have," he said. In the artificial light inside the store, his slightly-curly hair was such a deep black the light appeared blue shining on it. He walked past me as he followed Sanjay to the fishing section, and I got a whiff of his scent.

Oh, dear otter goddess.

He was the man from the night before, and he strode confidently behind Sanjay as if he wouldn't mind killing another six Krelk, just for fun. Broad shoulders stretched the black polo shirt he wore, his skin was the color of a warm latte and his voice sounded as if someone were pouring cream over gravel.

Whatever he was, he was no more human than Sanjay or I were. Sanjay would definitely notice the scent, too—every werewolf did.

Would he know what this one was?

"What's he looking for?" Aaron was back, holding the key to lock up.

"Waders and fishing gear, I think," I replied.

"That we have," Aaron sighed. "Damn, I wish we could get supplies in here faster."

"Do you really think the Blackhearts are heading this way?"

"I don't have that answer, but we need to be prepared."

"Yeah." Vampires were one of the reasons Aaron never kept the store open after dark. Most vamps were decent. A few weren't, and those few could kill in seconds if they wanted.

Werewolves weren't nearly as bad, but there were a few bad ones. Same with shifters, too, but only a few were big enough and dangerous enough to worry about.

"Ten-fifty in coin only," Sanjay said after setting chest-high boot waders next to the register.

"Got it," the man dug a coin purse out of a pocket and counted out dollar coins and change. No paper money worked in the buffer zone. Credit cards had died the moment the Krelk took over. It was all coins or barter, now, and coins were a lot of trouble to carry around.

"You live here?" Sanjay ventured to ask as he deposited coins in the till.

"Moved to Fairlawn Point two months ago. From up north," the stranger said. Sanjay had *definitely* noticed his scent.

"Got it. Enjoy the fishing."

"For sure." The stranger turned, gave me an eye-popping grin, hefted the waders over a shoulder and walked out the door.

"What the hell is he?" Sanjay mumbled.

"I was gonna ask you," I breathed, shaking my head. I couldn't get his grin out of my head, though—he may as well have said he remembered me from the night before, and that was impossible.

I hoped it was impossible, anyway. I didn't need to be outed to anybody I wasn't already outed to, and that was by choice as well as for safety reasons.

Otters were in high demand by the Krelk. They were either given as pets to children, or kept in special water cages to entertain Krelk diners.

I didn't want to spend the rest of my life with wet fur while Krelk kids slapped grubby hands against the glass walls of my cage.

"You think we ought to check him out?" Sanjay asked Aaron.

"People move all the time," Aaron sighed. "We can't be suspicious of everybody, can we?"

"If I haven't smelled them before, then yeah," Sanjay muttered as he walked toward the back room.

"Clare, what do you think?" Aaron turned to me.

"I think we ought to wait and see," I said. "He just bought waders. It isn't like he's gearing up to burn down St. Louis."

"At least not outwardly," Aaron said, moving to lock the door. "I'll see if Sanjay can walk me home. I kinda have the willies, now."

"I wish they'd get telephones hooked back up." My mother rose from a chair on my front porch.

"Why didn't you go inside?" I asked as she rubbed her left hip. She had arthritis, which was no surprise to anyone—she was one hundred sixty-two.

I was a late baby for her.

"The air smelled so fresh after the rain, I wanted to enjoy it," she said as I walked up the porch steps and pulled out my key. She had a key, too; she just hadn't used it.

"So the air was a trade-off for letting your hip stiffen and start hurting?"

"It'll go away. What are you doing for supper?"

"I have some bread and cheese," I said.

"Then it's a good thing I baked an extra pot pie."

"You made pot pies? I love you," I let the front door swing open as I turned to hug her.

"You can bring 'em in—they're in that bag by the chair."

"Will do. Go on in and get warm."

"I guess it's a good thing plastic lasts so long," I said as we washed up Mom's Tupperware later. We'd already had the discussion—multiple times—of where we'd find certain things when whatever we had broke, ripped or died.

"Armor-plated Krelk bastards," Mom grumbled as she handed me the lid to dry.

"Sheriff John says they live for eight hundred years or so, and they're looking for new places to take over because they've overpopulated their own planet."

"Well, they need to consider not having babies, then," Mom let the water drain out of the sink.

"I think so, too, but apparently that's against their religion or prime directive or something."

"If their religion says be an asshole, then they're following it too closely," Mom said. Both of us stiffened and went still the moment boots scuffed across my front porch.

"I'll go see who it is," I said, pushing her toward the broom closet.

"I'll come with you," Mom said, using the tone that told me not to argue.

That's how both of us answered the door to find Jessie standing outside it. "Jessie?" I said, waving him into the house.

Jessie was one of Sheriff John's night deputies—and a vampire. Actually, most of the night deputies were—with a sprinkling of werewolves thrown in.

"We found traces of Krelk, down by the river," Jessie said as he carefully studied Mom and me. "Where you go," he added, frowning directly at me.

He'd checked my cave down at the river bank; could probably scent it, actually. Vamps could scent as well as most werewolves.

"I saw 'em, but they went across farther south," I said, trying to keep the tremor from my voice. If Jessie thought I was hiding something, he had compulsion and I wouldn't be able to lie about the stranger.

Whom I'd seen twice, now.

"Did they take anybody?" Mom demanded.

"That's what we're trying to figure out, ma'am," Jessie said. "I'm glad they missed Clare; they came so close it's a wonder they didn't find her. Plus, two Krelk bodies washed up down the river. Don't know who killed 'em, but they did us a favor. The only way to kill that filth is to take their heads—bullets just bounce off the natural armor."

"Had to be a vampire, then," Mom sniffed. "We sure don't have what it takes."

"We think that, too, but all ours are accounted for and say they didn't have anything to do with it."

"You don't think the Blackhearts are here?" I squeaked.

"Hmmph. They'd stand back and watch 'em kill us," Jessie said. Jessie had no love for the Blackhearts—they'd kill him, too; they didn't take kindly to vamps, shifters or humans with darker skin, making Jessie a target for sure.

"Just our luck—to have a pile of white-supremacist vampires to deal with," Mom shook her head in disgust.

"We don't know for certain they're coming, but it don't look good. Reports came in from Arkansas yesterday." Jessie's voice turned grim.

"Be careful, all right?" I reached out to touch his sleeve.

"Oh, I'll be that for sure, Miss Clare, and you do the same."

Mom and I watched Jessie step off the front porch before he began to run. A running vampire was almost too fast for the eye to follow, and he would normally wait until he was out of sight to move so fast. Tonight, he had a lot of visits to make, both up and down the river, and time was short.

"Mom, why don't you stay here with me?" I turned to her. "I'll worry about you, otherwise."

"Yeah. Maybe I will," she sighed as I shut the front door and locked it. She lived closer to the river than I did—we were otters, after all, and being close to water made us feel safer, whether we actually were or not.

"They have those sounding devices," Mom waved a hand as she walked into the kitchen and I followed. "To find us in the water, you know."

She was right—the Krelk had all sorts of gadgets to find us in the water, and that's why I'd been so close to my cave the night before, rather than swimming the river.

Mom had a hole not far from her house—close to the water but not in it. "What will we do if it floods?" I whispered.

"Pray. That's all we can do."

Rajeon Dare

"Proceed with caution," Commander Forneel told me. "I don't want to lose another scout to those filth."

"Which filth? The Krelk or the vampire gang?"

"Either, although I worry less about the vamps."

"Understood. Did you receive the images?"

"We did. They're being discussed now."

"Look, I know this is a non-Alliance," I began.

"Do your job," he cut me off, his words blunt. "That's all you have permission to do right now. Is that understood, Captain Dare?"

"Understood."

I hated when he called me captain. And, he was reminding me that I couldn't interfere unless my life was in danger, or the Krelk were breaking their own laws, as was the case on the full moon.

The buffer zone was supposed to be a sanctuary for the life inside its borders, and no Krelk were allowed in unless they were pursuing a fugitive, either Krelk or human. Then, they only had permission to capture or kill the one they pursued and no other.

Lofty legislation, made by those who didn't really care whether the law was obeyed. There were no Krelk guards placed on their side of the buffer zone to keep poachers out, and there were plenty of poachers coming from both sides.

The ones I'd killed came from the east, but they could easily come from the west; there was nothing to stop them. Cage fights were a big draw among the Krelk, who ought to still be living in caves. Hand a child a computer and a star ship, pretty soon they'd figure out how to use both.

The Krelk still hadn't matured as a race, but they had advanced technology to beat others into submission if they wanted. It made them more than dangerous to D-Class worlds and below.

Stuffing my communicator in my pocket and sealing it in, I set about working on my meal of catfish. I'd tied the houseboat to an abandoned dock on the bank while I spoke with Forneel; I didn't want to be moving while cooking and having a conversation with my superior. *May as well stay here to eat my dinner, too.*

The vampire showed up just as I was putting the plate of fish and greens on the small table at the back of the boat; he likely smelled the cooking and came to investigate. If he were a rogue, he'd get no blood from me.

"Name's Jessie," he said, holding up a hand. "Deputy for the Fairlawn Point area. Just checkin' on the residents, makin' sure they're all right after the full moon."

"I'm fine," I agreed. "Want supper?" I offered a chair at the table.

"Nah, I'm good, but thank you for the offer," the deputy said. "Just a warnin', though, found a couple of headless Krelk floatin' in the water down Arkansas way."

Because I'd put them there.

"I heard that earlier, when I was in town buying waders," I replied. "You know what happened?"

"Nah, and the sheriff's kinda worried. Never seen more than one Krelk die at a time."

"I see. Do you suppose that vampire gang is closer than anybody thinks?"

"I sure hope not."

I understood his concern; it showed in his eyes before he lowered them. Any dark-skinned human, vampire or werewolf was in danger. The Blackhearts were governed by a vamp who'd led a band of confederate bushwhackers during the Civil War.

If I could find the one who turned him, I'd stake him and his protégé in daylight and not feel the slightest bit of guilt.

"I don't know what your background is, son," the vampire was looking at me again, "but your colorin' is right on the line, you know? Don't get close to the Blackhearts, and I mean it."

"If they get close to me, they may have to come to the middle of the river to do it," I told him. "If you ever need a safe place, you're welcome to join me."

"I thank you for the offer," he said. "I'll check on you again. Do you usually stay in this area?"

"Give or take a mile or so," I said.

"I'll keep that in mind. What did you say your name was?"

"Rajeon Dare," I said. "Friends call me Raje."

"Sounds Creole."

"It could be." I grinned to cover the lie.

"Well, you take care, Raje. I'll see you next time."

"You do the same, Deputy Jessie," I said.

He walked away fast, traveling up the bank and disappearing. I turned back to my dinner, then, contemplating why there were still vampires on Earth. The official word was that all the vamps had been removed or killed years ago, yet here I was, dealing with the Blackheart gang, who were among the worst, ever.

I suspected a powerful hand in this, and not a benign one.

Clare

"If you'll come to my house after work today, we can plant tomatoes," Mom told me as I was getting ready for work. "If there's any organic fertilizer left in that store, will you bring me some?"

"Sure. I think we have a couple of bags. I'll take my cart so I can haul it home."

"If we had gas, we could take the car."

"Mom, we haven't had gas in two years and that won't change. People are already riding horses into town and building wagons to haul their stuff. We're in the old west, now, without the shootin' irons."

"Oh, we still have shootin' irons, just no bullets," Mom sniffed. "Krelk shut that down real quick, even if those bullets wouldn't get past their damn, thick scales."

"If they'd been easier to kill, we wouldn't be in this mess," I sighed. "Look, I have to go or I won't make it to work on time. I'll see you at your place with the fertilizer tonight."

"Good. I haven't had a tomato since last October."

"Love you," I said, giving her a hug before heading toward the door.

"You, too," she said.

Sanjay and Aaron walked into the store together, five minutes after I got there. Aaron was scared enough to ask Sanjay to walk him to work and back home, now.

"I need to buy two bags of organic fertilizer for my mom's vegetable garden," I told Aaron.

"Want me to take it out of your pay, or pay up front?"

"I don't care. Whatever's easiest," I said. "We're planting tomatoes when I get home tonight."

"Tell you what," Aaron stopped for a moment beside the break room door. "Send me ten pounds of tomatoes through spring and summer and we'll call it even."

"Best idea I've heard all day. I'll tell Mom," I said. "She'll probably send some lettuce and carrots to go with them."

"Good. Julie will love that."

She would; Aaron lived in town and didn't have much of a yard for a garden, plus, Julie killed more than she grew.

"I'd pay your mom to get me a few pounds of clams from the river," Sanjay poked his head around a back shelf.

"When?"

"Whenever I can get them. Clam chowder sounds really good."

"Now you've made me hungry, and I just had breakfast," I made a face at Sanjay. I loved clams. On full moons, I ate them raw—when I went into the river. I hadn't been in the river long enough, this time.

Because of the Krelk—and the stranger.

"Hey, Sheriff John," I said as the bell tinkled over his hat-covered head.

"Jessie says your Mom is moving in with you?" He'd stopped in to see me. That was worrisome. John was in his forties and asked me out, once. I'd turned him down as politely as I could, but he still used any excuse to talk to me.

"Well, she is, but her land is better for growing vegetables, so we'll still be using it."

"We're trying to get those closest to the water to move farther in," he said, taking his hat off to reveal thinning, brown, hat-hair. He turned the hat by the brim in his fingers as he considered what to say next.

"I heard about the Krelk and the Blackhearts," I deadpanned. I didn't add that I'd seen a dead Krelk get dumped in the water.

"I didn't want to scare you," he said, locking eyes with mine. "Even with the two of you together, you could still be vulnerable."

"I know. We've done our best to be prepared."

"I'll make sure somebody checks on you regular."

"We appreciate that."

"I can go out that way now and then," Sanjay said. "I'd really go out there if I could pick up a bucket of clams."

"I'll tell you what," I turned to Sanjay. "I'll make sure one of us gets some clams for you tonight."

"Sounds awesome."

"Want some coffee, John?" Aaron asked.

"Damn, man, you have some?" John looked hopeful.

"Yeah. Come to the back. We'll sit and talk while Clare and Sanjay get the place open."

Half the coffee would be chicory, but that was understood nowadays. Coffee that we could get was grown mostly in greenhouses farther south; it had to be brought upriver by boat after it was roasted and mixed with chicory root.

"We really are in the old west," I said as the bell tinkled, announcing another visitor.

"Sheriff John here?" One of his werewolf deputies sounded out of breath, and that was unusual. Werewolves could run a long time without getting winded.

"In the back," I said.

"Blackhearts coming," he panted and half-ran toward the break room.

CHAPTER 2

"Where were they seen?" I'd helped two customers while the deputy spoke with John and Aaron in the back.

Sanjay, on the other hand, probably heard everything while I was selling gloves and garden trowels to two women; that's why I asked him about it. Otherwise, I'd have heard their conversation just as well as he did.

"Hickman Landing, Arkansas," Sanjay growled. "Not far from the Missouri border."

I'd heard the part about six farms hit, just as he did. "Probably looking for food to feed their slaves—can't get blood out of a turnip, or so Mom says."

"If they keep killing farmers, soon enough nobody will eat," Sanjay growled again.

"I've never heard that the Blackhearts were custodians of the future," I said. "At least it's daylight right now, and they're holed up somewhere."

"I wish we could find the bastards," Sanjay said. "I'd be happy to send them out to bake in sunlight."

"We all feel that way, but they have human slaves, remember, who protect them during the day. We have to get past that bunch, first."

17

"Wolves have a better chance at doing it," Sanjay pointed out.

"I hear that. I doubt anybody will tremble in fear when the otter brigade shows up."

"You guys are too cute for your own good," Sanjay grinned.

"Right. Cute enough that the Krelk are taking as many of us as they can."

"Hey, I didn't mean to bring that up."

Sheriff John and his werewolf deputy walked out of the backroom, then. John stopped on his way to the door and put a hand on my shoulder. "Think about what I said and consider moving into town. I don't like the way things are heading," he said.

Any other day, I'd have moved away from his touch. I didn't today, because his words scared me.

"I'll mention it to Mom."

"You do that." He dropped his hand and followed the deputy out the door.

"He thinks the Blackhearts have turned to the slave trade," Aaron mumbled as we watched them walk down the sidewalk. "The small shifters staying at those farms they attacked are nowhere to be found. The larger ones, along with the humans, are all missing or dead."

Sanjay cursed under his breath. I heard his words anyway and agreed with his assessment; *what the fuck were the Blackhearts getting from the Krelk in exchange?*

Rajeon

"Here you go." I lifted the stringer of fish from the bucket I carried and handed it to the man running the fish and game market in Fairlawn Point. Eight good-size catfish were on that stringer, and worth a few silver coins in exchange.

"Nice," Paul nodded and pulled fish off the stringer before setting them on a tub of ice. Paul's was also one of the few places in town that had an ice machine hooked up to a bio-fuel generator. Fish guts can run that kind of generator, actually, along with biological waste of just about any kind.

"Can I get a little ice from you, too?" I asked as he handed me four coins.

"Sure thing, on the house." I handed him my bucket, which he rinsed out before scooping some ice into it.

"Bring me anything you catch. I'll take mussels and clams, too, if you come across any."

"I'll do that." I gave him a half-wave and walked out the door, leaving the scent of fish and bait behind me.

"Ice," I set the bucket on the counter at my next stop, which was the closest place selling vegetables and eggs. Early spring greens lasted longer if they were cold; that's why I'd taken the ice.

"You are a godsend," Shelley, the middle-aged owner, grinned at me and went to dump the ice in a deep metal pan behind the counter. An entire bag of dandelion greens went on top of it immediately after; somebody would be having those for supper tonight.

"What can I get for you?" She was back, wiping her hands on the apron she wore.

"I'd like a couple of potatoes and some rice if you have it."

"I got a little of both." She set two baking potatoes on the counter and went to measure out rice for me.

"How much?" I reached for my coin purse.

"A quarter?"

"That's not enough."

"You brought me ice. Nobody else does that."

"All right." I handed her the coin and placed the potatoes and small bag of rice in my bucket. "I have a question, too," I said.

"Shoot," she said.

"I, ah, met the young woman who works at the hardware store, but didn't get her name."

"Oh, that's Clare," she waved a hand as if everybody ought to know who Clare was. "Truth is, Sheriff John has asked her out, but he's way too old for her, in my opinion."

"I see. Well, does Clare have a last name?"

"Coquina."

"Clare Coquina?"

"Yeah. Like those little, tiny clams at the beach? The ones that dig into the sand whenever the waves uncover them?"

"Well, that's appropriate," I said.

"Huh?"

"Nothing—just letting my mind wander, that's all. Thanks for the stuff." I lifted my bucket.

"You're welcome. Any time."

"You're the new one," I heard a voice behind me when I left Shelley's.

I turned to find the sheriff and a werewolf deputy walking the sidewalk toward me.

"I am. Been here only a couple of months. Saw Deputy Jessie last night," I offered, trying to make myself as familiar to local law enforcement as I could.

"Where from?" The sheriff apparently treated all strangers as a threat.

"North. Used to live in a houseboat community in Minneapolis."

"You're the one Jessie told me about. The one living in a houseboat on the river," the sheriff nodded. "Said you offered him dinner. Jessie don't eat normal food; he's a vamp."

"I got that idea after a while," I grinned. "Kinda hard to tell after nightfall, you know." *First rule of scouting; fit in and make yourself familiar to the locals.*

"I hear that," the sheriff agreed. "Said you was all right, too. Jessie's a good judge of character."

"I was about to say the same thing about Jessie. He's welcome at my place anytime."

"What did you do—when you were up north?" he asked.

"Well, before the squatters took over, I worked on computers. Nowadays, I fish and dig clams. Not much call for my expertise anymore."

"You're right about that. We've had warning from down south—the

Blackhearts are definitely headed this way. Be careful down by the water, understand?"

"I will definitely be careful," I agreed.

"I'll ask Jessie to stop by your place whenever he checks on the Coquinas."

"I'd appreciate that," I said. "If you need any catfish, let me know. I'll send you some when Jessie comes by."

"Sounds like a deal," the sheriff grinned for the first time.

Never hurts to bribe law enforcement with food. It was a well-known, unwritten rule. Besides, food and basic shelter were the highest-prized commodities in the buffer zone. Bio-fuel generators were better than gold, too, if you were lucky enough to have one.

My houseboat had solar power, so I wasn't in need, but everybody around me was—in some way. Now, my mission was to find where the Coquinas lived—at least the Clare part of that pair. She might need fish or clams, too.

Or protection—she and her mother.

A trip to the hardware store to buy more fishing gear was certainly in order.

Clare

"He's heading this way," Sanjay said, standing at the front window so he could watch the sidewalk. We'd turned away sixteen disappointed customers who were looking for pipe wrenches and shovels. We were currently sold out of hammers, too. Now, all we had to sell were woodcarving knives, so people could cut limbs and fashion clubs for themselves. Sandpaper, too, if they didn't want splinters.

"Who?" I looked up from sorting seed packets. There'd be a run on those soon enough; it was time for spring planting.

"The strange-scenter."

"Seriously? Is he coming in here?" I squeaked.

"Clare, don't get any ideas about him," Sanjay advised. "We don't know what he is." He moved back to allow the man inside the store, who gave me another of his jaw-dropping grins before asking for hooks and fishing line.

"What size?" I asked, taking him toward the fishing gear before Sanjay could do it.

"I'm looking to catch some of the bigger catfish—the line I have right now is twenty-pound test. Bigger fish are taking bait off my lines or eating the fish I've caught on my trotlines before I can get to them. Plus, you have no idea how well those fish fight, sometimes."

"She knows." Sanjay had joined us anyway and now stood nearby, arms crossed tightly over his chest, broadcasting his disapproval.

I caught catfish when I was otter; along with other fish that swam in the Mississippi. I loved the chase, and the freedom of movement the water offered. As for finding clams or mussels, that was any otter's specialty.

I'd never gone after anything that weighed more than five or six pounds, though. This guy wanted to go after the catfish monsters that lurked in the river.

"Planning a party?" I asked, after handing him a roll of one-fifty braided line.

"Huh?"

"What will you do with a sixty-pound catfish?"

"Sell it to Paul," he shrugged. "He says he'll buy whatever I catch, and a big one will feed a bunch of customers."

"How will you carry that into town?" Sanjay sounded skeptical.

"I have a cart. I just don't use it much, because I can carry the other stuff in my bucket."

He'd set the bucket at his feet to look at fishing line. It held two large potatoes and a small bag that probably contained rice.

It still had a slight smell of catfish about it, too, so he'd already talked to Paul before coming here. Shelley, too, because the potatoes and rice would come from her shop.

"Can I ask you something?" I said while he studied the roll of fishing line, reading the specs.

"Sure."

"What's your name?"

"Oh, the Sheriff hasn't told you? I'm Rajeon Dare."

He pronounced it Ray-jean, with the *jean* sounding French or Creole. I figured it was Creole; I hadn't seen any French people since the takeover.

"Friends call me Raje," he was grinning again as he handed the line back to me. "I'll take that and twelve big hooks."

"Is that it?"

"You could tell me your name."

"Clare. Come on, I'll ring you up."

Sanjay was still in a snit when Rajeon walked out of the store, the line and pack of hooks in his bucket. I'd gotten a look at his boots and jeans—both showed signs of wear and smelled of the river.

Two minutes later, Sheriff John walked in again.

"That boy don't smell right, according to my deputy," John said right off the bat.

"You mean Rajeon? I think the same thing," Sanjay grumped.

"I think he's fine," I frowned at Sanjay. "Our world is getting smaller, that's all. We haven't met everybody in it, yet."

I should have kept my mouth shut; John now wore a look that spelled jealousy to me.

"Jessie said he was all right, but I can't say I feel the same," John complained. "Lives on a houseboat on the river. How many people you know can survive like that?"

"I don't know anybody with a houseboat, but then they never caught on around here."

"Everybody in St. Louis pulled theirs in the last time it flooded, and they haven't gone back."

"Sheriff John, would you like some coffee?" I asked as sweetly as I could. The quicker we wandered away from the subject of Rajeon Dare, the better I'd feel about it.

"Sure. Can you sit with me for a minute while I drink it?"

"As long as I'm not away from the store too long."

"You think that's enough?" I stared at two long rows of tomato plants, which would have to be staked in a few days. We only used a small portion of the land Mom owned to plant our garden; before the Krelk came, she'd had a tractor and paid helpers to grow organic vegetables to sell. Nowadays, we only grew what the two of us could plow, plant and tend by hand.

"I sure hope it's enough," Mom answered my question. "Shelley will take everything we can spare, and I owe Aaron ten pounds of tomatoes for the fertilizer."

"I want tomato juice," I sighed. We'd used up or sold all we'd canned the summer before. "Potatoes and carrots look good." I turned to survey the rows we'd planted three weeks earlier.

"We may get lettuce for the table soon," Mom leaned back to stretch her muscles. "Want to help plant okra and squash tomorrow?"

"Sure. I'd gladly eat both those things."

"Good. I'll get the rows plowed while you're at work, and we'll plant when you get here."

I wished I could do the plowing for her—we only had a single-wheel, hand-pushed cultivator and it was hard work, forcing that thing through the dirt. "Your gloves holding up?" I asked Mom. She didn't need splinters from the wooden handles of the cultivator.

"Yeah. Those leather ones you got for me are fine."

"What's after the okra and squash?"

"Beans, bell peppers, cantaloupe and watermelon. Need to get them planted in the next ten days or so."

"Are we gonna trade with Barbara for onions, spinach and cucumbers again?"

"Yeah. And a few other things, too. She says her pear and apple trees are lookin' good this year."

"Good. Let's get this stuff back in your barn and go home. I'm starving."

"We ought to hurry; sun's going down," Mom frowned at the dimming light toward the west. "Clouds coming in, too. Fast."

"Yeah."

We didn't need heavy rains and a flood. Usually the garden was far enough inland that it would survive moderate flooding. A big flood, well, everybody worried about that.

Gone were the days of weather forecasts provided by local news stations. We were forced to rely on our senses and nature, and those weren't always the best predictors, especially for people who'd had limited practice at it.

The garden wasn't just a source of food for us; it was Mom's income for the year, too. A wiped-out garden meant scrounging and poverty. That's why we saved every coin we could, against a bad year of either drought or flood, although flood was by far the worst of the two.

We could get river water during a drought, and we'd done that a few times, to keep the plants alive in late summer.

It was back-breaking work, though, pushing buckets of water from the river to the garden and back again.

If we had the equipment and engineering skills, maybe we could build an aqueduct or a windmill, but neither of us were that talented.

Therefore, we relied on rain most of the time, and captured what we'd need for the house in big barrels.

We carried our hoes and trowels to the barn as the rain began to fall softly outside. We'd be as wet when we got to my house as we'd be if we'd gone swimming in the river. That's why I left my gardening boots on and carried my other shoes in a bag Mom gave me. I didn't want to clean muddy work shoes.

The sky darkened and the wind picked up as we began the two-mile walk to my place. Our straw hats would provide some relief from the rain, except when cold raindrops were driven into our faces by the wind.

We ducked our heads and dealt with it the whole way.

"Will you look at that," Mom said as she examined the contents of a familiar-looking bucket while I unlocked my front door. "There are clams and two catfish in here."

"Supper," my shoulders sagged in relief. "And Sanjay's clams, that I forgot about."

"Who did this?" Mom asked as she carried the bucket inside and shut the door.

"Raje. The new guy—he's come by the store twice, now, to buy fishing gear."

"He sure put it to good use." She pulled the catfish out—they'd already been cleaned, gutted and were ready to cook—after we rinsed them off.

"There's a note on top of the clams," she said. "How many does Sanjay get?"

"At least a dozen. How many are in there?"

"Two or three dozen."

"What does the note say?" I asked.

"I'll pick up the bucket at the hardware store tomorrow—Rajeon." Mom pronounced it Ray-John, but that was close enough.

"Thank you, Rajeon," I muttered and went to the sink to put water in a pot. "We'll fix a dozen clams for us and Sanjay can have the rest," I said. He lived with his brother, and werewolves liked to eat. Sanjay loved clam chowder so much he'd learned how to make it. Otherwise, the meal consisted of a hunk of meat barely introduced to the fire before consumption for him and Ishaan.

It's funny; I'd gone to school with Sanjay, and knew he was werewolf in grade school, just as he'd known I was a shapeshifter.

Once the Krelk took over, the shifters and vamps were outed, because they'd fought against the Krelk, hardest and longest.

Humans were finding that some people they knew were of the supernatural variety, and not only that, but the shifters, vamps and werewolves were willing to go to war for themselves and their human counterparts. It paved the way for a swifter acceptance than I'd ever imagined possible.

The Blackhearts, however, were working to tear down that acceptance. I hoped it wouldn't eventually paint a target on every vampire's back.

"You're awful quiet," Mom said as she set fried catfish on the table.

"Just thinking. About the Blackhearts and how they could damage the peace between vampires and everybody else. Clams smell good." I set the dish of steamed clams on the table.

"I didn't know we'd get a feast tonight," Mom smiled. "Tell that man thank you, next time you see him."

"I'll take his bucket to the store and tell him we're grateful. I wasn't looking forward to cheese and biscuits again."

"Fish is always welcome," Mom agreed and cut into her catfish first.

Sanjay eyed the bucket suspiciously when I carried it into the store the following morning, but he didn't say anything when I unloaded his clams into a bag he'd brought with him.

"I'll go get some ice," he loped out the door. The clams had been sitting in water overnight, so they were still alive. Sanjay's bag was made of burlap and wouldn't hold a drop of water. His only hope was ice from Paul's shop.

Actually, Paul probably owed him some ice; Ishaan, Sanjay's older brother, hunted rabbit, squirrel, deer and anything else he could catch that would make a meal, and often sold extra to Paul. The only meat they wouldn't eat was beef, but the werewolf in them required plenty of protein. They got it in other ways.

About an hour later, Rajeon walked into the store after leaving a pushcart outside.

"Did you catch a bigger fish?" I asked, smiling as he grinned at me.

"Sure did. Paul was happy to see it, too."

"I have your bucket in the back," I said. "Thank you for the fish and clams; Mom wants to hug you, I think. We were exhausted after planting tomatoes last night, and those catfish were more than welcome for supper."

"No trouble," he shrugged. I turned to get his bucket from the break room. At least Sanjay was helping somebody else at the back of the store and couldn't stare in judgment while I handed Rajeon's bucket back to him.

"So it's time to plant the garden, eh?" Rajeon asked.

"Yeah. We have to get the rest of the stuff in the ground in the next ten or fifteen days, so it'll be busy times. Worth it, though. There's nothing better than farm-raised tomatoes."

"I'd trade fish and clams any day for fresh vegetables."

"You may have a deal," I said. "Not much time to fish for ourselves when we're busy with the garden during spring and summer."

"Any word on the unwelcome guests coming this way?" He turned to a more serious subject.

"Nothing today, but then Sheriff John hasn't been by."

"I'm trying to gauge how far they can travel in a single night," he said.

"That would be useful information, for sure."

"Well, take care," he said. "I'm off to check my trotlines."

"Have fun," I called after him.

"Always," he gave me a final grin before leaving the store. I watched through the window as he set the bucket in his pushcart and trundled away.

Rajeon

The trouble with doing what I'd usually do to check on the encroaching vampire horde was that doing so could get me wounded or killed during the day. I'd have to go out at night if there was no reliable word on how close they were.

I wasn't here just to record what the Krelk had done to the planet so far.

I was also looking for signs of other things.

One of those things was a someone, actually, and he was half Krelk.

The other half?

Shelley would say the other half was the devil, but then she described most Krelk that way, too. If there were something worse than the devil, then Je'Dik fit that description.

The Alliances ought to be here, shoving the Krelk off the planet because it didn't belong to them. Instead, the bulk of their armies were fighting other enemies, and the most they could spare were the scouting ships, which were sent out to record everything for the Council to pore over and dismiss.

They wanted Je'Dik, though, and if he were here, hiding in all the chaos and squalor of a recently acquired world, then he'd have a relatively easy time of it.

As for the Blackhearts, until a few weeks ago, they'd been content to terrorize the area around the mouth of the Mississippi. That's where they were from, and they'd stayed there since the Krelk took over, roughly nine years earlier.

Only now were they working their way up the river. Besides, if there were ever a vampire whose temperament matched that of Je'Dik's, then Robert L. *"Bob Blackheart"* Williams fit that description.

Do your job. That's what Forneel told me. We'd lost two scouts already on this mission. They'd gotten close enough to the Blackhearts to send back reports, until they'd stopped reporting.

That meant one of two things; they'd either been killed by the Krelk or the Blackhearts, or they'd been made vampire by the Blackhearts.

Neither of those things would surprise me.

That's why I'd been pulled away from another assignment and sent here. I was the one who could fight either vampires or Krelk, and Forneel wanted Je'Dik.

Bad.

Really, really, bad. Dead or alive, didn't matter. He'd get a big part of the bounty on the bastard, if we took him.

Forneel and I had been good friends long ago; we'd gone through basic training together.

That friendship was unraveling. I wondered if he realized it, yet.

"Je'Dik, where are you?" I mumbled as I pushed the cart onto the deck of the houseboat and tied it to a rail. "Are you hiding behind a bunch of vamps, now? Are you selling shifters to Krelk, trying to ingratiate yourself? Hoping they'll take you in and hide your filthy ass?"

Soon enough, I'd make my way down the river to reconnoiter. If Je'Dik were hiding behind Bob Blackheart's double-breasted, confederate-style frock coat, I wanted to know.

Clare

"Sheriff John, Deputy," I greeted them as they walked into the store.

"Aaron here?" John asked.

"He's out today, it's his day off this week," I said.

"Well, I just wanted to pass along some information on the situation," John told me, leaning on the counter while I sorted more seed packs. They were selling as fast as we could get them in.

"What's that?" I tried to keep my voice even, although his words frightened me.

"Somebody with night-vision binoculars says they had eyes on the Blackheart bunch last night, right around Caruthersville."

"So they're in the state, then," Sanjay walked up and nodded at the werewolf deputy.

"Looks that way. About as far south as you can get in the state, but still be in it," John agreed.

"Will you send out messengers again tonight?"

"For sure. I've alerted as many as I can so far, and when Jessie and the others are awake, I'll have them do the rest."

Neither Sanjay nor I failed to notice that he was keeping his werewolf deputy by his side, now. John was all human, and afraid of what was coming. If I could see it, Sanjay could certainly smell it.

I didn't offer him coffee and he left after a minute or two.

"Scared to death," Sanjay whispered.

"Yeah. Maybe it's time to put a werewolf in charge during the day, and a vamp at night."

"You think they'd go for that?" Sanjay huffed. Some things might never change. Fairlawn Point had a human mayor, sheriff and judge.

"You're right," I said. "Too bad, too. Maybe they'd see we're mostly like them—until the full moon comes."

"How did they think we got along all those years before the Krelk showed up?" Sanjay grumbled. "They never knew anything about what we were."

"I miss going to St. Louis now and then," I said. "Mom and I used to go once a month, just to look around. That was back when I was making decent money, of course."

"Nothing but rag pickers and thieves on this side of the city, now," Sanjay said.

"It's too dangerous to go, even on the river. The hotel I managed between here and St. Louis is filled with the sick and wounded, nowadays, and Dr. Kim can barely take care of all of them."

"You been by there recently?"

"Not since last fall; I took some vegetables to Dr. Kim."

"Ishaan took a deer last week; it helped feed those people for a little while."

"Mom and I need some soap," I said. "You think your neighbor has any she can sell?"

"Probably. What kind?"

"Laundry and people soap," I said. "We're almost out of both."

"Good thing a few people still know how to make that stuff," he grunted. "Look, John's deputy is coming back this way."

"Now what?" I walked around the counter to watch as the deputy walked so fast it was almost a run.

"Sanjay, we may need you to help," he burst through the door, making the bell jingle furiously. "Somebody took Barbara's boy."

CHAPTER 3

*R*ajeon

By the time I arrived at Barbara Grant's farm, the werewolves were already there, changed and sniffing around.

I knew Barbara was a shifter bear; her son, a young bear cub, would be an attractive target for anyone looking to make money. He'd be sold to the Krelk and sent to the cage fights, once he was big enough.

"Which way were they headed?" I asked the first human person I found there. It was the sheriff; he didn't like me much, if I'd read him right.

"East, toward the river," he turned to frown at me. "About twenty minutes ago."

"All right." I took off running down the edge of Barbara Grant's tilled field, shifting as I ran.

Maybe the sheriff wouldn't grumble so much afterward, but that remained to be seen.

As a giant eagle, I could see the slightest movement on the ground, and if there were enough clear spaces, I could often catch movement through the trees, too.

I let out the loudest screech I could when I spotted the quarry;

three men were running; the boy was tied, gagged, and slung over the largest one's back.

Behind me, I heard werewolves yelp and howl; they were now on the scent. It was my job to keep the kidnappers from getting the boy onto a boat in the river.

I assumed they had one; heading east as they were, they'd have to cross the river to get to the Krelk in that direction, or merely travel southward, until they encountered others from the west side.

Now, to have a little fun while the wolves caught up. I dived like a rocket toward three running humans.

Clare

"Bird shifters are rare. A bird of that size has to be really rare," Sanjay told me. He'd made it back two hours after he left to look for Jeffie Grant, Barbara's son. I'd spent those two hours praying that the boy wouldn't end up in Krelk cage fights; that would kill Barbara, because that's how her husband had disappeared.

"He's a giant eagle?" I frowned at Sanjay. "For real?"

"Really. He just took off running down the edge of the field and turned on the run. Don't know how his clothes survived, but they did."

"Did you see the takedown?"

"Only part of it. Ishaan may have seen it; he was at the front. He said one man was lifted off the ground and dropped into the river, a tenth of a mile away."

"When the bird started flying toward those men again, they were almost happy to surrender to the wolves," the deputy was back, wearing a wide grin. "Now we know what a giant eagle shifter smells like." He gave Sanjay a fist bump.

"What happened to the poachers?" I asked.

"In jail, and John is giving them hell, too. Barbara was so happy to get Jeffie back, she offered Raje vegetables for the rest of his life."

So, not only was the deputy and Sanjay on board with what Rajeon was, they were at the nickname stage.

That was fast. Was that how Rajeon killed six Krelk? At night? How sharp were his talons? I shivered at the thought. Still, I didn't think it a good idea to share that information with anyone; I hadn't seen him kill the Krelk; I'd only watched as one was dumped in the river.

Rajeon had been humanoid and fully dressed when I saw him afterward. *It was the full moon. How was he able to change back?* Most shifters didn't have that kind of control.

"What kind of eagle?" I asked.

"Golden eagle, I think," Sanjay shrugged. "Not a bald eagle, for sure."

"Sanj, I need to check in with John. Thanks for the help." The deputy shook hands with Sanjay.

"No problem, Dan. Any time." Sanjay and I watched him leave.

"I like him better when John's not with him," I said.

"That makes two of us. Dan's a good guy; John uses him too much."

"Leans on him is a better description," I said.

"And there I thought you were sweet on John."

"Sanjay, I'm warning you," I snapped at him. "Honestly, John gives me the creeps when he tries to get friendly. I can't really tell him off, though, can I?"

"He's the sheriff, and he could keep Jessie and the others from checking on you and your mom."

"Yeah."

Sanjay mumbled something about selective law enforcement and walked toward the breakroom.

I wondered where Rajeon was. Had he gone about his business as usual, right after saving Jeffie and dumping a full-grown man in the river? He'd have to be a true giant eagle to carry that much weight.

I wish I'd seen it.

"Stupid poachers," Mom huffed as I told her what I knew later, while we planted bell peppers and yellow squash. "Any word on what they'll do with those three?"

"I didn't hear anything, other than they were in jail."

"I figure they won't live long; Judge and Mayor won't want to feed anybody they don't have to. Know where they're from?"

"No. Not from here is all I heard." I scraped loose soil around a fragile pepper plant before dribbling a little water on it from one of Mom's old watering cans.

Poachers weren't caught often. These might have gotten away without the wolves and Rajeon stepping in. Or, in Rajeon's case, flying in.

"Luck," Mom said, as if she'd read my mind. "Pure luck, that everybody was where they were when they were needed."

"I know. At least we're not going to bed tonight terrified or worried about Jeffie."

"Or for ourselves. Poachers are the lowest of the low, especially when they go after kids."

She meant shifter kids. Human kids were never a target of poachers. Kidnappers, maybe, but that was a stretch. There was no money to be made on humans. "All this excitement got the Blackhearts out of the conversation, for today, anyway."

"You don't think those poachers may have planned to meet up with the Blackhearts rather than the Krelk, do you?"

"I sure hope the sheriff asks them that," I said. "Because I'd really like to know the answer."

"These are good," I said, cutting into one of the king oyster mushrooms Mom had found earlier in the day. She'd caught a good-sized bass, too, that we were having for supper, and managed to find some wild onions growing not far from the river bank to go with it.

"Traded half the mushrooms I found for some butter," Mom told me. "Mushrooms and fish both taste better cooked in butter."

"Every time."

The knock didn't surprise me; I expected Jessie to come by. Instead, it was Rajeon. Suddenly, I was flustered as I invited him in.

"We have plenty of fish and mushrooms," Mom smiled as I introduced him. "Want to have dinner with us?"

"Sure. I brought this," he handed over a wrapped cloth. Inside were watercress and button mushrooms.

"Young man, you are a gift," Mom declared. She loved watercress.

"That fish smells really good. Is that bass?" Rajeon's nose was telling him what we'd cooked for supper.

"Yep. Caught today. Take a seat. I'll find a plate."

"You're lucky to have a bio-fuel generator," Rajeon took the chair adjacent to mine at the table.

"It only runs the lights and the stove," I sighed. "And the small cool-box. When I bought it back before, well," I waved a hand, dismissing the Krelk, "I got a small one. Only thought I'd need it when the regular power was out. Now, we use it every day."

"Lights, stove and cool-box are wealth, nowadays," Rajeon nodded as Mom set a clean plate in front of him. "You have a well, here, too, and that's another luxury."

"I like this house. Mom and I picked it out because it was within walking distance to her place, and not far from the river."

"Because you're otters," he grinned.

"And you're a really big eagle. We know that, now," I shot back.

"It's who I am," he said and lifted a portion of the bass onto his plate. "King oyster mushrooms? I love those," he helped himself to those, too.

"We were talking earlier about those poachers," Mom took her seat across from me. "About whether they were in it for themselves or had connections to the Blackhearts."

"Hmmph." Rajeon's mouth was full.

"You know something, don't you," I watched him carefully.

"Those three won't be answering many questions, I don't think. Vampire compulsion, most likely."

I drew in a breath. *How could he know that?*

"Deputy Dan had one of them on the ground and was growling in his face. The man pissed himself and his mouth worked, but he couldn't answer the sheriff's questions. A normal human would have spilled everything he knew at that point."

"That makes sense, then." Mom's voice sounded grim. "You think the Blackhearts sent them ahead, to scout the territory and see what they could find?"

"It's possible, or we could have another vampire faction coming from the north, hoping to take what the Blackhearts are aiming for before they get here."

"Oh, dear otter goddess," I shut my eyes and shuddered. "Please say that's just speculation."

"There are two vamp gangs from north of St. Louis," Rajeon said. "I figure they've banded together, to take a shifter now and then to sell for cage fights, but not enough to get feathers too ruffled, if you know what I mean. Now, they understand that the Blackhearts may be aiming to take their territory. I think they'll take what they can before the Blackhearts show up. I hope they head across the river when that happens. They can disappear into the eastern section of the zone. If you've noticed, Blackheart likes the western side of the river."

"You think this ah, faction wants the eastern zone, and are giving up on the western side?" Mom asked.

"It's possible—and it's what I'm hoping for—that they won't stay for a turf war with the Blackhearts. It was only a matter of time before the power play began for control of the zone. I'm surprised it hasn't happened before now."

"Now that you mention it, it does make sense," I agreed.

"The Blackhearts held sway in New Orleans. This other bunch is originally from Minneapolis, I think, and moved south the last year or two into the St. Louis area. Now that the Blackhearts are on the move, they've headed this way. I'm still keeping my fingers crossed that the other bunch will cut their losses and take the eastern side for themselves."

"Will the Krelk do anything?" I asked.

"The Krelk won't lift a finger, unless it's to buy what the vamps will be selling to them, and that will be big shifters for their cage fights and small shifters for pets."

"This is awful." I closed my eyes and blew out a breath.

"I'd like to say don't worry about it, but I think it's time that people knew what was coming," Rajeon said. "Keep your eyes and ears open, and don't trust anybody. Unless it's me," he grinned again.

"Does the sheriff know? About the other vamps?"

"No, but I think Jessie and a few others do. Word travels fast with the vamps."

"You think he'll tell John about them?"

"I don't know, and I'm not sure John will believe it. Sometimes, humans have a tendency to bury their heads in the dirt."

"John's focused on the Blackhearts, same as everybody else," Mom said. "Another gang or two may have to take a back seat. Plus, he may be hoping that Fairlawn Point won't be a Blackheart target. They don't hit every town or farm along the river."

"And yet other gangs can be just as dangerous to small towns and rural populations. Dead is dead, no matter how it happened."

"You're really not making this easy, are you?" I pointed my question at Rajeon.

"I'm just trying to make you aware. I'm flying down the river tonight, to see whether I can spot the Blackhearts or their vanguard. That means I'll be out all night and sleeping most of tomorrow to make up for it."

"You're telling us ahead of time that you can't rescue anybody if you're sound asleep." Mom studied Rajeon in speculation.

"Yes. Exactly."

He was worried about us. A part of that made me feel special. Another part of me was terrified. Was he right about all this? I really wanted it to be hearsay. I doubted it was anything other than the truth.

Rajeon didn't come across as anyone who'd lie about things like that. Just the opposite, in fact.

"How safe do you think those humans are in the lockup?" Mom whispered.

"I don't know how important they are to their vamp masters.

Humans are usually expendable in situations like this. They can't tell what they know, so there's usually no problem."

"Usually." My voice was flat. "Who's on duty at the jail tonight, I wonder."

"Probably one vamp and a wolf, if I know the sheriff. In most cases, that would be plenty," Mom replied.

Half an hour later, Rajeon thanked us for the meal after offering to help with the dishes. Mom shooed him out of the house, reminding him of the long night he had planned.

We watched as he disappeared into the night.

"He's a good one," Mom said. "I think he likes you."

"I don't know how I feel about that," I replied.

Rajeon

Eagles, giant or otherwise, don't see well at night.

Owls, however, see quite fine in the dark. As a larger-than-normal great horned owl, I swept my way along the western shore of the river, much faster than most owls could fly. There was a long way to go and plenty of ground to cover before dawn, if it took that long.

Clare

I didn't know what happened until I walked into the store the following morning. Aaron was already there with Sanjay; Sheriff John was there with Deputy Dan.

Vampires had broken into the jail the night before. All three prisoners were dead, as were the vampire and werewolf deputies guarding them.

"Blood and vamp dust everywhere," John shook his head. Standing nearby, Dan looked ill. He'd probably been good friends with the werewolf who died and wasn't happy about the circumstances, or the way John brushed off the death with blunt words and no emotion.

Rajeon was right—this wasn't the work of the Blackhearts; they were still south of us but coming this way. This was another gang from up north, and I felt sympathy for Dan as my stomach churned over this revelation.

"If you'd like to change jobs," John turned to Sanjay, "I've got an opening."

Aaron cleared his throat; he didn't like that idea any more than I did.

"I like where I am," Sanjay said. "For now."

"Tell your brother, then."

"I'll let him know."

Ishaan wouldn't work with the sheriff or anyone else, for that matter. He liked being on his own, hunting game and selling the extra. He only had to answer to himself; Sanjay told me that once.

Sheriff John would have to look elsewhere to replace two deputies. *What if he approaches Rajeon?* That thought scared me. Rajeon made me think of Ishaan, though. He was perfectly happy, in my opinion, anyway, doing things his own way.

John would be smart to ask, though, although Rajeon was much better at John's job than John was. Without Rajeon, Mom and I would still be guessing about the second gang from the north.

That's when I opened my mouth, when I probably should have left it closed. "Is there another vamp gang involved in this? Surely the Blackhearts aren't this far north yet," I said.

"We, ah, are beginning to suspect as much," John raked fingers through his thinning hair. "Jessie got word last night from someone else that they've seen strange vamps not far from here. The opinion was they were on their own and not part of the Blackheart gang."

"I sort of knew that after seeing those poachers yesterday," Sanjay growled. "No tattoos. Blackheart sheep have a black heart tattoo, usually on their arm or their neck."

"How do you know about that?" John's eyes narrowed as he studied Sanjay.

"Ishaan. Every now and then he sees someone passing through.

Got that description from somebody about a month ago. Somebody traveling north, to get away from the Blackheart threat."

He meant traveling werewolves. Ishaan had his ear to the ground, too, just as Rajeon did. Dan didn't appear surprised by Sanjay's words. John, however, lifted an eyebrow, indicating he'd been caught unaware.

It made sense that any fleeing humans or shifters would give the towns a wide berth if they could; strangers were often considered suspicious, and some regional law enforcement didn't allow them to come close enough to bargain for food or shelter. Somehow, Rajeon had gotten around most of that by taking up residence on the river and walking right into town with fish to sell.

I wondered how many strangers Ishaan had seen already. If there were a flood of people escaping northward, we probably needed to know about it.

Ten miles on either side of the Mississippi was all we had to work with; that's what the Krelk had given every survivor of the U.S. takeover. There wasn't a lot of space left for squatters except on the water; much of what was open ground had been turned into farming or grazing lands.

Government varied from town to town, too, and was often at the whim of the Mayor, the Sheriff and the Judge of those towns. Fairlawn Point certainly fit into that category.

Moving to another city or town often required that someone already there and respected by the current residents had to vouch for you. It usually made the resident responsible if the newcomers committed a crime.

There wasn't a lot of movement—that I knew of, anyway—until now. I needed to have a private talk with Sanjay—and maybe Ishaan, too. If shifters were coming northward, then they were running headlong into the Northern gang, and could face poaching from both directions.

Something needed to be done about that, if it were true. A week ago, my biggest worry was flooding. That was no longer true. If

Rajeon hadn't been there the night of the full moon, I could already be on a leash in Krelk territory.

"Do you think the Krelk are meeting these gangs—the new one and the Blackhearts—halfway during the full moon?" I blurted, causing everybody to turn and stare at me. "That could explain why six of them came across the river last time."

"Six? Where'd you get that number?" John asked right away.

Crap. "Uh, exaggeration," I floundered. "I was guessing."

"Don't scare us," Sanjay scolded.

"Yeah. We found evidence of three. Don't double it," John grinned.

"I'll remember that," I said, mentally relieved. Now wasn't the time to admit I'd seen six Krelk—or speculate on how they'd died afterward, although I was certain Rajeon deserved all the credit.

I hoped Rajeon was safe in his bed after searching for the Blackhearts the night before; I figured we'd need his talents soon enough.

Rajeon

I was slow to wake. Late afternoon had fallen on the river, fish were leaping from the water to capture flies and a werewolf sat on the riverbank, waiting patiently for me to notice him.

He was in wolf form; I could detect the scent from my makeshift bed on the boat deck.

"Waiting on me?" I asked, standing stiffly and leaning back to stretch muscles cramped from a long flight the night before.

The wolf yipped, telling me yes.

"Give me a minute," I held up a hand. "Want something to eat?" I added.

Another yip.

In twenty minutes, while the wolf watched, I had the grill going and three catfish gutted and slapped on it. I'd left the boat in deeper water while I slept; I was about thirty feet from the bank. Starting the motor, I moved closer in before dropping the anchor again.

"Come aboard," I invited the wolf. "If you want to change, I've got these," I folded a pair of sweatpants over the back railing.

Then, I went forward to turn the fish. They'd be done by the time the wolf was changed and dressed.

"Ishaan," he offered his hand before sitting down at my small table.

"Sanjay's brother?" I asked.

"Yeah. Sanjay told me what you did, yesterday."

"Wasn't anything," I waved off his words.

"I saw a giant, horned owl flying south along the river last night," he went on.

"Yeah. That was me, too."

"How?"

"It runs in the family."

"That all you can do?"

"For now."

"I'll keep that to myself."

"I'd appreciate that. Here, I hope you like catfish." I set a plate in front of him.

"I like catfish fine." He lifted the fork and knife by his plate and dug in.

"I found the Blackhearts—at least their vanguard, down by New Madrid last night."

"Did you take any of them?"

"That would be stupid. We don't need them on our doorstep faster than they'd normally get here. The last thing we need is a motivated Bob Blackheart. He doesn't take well to anyone using his own tactics against him." I didn't add that if Je'Dik was with Blackheart, then there was more trouble coming than the buffer zone could handle.

"You know who he was—before he was turned?"

"How well do you know your Civil War history?" I asked.

"Well enough."

"Recognize the name Robert L. Williams?"

"Blackheart Bob. That's why you called him that," Ishaan rumbled, shaking his head. "The master of guerilla warfare at the time."

"Exactly."

"Nobody could find him after that last raid he went on. Most people say he was killed and buried in an unmarked grave by his company. Becoming a vampire instead would explain a lot, wouldn't it?"

"It sure would."

"How do you have fuel for your motor?" Ishaan turned to another topic.

"Solar-powered. I used to be an engineer," I shrugged. "Mostly I worked on computers, but I can build other things, too. I was solar-powered before the Krelk showed up. If I had the proper pipe and tools, I could build a windmill system to pump water from the river to the local farms. Finding the pipe is the problem. Now, I have a question for you."

"What's that?" Ishaan spoke around a mouthful of catfish.

"How many shifters and vamps have you seen fleeing the Blackhearts? Just a general estimate would be good to have. I can't keep track of everything, and I figure you're out hunting most nights."

"At first, just a trickle. Maybe one or two a week. Now it's five or six a night, sometimes more. I get their scents while I'm hunting. I don't blame them for running; I'd do the same if the Blackhearts threatened me or my family."

"I'm worried that the Northern gang is taking whatever they can capture, and once the Blackhearts figure out that they're driving their quarry into someone else's pen, that'll mean a turf war. I like Fairlawn Point and I sure as hell don't want the turf war to come here."

"That makes two of us," Ishaan sighed. "I heard from Jessie that strange vamps have been seen nearby. After they tore into the jail last night to kill their sheep and two deputies, this news doesn't surprise me."

"Who got killed—deputy-wise?" I asked.

"Roger Pelletier—a werewolf friend, and Virgil—a vamp."

"That's not good. Means two or more vamps hit the jail, then."

"I think Virgil and Roger took down at least one of their attackers before they died. Too much ash to be only one dead vamp. I sniffed out at least four attackers."

"So, two or three got away."

"Sounds right."

"Who knows how many more gang members they have with them," I mused.

"I'll be looking into that diligently," Ishaan told me. "It may mean the difference in whether we can stand against this bunch."

"It must have been a slow day for them to target Barbara's son," I said. "Or there weren't enough big shifters coming through, so they figured they'd nab a young one."

"Could be," Ishaan agreed. "I've scented several smaller ones lately, and a lot of those have been undesirables—according to the Krelk, anyway. Skunk, armadillo, that kind of thing."

"That would make a difference. Skunk shifters don't make good pets."

"Hmmph." Ishaan almost smiled. "They make even worse enemies."

I laughed.

After promising to stop by again in two nights, Ishaan changed back to wolf and leapt off the back of my boat. I pulled anchor and moved the vessel farther into the water before dropping anchor again. I could get off the boat and onto dry land easily. Anyone else would have to swim to reach the boat, which was armed and alarmed against anyone I didn't invite aboard.

Time to go check on Clare and her mother. There was still an hour of daylight left, and they'd be working the garden, unless I was badly mistaken.

My nose told me rain was coming in. I hoped the Northern gang wouldn't want to be out poaching in such weather; if my guess were correct, it would be raining around sundown.

Nobody in the area needed to be out after sundown, human or shifter. Not with a vampire gang closing in. I hoped the sheriff was warning everyone to keep their weapons close at hand. Vamps didn't need to be invited into a home to attack; that was an old lie that should've never been told.

Stretching and flexing my arms, first, I became the eagle. Pumping my wings, I lifted off the deck, flying toward the Coquina farm.

Clare

"Well, look who the cat dragged in," Mom grinned as Rajeon walked up to us. We were ready to quit for the night anyway; it was nearly sundown and we didn't need to be out after dark.

"We're finished, we just have to put the tools in the barn," I told him when he turned a smile in my direction.

"Good. I'll walk you home, then, and we can talk about what I found last night over dinner."

"Now, how did you know we were having rooster for dinner?" Mom teased.

"I didn't, but I was ready to go find some fish, just in case."

"We're having fried chicken," Mom said.

"I ate not long ago, but I'd still take a piece of chicken," Rajeon declared. "I haven't had fried chicken in forever."

"We got lucky," I said, lifting the hoe and two trowels before walking toward the barn. "Two of Jacob's roosters got into a fight. Jacob gave Mom a really good deal on the loser."

"I take it he lost more than the fight?"

"Pretty much. He was on his way out, so we took advantage."

"We won the rooster lottery, I guess," Mom said as we walked inside the dim interior of the barn and set the tools in their proper places. "We'll need to hurry or we'll be wet by the time we get home."

We were wet by the time we reached my house. Mom and I changed clothes and cleaned up; Rajeon was forced to air dry next to the stove while we cooked.

"Do you buy your wheat berries from Shelley?" Rajeon asked as Mom dropped flour-dredged chicken legs into the frying pan.

"Oh, no, she charges too much," Mom told him. "We buy directly from Shep, just like she does. If you keep the whole wheat berries in a dry, dark space, they'll last for a long time."

"I learned not to grind up more than I needed," Rajeon admitted. "Fresh flour goes bad after a few days—especially down on the river."

"I'll bet you didn't do a lot of cooking before the Krelk came," Mom said.

"Not if I could help it," he laughed. "I was forced into it."

"A lot of people were."

"So, what did you find out, last night?" I asked.

Rajeon's smile disappeared. "The Blackhearts are coming," he admitted. "I saw their vanguard down by New Madrid, last night."

CHAPTER 4

*C*lare

"It's my day off, tomorrow, so we'll be in the garden early," I said when Rajeon asked. "You really ought to pass the information you have to the sheriff."

"I told Ishaan earlier. I figure Sheriff John will hear it soon enough."

When the tap came on the door, Rajeon rose when I did to answer it. "I hope it's Jessie," I mumbled as we made our way to the front door.

It was Jessie, and my shoulders sagged in relief as I let him in. He was wet from the rain, too, although he was dressed better than we'd been. He had a slicker and a hat on, to keep his clothes as dry as possible.

"Come into the kitchen for a minute," I invited. Jessie nodded; even though he'd never eat human food, he liked being warm as well as anyone else.

"I have some news for you," Rajeon told Jessie as we walked toward the kitchen.

"I reckon you do. I already talked to Ishaan."

"Good. I was hoping he'd see you or one of the others," Rajeon replied.

"Can you tell me exactly what you saw? Ishaan said vanguard. Tell me about that," Jessie said.

"Human and shifter slaves," Rajeon replied. "Sent ahead to scope out the territory. If they come across friend or foe, one of the vanguard runs back to tell Blackheart. They're like a scouting party, I suppose."

"These the shifters he's planning to sell to the Krelk?" Jessie asked.

"I don't believe so. These are the ones that are expendable, in my estimation. He uses them as a disposable shield; the ones for sale will be left in camp in cages, where they're guarded. They need to be in good shape to sell to the Krelk."

"Ishaan said you didn't take any of them—for a reason."

"We need Blackheart on a steady pace, rather than an accelerated one," Rajeon pointed out. "He's vindictive and we don't need to be enemies with him faster than normal."

"Good choice. I know a lot of folks who might not have thought that through."

"What does the sheriff have planned for the other gang—the one from the north?" Mom asked Jessie the pointed question.

"He doesn't have a plan," Jessie snorted. "We lost two good deputies last night, and the only thing on his mind is getting replacements instead of making a plan of defense. Armageddon is coming, and he's ignoring it. We'd be better off if he'd just ordered those poachers' executions after they were caught, yesterday. John doesn't know which way is up, right now."

"You think it's that bad?" Mom stifled a gasp.

"Yeah. I've heard rumors, and Ishaan is out there now, sniffin' the ground. Nothin' good will come of this, Miss Doreen."

"Jessie, do you know where there might be felled trees or logs to be had?" Rajeon asked. "Barring that, are there boats out there? I've seen a few on the river, but not many."

"Nobody has gas. The ones you've seen are paddle boats and they don't get far from the shore."

"So there are boats out there, but they're not being used?"

"I've seen some boats turned into planters for vegetables," Jessie said. "Others are just layin' out in yards or in garages, takin' up space."

"Why do you want boats?" Mom turned to Rajeon.

"I'd rather take my chances in the middle of the river, than take my chances on dry land when two rival vampire gangs clash. Wouldn't you?"

"Now there's a thought," Jessie leaned back in his chair, making it creak beneath him.

"Well, it sounds like a temporary fix, maybe," I pointed my fork at Rajeon. "But for the long term, we need another plan."

"I'm working on that," Rajeon sighed.

"Weeds already sprouting," Mom grumbled as she bent over to pull two from the row of potatoes. "Hope the bugs don't show up early this year."

She and I'd left the house right after sunup, heading for the garden. We'd get the last of it planted today, if nothing interfered and the weather stayed good.

Sheriff John likely had all the news Rajeon reported before daybreak. I was waiting to see how he reacted to it, but that wouldn't come until the following day, when I went back to work.

Was Jessie right, and there was no plan to protect Fairlawn Point? Would it be everyone for himself?

I didn't like that idea. This was our home, and I liked living here. Even a silver-plated pipe wrench wouldn't fend off an entire vampire gang, no matter how well you could swing it.

Secretly, we'd thought—hoped—that the Blackhearts might pass us by.

That hope was now gone.

"It makes me mad enough to spit, thinking that the Blackhearts may have shifters chained up and traveling with them, just to sell them off to the Krelk," Mom said, pulling more weeds out of the potato rows.

"That could be us," I agreed, searching through the box of seeds for the cantaloupe and watermelon packets. These we hadn't bought; we'd saved seeds from some of our best last year, hoping to have a good crop of them again.

"It would have been Jeffie, too, with that Northern gang, if their human poachers hadn't been stopped."

"I know. I wish I knew more about when the Krelk show up to buy, and where. Somebody, somewhere, has to plan those things, don't you think?"

"I want to know how they communicate," Mom said. "It's not like they have a cell phone or anything."

I went still. "What if they do?" I stopped and turned toward Mom. "The Krelk have communication devices. If they've given some to the Blackhearts and this other gang, they could talk whenever they wanted."

Mom froze, a two-inch weed clutched between a thumb and forefinger, a tiny bit of dirt still clinging to its roots.

"I think we need to have another talk with Rajeon," Mom breathed and dropped the weed between rows.

"You don't want to take this to John?"

"You heard Jessie last night, just like I did. John doesn't know what to do in this situation. I really don't either, but Rajeon is thinking about it, that's for sure. He's looking to get people out of danger, first, and that's what John ought to be doing, you know?"

"I know. It won't solve the ultimate problem, but it's a start."

"Then you start thinkin' about the ultimate problem solving and help Rajeon. Damn, I wish I were younger. Hand me those cantaloupe seeds. Let's get going on this."

"Younger?" I asked.

"I swear, my otter would sneak into that Blackheart camp and let as many shifters loose as I could. Nobody deserves to be chained up like that."

"They'd have you in seconds, Mom," I pointed out. "Then you'd be chained up, too. Let me think about that for a while, all right?"

"We'll both think while we're planting."

"Sounds good."

Rajeon

I showed up at the Coquina garden an hour before sundown, to find them finishing up for the day.

"Everything's in the ground," Doreen smiled at me. "Now, we need rain but not too much, no floods and fewer bugs. What's in the bucket?" She nodded at the bucket in held by the handle.

"Clams, fish and four potatoes. What else would there be?" I grinned.

"We have some lettuce ready to pick," she said. "We'll have some of that, too."

Clare was at the bottom of the garden, gathering tools. "She looks serious," I told her mother.

"She's been thinking about the big problem all day. If Clare puts her mind to something, she doesn't let it go until she has an answer. She can be pretty stubborn at times."

"Is that a warning?" I asked.

"Just the truth. That's all I'm sayin'," she held up a hand.

"I'll keep it in mind, then." I watched as Clare walked our way. I'd be lying if I said I didn't enjoy the sight of her, even when she was covered in dirt.

"I have an idea," she told me the moment she came close enough.

"What idea is that?"

"Well, there used to be some snake shifters west of town. I never got to know them very well, but they used to come into the store now and then. If we could send snake shifters into that camp," she turned toward her mother. "You think vamps are scared of snakes?"

It took me several moments to decipher what she meant.

"You're talking rescue?" I frowned at Clare and her mother.

"We are." She gave me a defiant look.

"I'm not sure the snake shifters are still out there," Mom said. "I haven't seen them in a long while."

"I may have an alternate suggestion," I offered.

"What would that be?"

"Vamps may or may not be afraid of snakes," I said. "But they sure as hell won't stick around if a skunk shows up. Their noses are too sensitive."

Clare and her mother exchanged glances before turning to stare at me. "Make it happen, please," Doreen begged.

"It makes sense that they'd have some sort of communication device, and likely Krelk in origin," I agreed with Clare's suggestion while we talked and ate later at the dinner table. "They'd waste too much time, otherwise. This means the Krelk slavers have worked this out ahead of time. Not only that, but they've likely been in contact with both Blackheart and the Northern gangs. At this point, I'm pretty sure the Northern gangs have consolidated, to take on the Blackhearts if they're forced to. They want control of the zone, I think, just as much as Blackheart does."

"The Krelk slavers are probably egging them on," Doreen speared a piece of fish onto her plate.

"More than likely," I said after considering that for a moment. "If they can whittle it down to only one gang in control, they can do all their shopping at one place."

"Like Walmart?" Doreen frowned as she named the now-defunct shopping center.

"Cuts down on the chances of getting caught. What they're doing is illegal, according to their own laws, but once a shifter is forced to stay in his other shape, he's an animal, and they're more willing to overlook inconveniences in the law."

"Bunch of bloodthirsty bastards," she grumbled.

"I'll give you that," I agreed.

"Where will we find skunk shifters?" Clare came back to the immediate problem at hand—in her mind.

"Ishaan mentioned that some were passing through. Now, if

they've run into the Northern gang, they may need a place to go if they've turned back this way. I'll ask Ishaan to look. It's the best we can do," I shook my head at her. "Plus, we have to consider how to keep everybody safe, if and when these two gangs collide."

"Well, I don't want the shifters they've captured to be caught up in all that," Clare insisted.

"Darlin', I don't want that, either."

Clare went still and almost dropped her fork, while her cheeks flooded with color. *Because I'd called her darlin'.*

I'd bet money she hadn't had that reaction when the sheriff asked her out.

"What can we do?" She ducked her head to hide the blush. I considered calling her darlin' again.

"If we put our heads together," I teased gently, "we may be able to come up with something."

"We have two vamp gangs to contend with, and Je'Dik could be with either one," I reported to Forneel when I got back to the houseboat. "I may need to do closer reconnaissance to determine that."

Forneel would say yes, if he thought Je'Dik's capture was in the near future.

"Do what you have to," Forneel made his decision immediately.

"On it," I said and ended the communication. No need to tell him what else I was thinking of doing. He didn't give a damn about anyone born on Earth. He wanted the bounty on Je'Dik's head. Everything else came in a distant second, including his own duty as Commander.

Now, I needed to find Ishaan and Jessie. I needed skunk shifters and vampire ash, and those two might know where I could get both.

Clare

Aaron was at the store the following morning when I got there. "Where's Sanjay?" I asked, first thing.

"Sanjay took the deputy spot with John." Aaron sounded far from happy. "Offered more money. A lot more."

"Oh, no," I closed my eyes to let the news settle into my brain. "He's walking right into danger, you know that?" I opened my eyes and stared at Aaron.

"I tried telling him that. He said he didn't feel right, standing back and doing nothing."

"What did his brother say?"

"I got the idea that Ishaan wasn't happy with his decision, either."

"Yeah. Are you going to look for a replacement?"

"I already talked to Willie."

"Willie would be a good choice," I said. "He knows everything."

He did, but he was ancient and arthritic. I hoped standing on his feet wouldn't become a problem for him. Nobody had a retirement plan nowadays. If you didn't have a family to support you, you worked until you dropped. I liked Willie; I had no desire to see him die by working himself to death.

"He's coming by after lunch. If you could show him how to count change back, I'd appreciate it."

"I can do that." I also resolved to get a chair or a stool to put behind the counter—Willie would need it. He could sort out seed packets that way and write up inventory sheets for Aaron.

"We'll make this work," Aaron promised. "And, since Willie will only be part-time, I'll give you a raise."

"Thanks, Aaron." I walked toward the break room, thinking the whole way that I'd rather work with Sanjay than get a raise because he was gone.

"There, all sorted," Willie offered me a grin later as he pushed the box toward me. Sheriff John chose that moment to walk into the store, followed by Deputy Dan.

If he thought I was going to be civil to him after Sanjay, he ought to think again.

"I didn't think I was in for a warm welcome," John said when I didn't say anything. "Willie, good to see you," he turned toward the old man. "Good to see you working."

"Hmmph. I'll be working until noon on the day of my funeral," Willie cackled. It was an old joke with him. He'd done farming until his arthritis worsened. His hands showed signs of permanent crookedness, and he always walked with a limp.

"Aaron here?" John asked.

"In the back," I said.

John walked toward the break room; Dan stayed behind.

"I know how you feel," Dan said softly. "I wasn't sure about it, either, but John will be John."

"I know. I want to know what Ishaan said about it."

"I'm not sure they're talking, right now."

"I can understand that," I said. "John come up with a plan, yet?"

"Hide."

"That's it? Vamps can sniff us out, just like the wolves can."

"Jessie told him that."

"At least Jessie has some sense. How many boats do you think might be found in the area?" I thought to ask. May as well consider Rajeon's idea of keeping folks safe if John's only suggestion was to hide.

"Jessie mentioned the same thing. Taking to the river might not be a bad idea. Especially if there's a gang war between vamps in the works. We could float downriver a couple miles, get out of the way while the battle is happening, then make our way back, after the war is over."

"If there's anything to come back to."

"They'll be looking to kill each other first. Besides, they like safety and comfort just as well as anybody. I can't guarantee they'll let us have the town back, but at least we'll know where we stand afterward."

"I just hope we're still standing," I said.

"Getting most folks out of the way is a good idea," Dan said. "Trust me."

Rajeon was right. I thought the boats were only a temporary fix. They might be the only fix—to save lives. He'd known that the town might need relocation. I hadn't considered it.

Until now.

"We have a lot of work to do," I told Dan. "And not much time to do it in."

"John might not go for whatever it is you're thinking."

"John can go soak his head in the river."

"He won't go for that, either."

I cleared my throat to let Dan know John and Aaron were walking toward us. It probably wasn't necessary; Dan probably heard them breathing from where he stood. John and Aaron said their good-byes while Dan and I stood by.

Once John and Dan were out the door, Aaron released a sigh. "I don't know what's going to happen," he said. "But I don't think we're gonna like it."

"I hear that," I agreed.

"Times are changin' again," Willie said from his seat behind the counter. "I don't expect 'em to ever get better."

"We may have to move the whole town, or as many as are willing," I told Mom when I reached the garden after work. It was time to pick weeds and stake tomato plants.

"So Rajeon was right about the boats," Mom grunted as she bent down to pull up a newly-sprouted weed.

"It looks that way. I'm worried about getting the whole town evacuated, though."

"I'm worried about where we'll go. We'll need gardens and game, baby girl. We'll keep working this one, in case a miracle happens," she added.

She never called me baby girl unless she was really worried or feeling emotional. This time it was worry, and that ramped up my own worry. Gardening was something to keep us busy while we worried together, so we kept at it.

Was there a way to safely get the cows, chickens and other farm animals belonging to the residents away, too? I really needed to talk to Rajeon again and ask him about that.

"John showed up at the store today, and he still doesn't have a clue how to handle this mess," I told Mom as we worked our way down two long rows of tomatoes, tying the tender plants to stakes with string. "And Sanjay went to work for him." I didn't bother keeping the bitterness from my voice.

"He what?" Mom straightened up and blinked at me in shock.

"Sanjay went to work for John. John offered a lot more money, so Aaron had to hire Willie part-time to help cover the hole. That means Aaron and I will be working half-days on what used to be our days off."

"Did he give you a raise for that?"

"He said he would. I'd rather not have the raise and have Sanjay back."

"I'll bet Ishaan wasn't pleased with Sanjay's decision." Mom went back to staking tomatoes.

"He wasn't, according to Deputy Dan. Sanjay took the job, too, right after hearing how a werewolf deputy died in that attack on the jail."

"Too many people think they're indestructible," Mom grunted as she moved to the next plant. "John's lucky he wasn't at the jail when all that happened."

Rajeon

Ishaan was on the lookout for skunk shifters. Jessie would help him after nightfall. I needed more help than that, if I expected to save the lives in Fairlawn Point.

I wasn't supposed to do that. I was supposed to do my job, as Forneel so bluntly put it. I'd done my duty many times before, but this time, things were different. I was tired of sitting back and watching Krelk take over one planet after another, with nobody stepping in to stop them.

If the world was non-Alliance, the Alliance evidently didn't care. Somebody, somewhere, obviously *did* care, and that's why I was here, now.

I need help, I told myself. Help that Forneel wouldn't give. He expected me to hand Je'Dik to him if Je'Dik were here, somewhere, but as for getting to Je'Dik and fending off two vampire gangs, well, that was all up to me.

Stabbing my thumb against the recognizer beside the door, I waited for the door to swing open before striding into the wheelhouse of my boat. The door shut behind me automatically.

Digging through a bottom drawer of the small desk in the back, I found my comp-vid. I'd ask for help; the people who cared enough to send me had made the offer. I'd see what help they could send.

Clare

Rajeon didn't come for supper, and I was more than disappointed. It made for a bad day all around, I suppose.

We still had the clams Rajeon brought the night before, so those were steamed and paired with fresh lettuce and leftover cresses and mushrooms. I had no idea where Rajeon found the watercress; I hadn't seen any on the western bank on any full moon.

He's an eagle, I reminded myself. He could travel up and down the river on both sides if he wanted. No wonder he had wide shoulders and big, dense muscles on his arms and back. He'd need those to fly long distances.

Mom and I answered the door when the knock interrupted my thoughts. I hoped it was Rajeon or Jessie. It turned out to be both—plus Ishaan.

"We have this," Rajeon set a bag on the table. Inside, we found a fresh loaf of bread, cheese and a warm container.

"That's gumbo," Rajeon said. "I cooked it earlier. Sorry I didn't get here sooner."

"That's no trouble," Mom went to find bowls. Food was welcome, no matter where or when it presented itself.

"We have to move the town, don't we?" I blurted once the food was on the table and everybody except Jessie was eating.

"I think so," Rajeon agreed. "I just can't gauge exactly when, but it ought to be soon. First, though, we need a place to go. Somewhere that we won't be seen as squatters or interlopers."

"Harder than it sounds, too," Jessie nodded his agreement. "Folks are mighty attached to ground that's attached to their ground, and so on."

"Whatever we find, we can't be particular about which side of the river it's on, either," Rajeon pointed out. "I'll be looking, but we need to settle on a place soon. Jessie is going to ask the sheriff for a town meeting, but we don't know whether he'll agree to it."

"John's scared; he just doesn't want anybody to know it," Ishaan offered. "Sanjay has no idea what he signed up for."

"I've asked a friend for help," Rajeon sighed. "I haven't heard yet if he has someone available to send."

"Your friend can't come himself?" I asked.

"He has his own irons in the fire, you understand. If he sends someone, you can place your life in his hands, though. I trust him that much."

"From up north, where you come from?" Ishaan asked.

"Close," Rajeon nodded. "He owes me a couple of favors."

"No luck on skunk shifters today," Ishaan answered Mom's question next. "I'm hoping we'll see some soon enough."

"Or find a substitute," Rajeon bit into his toasted bread.

"Who made the bread?" I asked. "It's really good."

"I did. I can bake," Rajeon said with a grin. "I don't do it often, but I can."

"A man who can cook gumbo and bake bread," Mom sighed. "That's wonderful."

Another knock sounded on the door, startling all of us.

"I'll go," Jessie offered.

"I'll come with you," Rajeon rose from his seat. I blinked at Mom; anybody we may have expected was sitting at the table with us. Jessie and Rajeon's feet trod lightly as they strode out of the kitchen toward the front door.

Ishaan held up a hand; he was listening.

"Thank the stars," we heard Rajeon say. Ishaan relaxed immediately; apparently Rajeon's friend had found us.

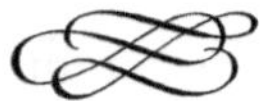

*R*ajeon

"This is Nyarr Blackmantle, and his ah, associate, Cle-Anne Black," he introduced both our guests. He'd been expecting one person. Two had come instead. I blinked at Cle-Anne; she looked to have some Asian ancestry, wore black leather clothing with two blades strapped to her back, and had a black leather pouch slung over a shoulder.

Nyarr was dressed almost casually in black, with a black polo, black jeans and black boots. Both had dark hair; Cle-Anne's was long and braided down her back. Nyarr's eyes were also dark, whereas Cle-Anne's were blue.

Nyarr smiled at Cle-Anne.

Often.

"We're here to help," Cle-Anne said. "And, I have something for each of you, that my Auntie Zaria sent."

Clare frowned for a moment.

"Don't worry," I held up a hand. "If you knew Zaria, you'd be anxious to have whatever she sent."

"She sent one for you, too," Cle-Anne dimpled as she pulled a small box from her pouch and handed it to me.

"Really? I feel special," I mumbled, opening the box and lifting the medallion out of it. Without hesitation, I placed the necklace over my head and tucked the medallion beneath my shirt.

Zaria was taking interest in the plight of these people. I hoped it was enough to save some of them.

"Your names are on the boxes," Cle-Anne said as she set more boxes on the table. "Put these on and don't take them off for any reason, unless Zaria tells you to."

"Where is she?" Doreen asked. "To tell us whether to take them off?"

"You'll know, don't worry about it," Cle-Anne said. "Just be sure to keep these on always, even if you're in the bath or the river."

"I have one?" Jessie lifted the box with his name on it.

"I wish I could tell you exactly what that means," Nyarr smiled. "I've had mine for a while, now." He lifted his own medallion from beneath his black polo.

I wasn't sure I'd ever seen a vampire's hands tremble; Jessie's did when he lifted his gift from the small box and placed the medallion over his head.

Doreen followed Jessie's lead, then Clare and Ishaan did the same. I breathed a relieved sigh; this was some sort of protection for all of us, and I was more than grateful. Tamp had come through for me in ways I couldn't imagine.

"Have you eaten?" Doreen thought to ask the newcomers.

"We have, but we appreciate the offer," Nyarr dipped his head to Doreen. "We've parked our houseboat next to yours on the river," he turned to me. "We can discuss things here or there, if you want."

"We were talking about calling a town meeting, but may get resistance from the sheriff," I said. "I believe we'll be ground zero when the vamp gangs get here, and if we don't do something, many will die."

"Rajeon, Jessie and I think that one gang or the other will have control of the entire zone afterward," Ishaan said. "That gang will have ties to the Krelk black market, and that doesn't look good for shifters or humans."

"Krelk are a virus," Cle-Anne shook her head. "They just keep growing and spreading, with no cure in sight."

"Their barbaric practices are getting worse, too," Nyarr said. "We were given information regarding the ah, cage fights."

"I've scoped out two boatyards in St. Louis," I said. "With Nyarr's help, we may be able to get several houseboats from drydock and send them here to help carry the load."

"You're just going to take them?" Clare asked.

"Those things no longer have a way to get back in the water," Nyarr explained. "No gas to run motors, and they're too far inland to do it another way. They could have hooked up horses, but there's no meat stock left anywhere within city limits, and that includes horses."

"In other words, they've been abandoned," I explained.

"Then how are you going to get them to the river?" Doreen asked.

"We have our ways," Nyarr shrugged and smiled.

"You'll have to trust me—us," I said. "If all goes well, we could have them down here sometime tomorrow. We may have to do some renovation, so Jessie and others like him can travel safely that way."

"You may have to do renovation before setting them in the water," Ishaan said. "If they've been drydocked for a while."

"We'll be checking on that before we take them," Nyarr agreed.

"When are you going?" Doreen asked.

"Tonight, if Raje isn't too tired," Nyarr said.

"I'm not," I said. "Jessie, Ishaan, if you'd like to come with us," I offered.

"I wouldn't mind seeing this," Jessie agreed.

"What about us?" Clare demanded.

"Sweetheart, if I could, I'd like to take you and your mother to my houseboat before we leave," I told her. I have an extra bedroom you can share. Just bring clothes and shoes; I worry about you in this house by yourselves. Especially at night."

"Mostly because the Northern gang is closin' in," Jessie nodded.

Clare and Doreen exchanged glances.

"Baby girl, go pack your stuff," Doreen reached out to pat Clare's hand.

Clare

The bedroom wasn't huge, but it held two twin beds, a dresser, a tiny table and two small nightstands. A small closet and a bathroom with a shower was attached; Rajeon said we could shower if we wanted, and that sounded like a luxury to me.

"Kinda like a cruise ship cabin," Mom said, setting her battered suitcase on the bed.

"Well, houseboat or cruise ship, they both float," I said. "Space is a premium, either way."

Rajeon and the others left shortly after showing us to our cabin. I hoped they got what they were going after—without getting killed.

"I'm going to shower. Lord knows how long it's been since we were able to do that," Mom yawned. We were both tired, it was getting late and dawn would come too soon for both of us.

"Clare," Mom yelled moments after she turned the water on.

"What?" I jumped off the bed and ran toward the bathroom, worried that something was wrong.

"Hot water," Mom said, almost doing a jig on the tiled bathroom floor. "He has hot water."

"Thank the otter goddess," I sighed and leaned my head against the open bathroom door. We'd been taking tepid baths for years.

Rajeon

"I don't suppose you'll be explainin' how we got here like we did?" Jessie lifted an eyebrow at me.

We stood between huge houseboats sitting on rails in the boatyard, while Nyarr scanned them for problems.

I hesitated to tell Jessie what Nyarr was; people from Earth had an aversion to the word *warlock*.

"Zaria said to tell you he's Roma—some people call them Gypsies,"

Cle-Anne walked up to us. Ishaan, listening intently, pursed his lips at Cle-Anne's explanation.

"Ain't never see a Gypsy do that," Jessie observed.

"He's special. It runs in his family," I said.

"What else can he do?"

"I don't want to scare you. Just keep in mind that he's on our side."

"I sure do appreciate that," Jessie huffed.

"These two are good to go. What else do you want?" Nyarr asked.

"Let's find another two or three that are similar," I said. "If we need more, we can hit the other boatyard later."

"There are three big ones at the back," Cle-Anne said. "I'm glad nobody thought to hole up in them." Nyarr followed her toward the back of the lot.

"Lucky, or just too far away from food or water," Ishaan said. "This isn't the best place for either of those things."

"Ready," Nyarr and Cle-Anne were back.

"Let's go, then."

Nyarr raised his hands, which, in turn, raised five houseboats above the others. Ten minutes later, we floated gently into mooring spaces beside my boat and dropped anchor on all five.

If Forneel were paying attention, he'd know something was going on. I depended on his usual tactic of ignoring his scouts.

Two were dead on his watch—on this planet alone.

Clare

"Want coffee or tea?" Rajeon was already on deck, leaning on a rail and studying five large houseboats lined up between his and Nyarr's. The cup in his hand was steaming in the early morning mist on the river; he'd already made something for himself.

"What are you having?" I asked, ignoring the question hammering in my brain—*how did they get all those boats down here without waking Mom and me?*

"Coffee it is. Want milk or honey in it?"

"You have those things?" I squeaked.

"I get around," he grinned and straightened up. "Come into the galley; you need breakfast before going to work."

"Duck eggs," he told me, tipping scrambled eggs onto my plate. "Got 'em from a farmer south of here. He sometimes has bacon or chops, too."

"He has pigs?"

"Yes. And ducks, geese and chickens."

"How far away?" I placed scrambled eggs in my mouth and closed my eyes in pleasure at the taste.

"Twenty miles. I carry my clothes in my bucket when I fly, just in case." He was grinning as he watched me eat. "If I get there early, I get first pick of what he has."

"Flying would solve a lot of transportation problems," I said before dipping up more eggs.

"It does. Wings and a bucket. Who could ask for more?" he teased.

I laughed.

I reached the store before Aaron did; Rajeon saw me off early enough to make it to town on time for work.

The bell tinkled when Aaron walked through the door. I was already straightening the gardening tools we had left. "Almost out of trowels," I told Aaron when he stopped beside the shelf where I was working.

"I see that," he said. I looked up at him; he was worried, that was plain.

"What's wrong?" I asked him.

"John stopped by the house early this morning. Sanjay was out with another deputy last night. Neither one reported in. Dan is out hunting now, as is Ishaan."

"Oh, no," I breathed, standing up so quickly I wobbled. Aaron steadied me with a hand while I scrambled to sort reality for a moment.

"John says he was with another werewolf; we're worried both were taken—or killed."

"This is awful." I felt like crying, but that wouldn't do any good. "What can we do?"

"I hope Ishaan can convince Rajeon to help."

"Rajeon will certainly help," I said. "As soon as he knows about this. Do we know when they ah, disappeared, last night?"

"No idea. They were supposed to cover the western edge of town. That's all I know."

"John needs to get the people out of here," I said, my voice trembling. It was only a matter of time until one gang or another showed up to take what they could and get rid of the rest.

"That's not as easy as it sounds," Aaron pointed out. "People's lives are here. Their homes are here."

"I know all that, Aaron. My question is this; how badly do they want to stay alive? Those gangs won't have any use for humans—admit it. The shifters they'll poach and sell to the Krelk; the vamps who won't side with them will be killed. I think options need to be presented to the people of Fairlawn Point, so they can make a decision."

"John doesn't want to cause panic," Aaron held up a hand.

"Aaron, Sanjay has been taken—or worse. Don't you think it's time to panic?"

Aaron turned to stare at the front door, as if a solution could walk through it any moment. He'd inherited this store from his father, who was also named Aaron. He'd be forced to leave it behind, in exchange for something less, in his mind. "I have to think about this," he mumbled before walking toward the break room and his office beyond.

When John walked through the door half an hour later, I pointed him toward Aaron's office. Aaron still hadn't come out again and I had no desire to share small talk with the man who'd set Sanjay up for capture.

I had to believe my friend was still alive.

Had to.

Rajeon

"I have this." Ishaan handed one of Sanjay's shirts to me. Nyarr stood at my back, waiting for something to link to Sanjay, which would make it possible to scry for his location.

"Don't be afraid of what you're about to see," I warned Ishaan.

In minutes, Nyarr had a luminescent scrying wheel hanging in midair, while he handled Sanjay's shirt with his eyes shut.

Ishaan didn't miss the map of the area outlined in blue on the scrying wheel. No better map could have been drawn in so little time.

Seconds ticked by, each one lasting forever, in my mind. If the news of Sanjay's disappearance had reached Clare, she was likely more than upset. I had to shove my worry for her aside and concentrate on getting Sanjay back—for her and Ishaan.

"The trail disappears here," Nyarr tapped a point on his floating map. "Now, there's only one reason for somebody to disappear like that."

"He's dead, isn't he?" Ishaan looked as if he were ready to turn and howl his grief to the sky.

"No. If he were dead, I'd find him," Nyarr held up a hand. "We have interference—from bone dust, more than likely."

I went still while Ishaan frowned. He had no idea what this news actually meant.

I did.

Somehow, the Northern gang had been given Sirenali bone dust, to hide from Nyarr and others powerful enough to search for Sanjay using supernatural means.

"Can you get us to the place he disappeared?" I asked.

"I can."

"Get Cle-Anne and let's go."

They could hide Sanjay from Nyarr with bone dust. They'd have a harder time hiding him from Ishaan's nose. For a moment, I considered letting Forneel know that bone dust had made its way to Earth.

Instead, I might go over his head with this.

Way over, actually.

Clare

Dan walked into the store, looking for John. "He's in Aaron's office," I pointed toward the break room.

"Ishaan went to get Rajeon," Dan said as he strode past me, heading for Aaron's office. "I met them at the place where Sanjay and Frank were taken. Vamp scent everywhere, along with some of Frank's blood."

"Of course," I sighed. Sanjay was in enemy hands, along with the oldest werewolf deputy John had. Would they even try to keep Frank alive? He was too old for the cage fights—too old to be working for John, too.

Especially at night. Had we become so complacent that we'd stopped thinking about our vulnerability? Why wasn't John working out where his strengths lay in keeping nights and days as safe as he could?

Pairing the newest werewolf with the oldest might have worked on the day shift, when there were no vamps to worry about. At night, it became a different story.

My frustration needed an outlet, so I tackled the shelves that held old merchandise that nobody wanted or needed any longer, like the flat-tire fixers, windshield cleaners and such. Cleaning them would take my mind off my building anger, or so I hoped.

Aaron left all those old, former necessities where they were to make the store look fuller, but that was the only purpose they served, aside from collecting dust.

While I cleaned dusty shelves and the sheriff and Aaron talked, I reflected on the fact that I'd never felt so small and helpless in my life.

Rajeon

"If we take them, we only get the lesser part of the gang," I pointed out to Ishaan. Nyarr had a shield around us, keeping us invisible to sight and scent of the human and shifter elements of the Northern gang.

"The vamps will be scattered and buried in the ground somewhere, and that won't be so easy to find," Cle-Anne said. "If your brother is here, he'll be in one of those cages back there." She meant the ones covered in canvas tarps.

"I say we take the cages and let the rest answer to the vamps come nightfall," Nyarr suggested.

"Let's hope they don't have compulsion laid to come right back to the vamps," Cle-Anne snorted.

"There's that," I agreed.

"I'm willing to take my chances," Ishaan growled. "Why keep them in cages if they have compulsion laid not to run away?"

"Also a good point," I acknowledged.

"So, we're agreed on taking the cages? I warn you, this will infuriate the vamps when they wake," Nyarr said. "It could precipitate an attack on the town—earlier than intended."

"How can we make it look like the Blackhearts did this?" Ishaan asked.

"Good question. I may have an answer," I said. "We just need a little of Nyarr's ability, I think. That, and a few dead animals."

"This probably won't fool anybody for long," Nyarr studied six dead alligators lying on the bank of the river.

"We'll take whatever time you can buy us; we need to get the people out of town—or as many as are willing to go."

"All right."

"We can't turn you or Cle-Anne loose," I whispered. "The Krelk will notice, and we don't need Armageddon on the Mississippi. They'll kill everybody if they even imagine we have any firepower."

"Understood."

"The Blackhearts tattoo their recruits with a black heart—either on an arm or the neck," I said. "When you change these alligators to resemble humans, they need the ink and substantial wounds to account for their deaths."

"No problem," Nyarr flexed his arm muscles. "Let's get this rodeo started."

Clare

"John says he thinks we can take a stand, and the Mayor and Judge agree with him," Aaron stood over me while I cleaned a bottom shelf.

"Aaron, I don't know how they plan to take a stand. The vamps from either gang can likely mow us down whenever they feel like it, right after nightfall."

"He's going to send his wolves out to sniff around for vamp sleeping places," Aaron said. "He already has noses to the ground, although they laid a few false trails that lead into the river just north of town."

"So they're wading or swimming in the river and coming out at a different place to dig in for the day?" I shook my head at Aaron.

"That's what Dan said. All they have to do is find where they came back ashore to bury themselves."

"Right. Aaron, I think we need to get away from here while we still can. John needs to call a town meeting right now, and discuss pros and cons."

"John says he'll need everybody to stay to make this work; it may take all of us to dig up vampires during the day. Once they're exposed to daylight, it's over for them."

"You have to find them first, Aaron. You don't have a guarantee you can do that; or that we can do it in time before they wake and hit us from two sides. You know yourself that some of these people aren't able to go out and dig up vamps. Willie had to stop gardening, remember?"

"Granted some of them are too old," Aaron said. "And a few of them are too sick or pregnant."

"Now see—those folks can't do anything except wait for them to come take us. The people need to know what they're up against—all of it, Aaron, so they can decide for themselves. Rajeon thinks we need to evacuate, and I agree with him."

"Rajeon is a relative stranger," Aaron huffed. "Why should we listen to him?"

"Because he knew what was happening before John ever considered it."

"Where is he now, then? Maybe he should be here, talking to John."

"He and Ishaan are out hunting for Sanjay," I snapped, standing up and throwing down my cleaning cloth. "Aaron, I love you. You've been a great boss and at times, I even love your stubbornness. Just not today. I'm quitting. Find somebody else who isn't worried about the coming war, because I feel in my heart that one is coming."

Aaron followed me toward the breakroom, where I was headed to gather my things. My sweater was slung over an arm and my lunch tote was crushed against me as I marched toward the door.

"Clare, please reconsider," Aaron begged as I stalked past the counter at the front. Both of us ducked when the bullet smashed the front window, flinging glass everywhere.

Rajeon

When we got back to the gang's camp with spelled alligator carcasses, all the humans and shifter minions had disappeared, leaving only the tarp-covered cages behind.

"No perimeter spells," Nyarr said after taking a moment to check.

"They're headed for the town," Ishaan mumbled after sniffing out their trail.

"Fucking hell, what are they planning?" I asked.

"No idea. Let's get the tarps off those cages and see what we have to work with."

"Somebody needs to go warn the town," Ishaan said.

"You want that job?" I turned to him.

"I'll go with him; I can transport," Cle-Anne offered. Well, she could fold space just as well as Nyarr could.

"Good. I don't like the looks of this," Ishaan growled.

"Let's go." Cle-Anne gripped Ishaan's arm and both disappeared.

Nyarr employed power to uncover the shifter cages. I didn't like what I saw when he did. They'd all been given compulsion to sleep, all were in their animal form, and all of them already had the tags on their necks to prevent them from changing back to human.

"Can you get those things off?" I turned to Nyarr, who was assessing the situation.

"Yes, but I can't circumvent the compulsion. It's obvious they've been told to sleep during the day, so they won't give the day crew any problems."

"Damn."

"Agreed."

Clare

"We can't go out there," Aaron hissed, pulling me down behind the counter again. Bullets had riddled the door and other windows of the store while we remained on the floor, avoiding flying glass.

"Where did they get bullets?" I demanded. "Nobody has any."

"Somebody does."

"Ya think? Who is it, anyway? Northern gang or the Blackheart bunch?"

"No vamps from either, that's a sure bet, it's still daylight," Aaron said while a fresh spate of bullets hit shelves inside the store, blasting merchandise into pieces that dropped all around us.

"Why are they wasting bullets if they have them?" I asked. "This makes no sense."

That's when we heard the scream—from Shelley, before it was cut off abruptly.

"Oh, no," Aaron dropped his forehead to the floor. I drew in a breath as we heard boots crunch on glass inside the store.

We should have crawled into Aaron's office and barricaded the door, but we didn't. I have no idea why.

"Come out," a rough voice growled. "Maybe we'll let you live if we find you useful."

Yeah—they'd let me live so the could sell me to the Krelk. I'd rather die than suffer that fate.

"Fuck off, you asshole," I leapt from the floor. If he shot me before he figured out what I was, then my worries would be over.

I never expected to see what I did, though, when I came face to face with my would-be murderer.

His eyes widened and he dropped the rifle he carried, before his head toppled from his shoulders.

When he fell face-first onto the glass-littered floor amid a splash of blood, Cle-Anne stood behind him, both blades in her hand. She'd relieved him of his head without him knowing.

More gunshots sounded down the street. "Got anything to protect yourselves?" Cle-Anne demanded.

"His rifle," I jerked my head toward the gun on the floor.

"Good. Grab that and shoot anything you don't recognize. I'll be back." She disappeared like the best magician, and without a subsequent puff of smoke.

"What the hell?" Aaron breathed.

"That's Cle-Anne. She came to help. I got this," I swung the rifle into my arms. "I was a pretty good shot while I was in the army."

"I have a pipe wrench in my office," Aaron said.

"Get it. We need everything we have, I think."

While he was gone, I checked the magazine on the rifle; it was still half-full. I also checked the dead man's clothes and found another magazine in a side pocket of his trousers.

"Good enough." I shoved the extra magazine into my jeans pocket, looked both ways before leaving the store and headed for the eastern edge of town, where gunshots were still going off.

Rajeon

"These are outlawed just about everywhere, including non-Alliance worlds," Nyarr waved a hand to destroy the tags he'd removed from shifter necks. Sanjay was one of the sleeping werewolves, I think, but I couldn't say for sure until he turned back.

Ishaan would know by scent. I wondered how things were going with him, Cle-Anne and the missing minions.

Nyarr frowned; it took a moment to realize he was receiving mindspeech from Cle-Anne.

"The minions attacked the town—with guns," Nyarr said, anger in his voice. "Cle-Anne and Ishaan have taken down most of them, but there have been casualties."

"Fornication," I hissed. "Get us there. Quick." Clare was in town. If she'd been hurt, I might take both gangs apart myself, and be damned with the Krelk.

Nyarr had enough sense to bring the sleeping shifters with us; he set all of us down near the hardware store, which had been demolished by gunfire. My heart, nearly beating out of my chest, raced far faster than I did as I ran toward the store. I was praying the whole time to anyone listening that Clare was alive.

I found a dead minion just inside the door; Cle-Anne had removed his head, which lay nearby. Blood was everywhere; I had no idea whether all of it was his.

"Clare," I shouted. "Clare!"

"Keep your shirt on, we're okay." Clare, her boots crunching on broken glass, stepped into the store, followed by Aaron and Cle-Anne. Clare had a rifle slung over her shoulder, military-style.

I didn't waste time. I walked straight toward her, crushed her against me and kissed her.

Hard.

"I missed you, too," she said, sounding breathless when I let her go.

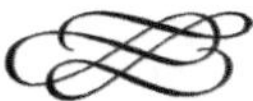

CHAPTER 6

*C*lare

"Sixteen people, dead," Rajeon argued with John and Mayor Stephens. "That includes the Judge, by your own admission. We need to evacuate before the vamps rise tonight."

He didn't add that John had been hiding out in the Mayor's cellar, with the Mayor and a couple of others.

"We don't have time," John waved his hand.

"Look, you can choose your life, or your property. I have five empty houseboats on the river, waiting to take people elsewhere. Tell everybody to bring what food they have and get onboard. I'd rather take my chances on the river than here in town."

"We have the rifles from the dead attackers," John countered. "Eleven of them, with extra bullets."

"There's something my great-aunt says," Cle-Anne ventured into the argument between Rajeon and the Sheriff.

"What's that?" Yes, John was as polite as he could be; without Cle-Anne and Ishaan's help, those guns wouldn't have been captured and a lot more people would be dead. Some shifters would be poached, too, if they survived the attack.

"My great-aunt says *never take a gun to a vampire fight*," Cle-Anne shrugged at John. "Bullets only piss vampires off. You'd be better off firing wooden stakes with a crossbow."

"Look, stay if you want," Rajeon said. "Just give your townspeople the option of staying or going."

"Fine. You tell them what they'll face if they leave, and that includes being outcasts in the zone and facing starvation because of it."

"There are plenty of fish in the river," I said. "Some of us can forage on land without raising too many eyebrows."

"Fine. It'll be nightfall in three hours. Tell everybody you want. I doubt you'll get much cooperation," John flung out a hand.

We'd held our meeting in the Mayor's office; a small building that also served as the town court. *Which no longer had a judge.*

"All right. We'll go knock on doors," Rajeon unfolded long legs and slid off the chair he'd been sitting on.

Somehow, he and Nyarr had already delivered sleeping shifters from the gang camp to the houseboats; he'd said they'd probably wake come nightfall. That was after he'd kissed me. Several times.

Rajeon also thought one of the werewolves was Sanjay, but he couldn't say for sure until Ishaan identified his wolf, or he woke and changed.

I worried about Jessie, too. I wanted him to come with us, and that meant waiting until nightfall, when he'd wake.

We'd listened to John's bluster about digging up vamps in the daytime; I worried he wouldn't live past dawn tomorrow morning, or, failing that, could find himself under a vamp's compulsion and forced to work for them.

"Let's go. We have plenty to do," Rajeon said, walking toward the door. We weren't expecting to see most of the townspeople outside, waiting on the outcome of the meeting.

Rajeon's footsteps creaked on the wooden riser as he stepped off the Mayor's porch. "I suppose you're all wondering what's going on," John called out from behind us. "I think we should stay put and defend ourselves until tomorrow, when we have plans to find where the vampires are buried and dig them up. We've already eliminated their minions, today," he added. "We lost some of ours, that's true, but we took down their gang and now have their guns."

"What the Sheriff isn't telling you," I stepped forward to stand beside Rajeon, "Is that the people who took down the attackers are going with us to the river. We know what's coming; the vamps will want revenge for killing their human and shifter slaves. They'll hit this place like a storm. It's up to you whether you want to stay here with John or follow us to the river. All we're trying to do is save lives."

"How soon do we have to decide?" someone asked.

"Now," Rajeon said. "At nightfall, we pull the boats into the river. Be there before then or be left behind."

Rajeon walked through the crowd, who parted to let us through. The rest of us followed in his wake. Deputy Dan stepped off the Mayor's porch and followed Ishaan, who'd taken up the last place in line.

"I'll fire you if you go," John shouted after him.

"Don't bother. I quit," Dan yelled over his shoulder.

By the time we reached the river, Barbara and Jeffie had joined us. At least she knew what we were facing and was willing to leave her tilled land behind in favor of saving her and Jeffie's lives.

"I've been busy," Mom said, when Rajeon, Ishaan and I stepped aboard the houseboat.

"You sure have," I breathed.

Every open space she could find now held pots of tomato plants, and three larger planters held potatoes. "It's all I could handle today," Mom said.

"You did well," Rajeon smiled at her.

"Any more comin'?"

"I don't know. If they do, they have to be here before nightfall. I hope Jessie knows to catch up to us; we can get him aboard when he reaches the shore."

"Where will he sleep?" Mom asked. "It has to be light-proof."

"I think there's a big cooler on one of these houseboats," Rajeon said. "If Nyarr turns his mind to it, he can make sure its light-proof and spelled against anybody opening it except Jessie."

"He can do that?"

"I believe he can."

"He's as handy as a pocket on a shirt, isn't he?"

"I'd say so. Is that dinner I smell?"

"I'm cooking fish chowder. I found some rice in your kitchen, so I went to work with the fish and crawfish in your cold-box."

"How many can you feed?"

"Well, if we feed everybody that's here, now, I'll need more fish and crawfish."

"I'll see you get it. Nyarr," Rajeon called out.

"You need something? Is that gumbo I smell?" Nyarr was already on the scent of food.

"We need more fish and crawfish to feed everybody. Can you and Cle-Anne help with that?"

"I can get fish," I offered. "If they can get crawfish."

"What are you waitin' for?" Mom shooed me toward our cabin. I'd have to change to get fish, but it would be simple, once I was in the water.

Rajeon

"She can handle a gun," Doreen said, while examining the rifle Clare had stolen from a dead minion. "She was in the military. Worked as military police on the base. That's how she paid for college —with military benefits."

"She took out four of those assholes," Cle-Anne appeared with a large bowl full of crawfish. "Nyarr says he can get these shelled for you after they're cooked, if you want."

"I'd take the help," Doreen agreed.

We'd already gotten four fish from Clare's efforts. Nice-sized ones, too. Doreen asked her for six, so she was looking for two more.

Her otter was more than cute, but I didn't know whether I should say that. So far, too, nobody had come to join us on the river. I wondered why that was.

"John's probably brainwashing the people left in town," Ishaan stepped aboard from the boat just north of mine. He and Dan had taken it, then went to work bringing three sleeping werewolves onto it. "Sanjay's out. I hope he has his mind left when he wakes."

"At least it's Sanjay," I said. "Glad to hear it, by the way. Clare will welcome that news."

"The older deputy isn't one of the captives," Dan followed Ishaan on board. "Killed in the line of duty. Dumped in the river afterward, most likely. I told Barbara and Jeffie that dinner was cooking. They'll be here after they settle in."

They'd taken the boat on the other side of the werewolf boat.

"I think it's a good idea to string the boats together," I said. "Yours and the other five we brought in don't have power. Nyarr's and my boat have solar power. If we hook up those two on either end, we'll have rudder and steering, no matter which direction we want to go."

"That sounds logical," Clare was back and dressed, with damp hair. She handed three more fish to her mother.

"Why didn't I know you could shoot a rifle?" I grinned at her.

"You didn't ask."

"Can you shoot a pistol, too?"

"I've trained to use a pistol. Why do you ask?"

"No reason." I couldn't help grinning at her anyway.

"I'll clean the fish," Dan offered. Doreen handed the latest fish to Dan before dipping steaming hot crawfish from the boiling pot and dumping them on the table. "Go find your magician," she told me. "It's time to shell crawfish."

"He's a warlock," I patted Doreen's back. "You may as well know. Calling him a magician is like calling a dragon an oversized gecko."

"I didn't know there were warlocks here," I heard Doreen whisper to Clare as I walked away to find our magician.

Clare

"I thought some of them would come. I was hoping Aaron and

Julie would come; the store was destroyed in the attack, so there's no real reason for them to stay," I said as the sun lay low on the horizon. Light filtered through the trees lining the western bank of the Mississippi, while evening insects began to venture out.

"We can't make up their minds for them. We offered safety. We can't make them accept it," Rajeon's hands dropped onto my shoulders.

"They could die," I whispered.

"I worry about that, too. If the vamps show up, and I think they will, the bullets will run out fast enough."

"I know." I brushed moisture from my cheeks as I watched the sun drop below our line of vision on the bank.

"Time to pull anchor," Nyarr was suddenly beside us. "I'll connect all the boats once we get farther out."

"Do it," Rajeon said. "Jessie will find us if he wants to come."

"Clare?"

I recognized that voice. Sanjay was awake.

"Sanjay?" I turned toward the boat next to ours as we began pulling away from the shore. "Are you all right?"

"I hope so. I hope they only commanded us to sleep during the day. I don't feel anything else," he called out.

"We'll talk when we get away," I said softly. I knew he'd hear me.

"Yes. I need to hear what happened after they caught me."

"I need to ask you about that, too," Rajeon said.

I turned my eyes back toward the bank; I could see well enough at night to notice the movement.

"Jessie's on the bank," I gripped Rajeon's hand.

"I'll bring him in," Nyarr said. Seconds later, a worried Jessie was deposited on Rajeon's deck.

Rajeon

The night was a busy one. Nyarr lined up the houseboats in order, with mine leading southward and Nyarr's at the rear. Everything else was connected in between, with a gangway of sorts between boats to get back and forth.

"We may have enough space to make one boat a kitchen and dining vessel," Cle-Anne pointed out.

"We should table that for now," I said. "It's a great idea," I held up a hand, "but we don't know what kind of space we'll need in the long term."

"I wish we had the equipment to put solar panels on all the boats," Nyarr said. "I can't make something from nothing; I need raw materials, at least. You could hook them up, though, if we had them."

"I know. You have no idea how many times I wanted to put up an aqueduct or a windmill system to pump water into the town," I said. "But I needed pipe and tools, and I didn't have either."

"It's moot, if the vamps show up tonight," Cle-Anne snorted gently.

"I know." I was glad Clare and Doreen had gone to bed earlier—it was long after midnight, and we still hadn't had a conversation with Sanjay and the others. At least Dan and Ishaan had taken the job of reassuring the shifters who were strangers; it terrified them that they'd been asleep while we moved them.

I understood; not being able to wake during the day would frighten anyone except a vampire.

"I'll need to feed," Jessie stepped onboard and came to sit beside us.

"I know. We're working on that, all right?"

"I sent a message to Aunt Zaria. I hope she can help," Cle-Anne said.

"I hope she can help, too." A few cases of blood substitute would more than make me happy and keep Jessie from having to feed from the rest of us.

"Did you feed tonight?" I asked.

"I got enough," Jessie said. "I smell smoke," he added.

"Me, too." I stood, sniffing the wind, which was coming from the northwest.

"They're burning the town," Nyarr said after his eyes lost focus for several seconds.

"May the Lord be merciful," Jessie breathed.

"Take me," I stood immediately and nodded to Nyarr.

"I'll come," Cle-Anne *Pulled* in her blades.

"Take me, too," Jessie said. "That's my town."

Nyarr transported us to Fairlawn Point—or what was left of it.

For a moment, I thought everything was on fire, the flames were so high. Only a few buildings were left untouched; I scented no life, the smoke was so thick. Nyarr wasn't relying on his sense of smell; he was performing a swift, scrying spell for any life remaining in the small town.

"The cellar," he shouted at me, as intense heat and fire-whipped winds blew around us.

"What about the vamps?" Cle-Anne shouted to make herself heard above the roaring fire.

"Gone already," Nyarr shouted back. "They left most of the dead inside those burning buildings."

"Damn and tarnation," Jessie said. "Let's go to the cellar and see who's there." I got the idea that if he found Sheriff John hiding below ground, he wouldn't feel charitable toward the man.

"I'll put up a bubble shield," Nyarr said above the roar of flames and collapsing structures. Once the shield was in place, it was like a haven in the middle of the maelstrom.

"That's different," Jessie looked about us; we were inside a soundproofed bubble; the noise, smoke and fire had been left outside it.

"Let's go see who's left," Nyarr didn't sound pleased. He and I expected to find the Sheriff and the Mayor holed up there, just as they'd done earlier in the day.

We weren't wrong. John and Mayor Stephens stepped out once Nyarr forced the inside lock to open with power.

Behind those two, however, were Paul, Aaron and Aaron's wife, Julie.

Five survivors out of sixty-seven.

The town should have followed us to the river, and I think the Sheriff knew that when I cast an accusing glare in his direction. I thought about telling him and the Mayor to make their own way; that I was done with them.

I didn't.

"Are you ready to go, now?" I asked them.

"Yeah." At least John had the good sense to hang his head.

Clare

Mom and I got out of bed after Rajeon brought the only survivors of Fairlawn Point to our small, floating town before daybreak. We put something together for them to eat, then allowed Julie and Aaron to clean up in our shower.

I loaned Julie some clothes; Nyarr came up with something for Aaron and the other men.

"I haven't had hot water from a shower in years," Julie sighed as she sipped the tea Rajeon made for her and the others.

"Solar power," Rajeon told her gently. "I wish I had the panels and equipment for the other boats. I'd make all of them solar-powered."

"You know how?" Aaron stared at Rajeon.

"I was an engineer," he shrugged. "I can put almost anything together, if I have the proper components."

John and the Mayor sat in silence at Rajeon's table, drinking their tea. I hoped guilt nagged at them, but I wasn't a mind reader. In my opinion, they were responsible for the deaths of a lot of people. I wanted to ask John if he still wanted to look for vamps to dig up, but that would just be nasty on my part. Mom raised me better than that.

Jessie was so mad at both of them, he'd gone to talk to the werewolves while Nyarr set about spelling the large cooler on the last boat. He said he'd make it tamper-proof, light-proof and water-tight, too, in case the cooler got dumped in the river during daylight.

Jessie would be safe from harm, no matter what.

"There are two bedrooms on the next-to-last boat," Rajeon told the sheriff and Mayor. "Paul, if you wouldn't mind staying there with them; one of the bedrooms has two beds in it, the other only has one. Aaron, you and your wife can stay on Barbara's boat with her and Jeffie."

"Be happy to," Aaron nodded. "Thank you for coming back for us," he added.

"You're welcome."

John and the Mayor exchanged glances but didn't say anything. Rajeon should have dumped both of them in the water right then, for their lack of gratitude. He didn't. I guess his mother raised him better than that, too.

"Clare, can I talk to you for a minute?" Rajeon asked.

"Sure." I rose from my chair and followed him toward the back of the boat.

"Sweetheart, Nyarr, Cle-Anne, Ishaan and I need sleep. Can you take charge while that happens? We'll be up by late afternoon at the latest, but if anybody gets out of hand while we're asleep, shoot 'em with your rifle, all right?"

"You don't mean that," I huffed.

"I do. John and the Mayor may have witchcraft on their minds ever since Nyarr got them to the boats like he did. If either make a wrong move or suggest anything other than enjoying the scenery, well, you take care of it."

"I'll take care of it," I agreed. If Nyarr hadn't helped us out, even more people would be dead. We didn't need to argue amongst ourselves. If they thought they were in charge, I'd dump them in the river myself, and told Rajeon as much.

"Good thinking." he leaned in to kiss me, then took one of my hands and kissed it, too. "Been a long day and a longer night, baby, and I need some sleep. Help yourself to anything in the kitchen, and we'll take stock of the situation when I wake up."

"All right. Sleep well. I'll go find my rifle and stand watch."

"You do that." He chuckled before walking into his cabin and shutting the door behind him.

At least John and Raymond, former sheriff and mayor of Fairlawn Point, kept to themselves on the boat until it was time for lunch. Mom, Barbara and I fried catfish we'd caught while floating the river.

All the shifters had fallen asleep at daybreak, willingly or not, so we didn't have to worry about feeding them during the day. They'd wake hungry, though, come nightfall, and we needed something to feed them when that happened.

Two things happened roughly three hours after lunch; Rajeon came out of his cabin, as did Nyarr and Cle-Anne. Ishaan and Dan were already awake and discussing how to feed all of us.

That's when we rounded a bend in the river to find four houseboats sitting there. They had to be anchored, or they'd be floating downriver, like we were.

"Thank you, Zaria," Cle-Anne came aboard our boat and waited for Rajeon to stop the boats and drop anchor.

"How do you know?" I began.

"She told me." She disappeared from our deck and reappeared on the deck of the closest houseboat.

"We can attach those four to our center boats," Nyarr suggested to Rajeon, who nodded his agreement. "It won't be any different from driving a barge down the river."

"Let's get to work. I hope she sent supplies," Rajeon said.

"If I know her, she sent anything we might need now and in the near future," Nyarr replied.

At that moment, I wondered who Zaria was, how she'd known where and when to find us, and what we'd need when we came across the gift she left us.

"Come on, let's go see what we have," Rajeon grabbed my arm before Nyarr transported us to the boat Cle-Anne was on.

Rajeon

"I don't believe this." Clare blinked at the houseboat that was all kitchen inside it. Everything was solar-powered, and an industrial-sized refrigerator and freezer were fully-stocked, as was the pantry.

Another boat held nothing but showers, a laundry room and a lounge with tables and comfortable chairs. The third boat was all cabins, with stacked bunks in each. The last one held a big dining room on one end, with a large, furnished cabin on the other.

Loaded on the deck of that boat were solar panels and a metal chest filled with tools. I'd wanted to add solar power to the other boats; Zaria had read my mind.

"The kitchen and dining room need to go on the same side," Nyarr said. "The cabins and laundry boats can go on the other side."

"This will give us enough room for the shifters, and still have some left over," I agreed. "They're asleep all over the deck of their boat right now, because the cabins weren't big enough to cover all of them."

"Let's get started, then. The new boats are solar-powered, and we can use their engines to get us back up the river if necessary."

"I was thinking the same thing," Cle-Anne said.

"Now that we don't have to forage for food for a little while," Clare walked up to me, "maybe we can rescue the shifters the Blackhearts took."

"Maybe," I told her. "We have to plan it carefully, though. We don't need more people dying because those vamps want revenge."

"I know."

"Come on, let's get this floating city put together," I said. "Then you and your mother can go through the kitchen and decide what we'll have for supper. I'll even help cook."

"Mom will kiss you for that," Clare grinned. That smile was worth everything I ever owned.

"I'll make us invisible afterward," Nyarr promised. "Nobody will see us unless we want them to."

"Mom was right—you are as handy as a pocket on a shirt," Clare told him. Nyarr laughed.

Clare

"We have a bear shifter, two wild boars, a horse and three gator shifters, in addition to the two extra werewolves," Ishaan sighed as he seated himself at the small table in the new kitchen boat. "We just got them into their new quarters. We found a closet full of clothes, so they're washing up and getting dressed."

"Want coffee? We have the real thing," Mom offered.

"Yeah. That sounds wonderful," he said. "Is that chicken I smell?"

"We're having chicken and dressing for dinner," Mom said, setting a cup of hot coffee in front of Ishaan. "How's Sanjay?"

"Sanjay's fine; he's just grumpy about sleeping during the day."

The sun had set minutes earlier, and that meant Jessie would probably be out and about shortly. The new shifters had also awakened. "Food should be ready when they're done cleaning up," I said.

"Good. I think we're all about to cave in."

"We need to assign duties while we're on the river—everybody needs to pull their weight," Rajeon walked in, followed by Nyarr and Cle-Anne. "That can be cleaning, laundry, dishes, cooking, whatever. Wait," he tapped the front pocket of his jeans. "I'll be back."

I watched him walk out of the kitchen swiftly, wondering what it was he'd suddenly remembered.

Rajeon

"Forneel?" I tapped the communicator.

"It's not Forneel," his assistant, Ginter, answered. "We ah, don't know where Forneel is, or the landing party he took with him."

"What?" I stared at Ginter in alarm. "What the hell is he doing, coming to the surface?"

"He—thought he found evidence of Je'Dik, so he went after him."

"Without telling me?"

"He wants the bounty for himself," Ginter lowered his eyes. I cursed. "We lost communication with him last night. He said not to tell you that he was on the surface, too."

"What kind of weapons did he bring?" I snapped.

"Laser pistols," Ginter winced as I cursed again.

"So. Forneel and how many others are missing?"

"Five."

"And they were all armed with laser pistols, which may or may not be in the hands of the enemy, right now?"

"Yes." Ginter's face flushed and he refused to meet my gaze.

"Well, Ginter, I may have information that should have gone to Forneel, were he where he was supposed to be rather than chasing after a bounty on the surface, which is not in his job description, by the way."

"What information?"

"I think Sirenali bone dust has found its way here, that's what. I'm working on that angle for now, to make sure before we go higher up the chain with this. Can you get a lock on Forneel anywhere?"

"We've had no sign of any of them, once Forneel's communicators stopped sending a signal."

"We don't know if they're dead or alive, then."

"Yes. I'm sorry this is complicating the entire mission, and I should have told you sooner," Ginter looked as if he were about to burst into tears.

"Tell me this, did Bender go with him?"

Ginter hung his head again. Bender was second-in-command and should never have left the ship. "Who the hell is in charge, now?" I demanded.

"That would be uh, Mirlund."

If Forneel were alive and in front of me at the moment, I'd have choked him to death. He'd taken his second and third-in-command to the surface with him, violating every rule and protocol he was supposed to uphold to do it. Mirlund was fourth-in-command. At least she was reasonable. The other three obviously weren't.

"Does she know she's now in command?"

"I called you first," Ginter squeaked.

"Call her. Now. The three of us need to have a talk, and then I need to know where Forneel and the others set down. I can go from there and try to track him."

I waited for several minutes while Ginter placed an emergency call to Mirlund, who was undoubtedly at the opposite end of the ship.

When she arrived and saw my face on Ginter's screen, she knew something was wrong. "Tell her, Ginter," I ordered. "Tell her where Forneel and the others went, and then explain why she's now in charge of the ship."

I outranked both of them and they knew it. For the record, I was now in charge of the entire operation, and I had to find the whereabouts of six idiots.

Dead or alive.

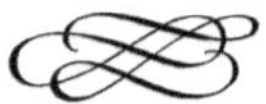

CHAPTER 7

*C*lare

The alligator shifters were brothers, and they'd been caught on the last full moon. The bear, the boars and the others told the same story—all of them were caught on the last full moon.

That meant the Northern gang was handing off shifters once a month to the Krelk. The Blackhearts likely had a similar schedule.

Rajeon came back, then, sitting heavily on the chair beside mine.

"I left your plate in the oven, so it would be warm," I told him and rose to retrieve it. Rajeon had a set look to his face, as if he'd gotten bad news or something.

"Thanks," he sighed when I set the plate down. He lifted his fork and began to eat. Sanjay and Ishaan sat on the opposite side of the table; they'd finished their meal, as had I. "Did you ever see the vamps using any kind of communicator?" I asked Sanjay. "They have to have some way to contact the Krelk."

"I think they had something, but I never saw it," Sanjay said. "I only heard it going off once in a while. The vamp in charge of our cages—everybody called him Tark. He'd leave the area at a run whenever that thing jingled. Probably so we wouldn't hear anything after that."

"Tark, eh?" Rajeon stopped eating for a moment.

"Heard of him?" Ishaan asked.

"No. Figure it's a nickname, like Blackheart." Rajeon went back to his food.

"Will you recognize his scent—or any of the others?" I asked.

"Yeah. I won't forget that in a hurry. He killed Frank and laughed, because Frank was too old to mess with."

"Did you see any Krelk while you were held?" Rajeon stopped eating again.

"No, but that wouldn't mean anything; we were dead to the world during the day, and kept in covered cages most of the time, too."

"Did you ever hear when they planned to sell their captives?"

"I never heard them say anything about that."

"They may not have known," I laid my hand on Rajeon's arm. "Tark may have been the only one to know until the actual time arrived."

"The less people know, the less they can spill," Ishaan nodded.

"Ishaan, I need to talk to you, Dan and Jessie after a bit," Rajeon said. "We need to do some reconnaissance."

"Any time you're ready," Ishaan said and scooted his chair back. "I'll let Jessie know."

"I'd like you to hear what I have to say, too," Rajeon patted my hand, which still rested on his arm.

"What do you want me to do?" Sanjay asked.

"This is going to sound strange," Rajeon told him, "but I don't trust John or Raymond. Keep an eye on them for me whenever you can, all right?"

"Yeah." Sanjay nodded and scooted his chair back. He had words he wanted to say to John, about putting him and Frank in the line of trouble without a second thought. Sanjay's mother raised him right, too, though, so I figured Sanjay would keep those words behind his teeth.

"I know how you feel, Sanjay," Rajeon said softly. "Don't let it ruin a good meal."

"It was very good," Sanjay turned back to tell me. "I sure haven't had anything that good in years. Thank you for coming for me—and the others," he nodded to Rajeon.

"You're welcome," Rajeon replied.

Rajeon

"I have it on good authority that heavy rain is coming this way," I began. Clare, Jessie, Ishaan, Dan, Nyarr and Cle-Anne were all aboard Nyarr's boat, inside the galley. I'd asked Nyarr to put up a sound-proof shield so we wouldn't be heard.

"How heavy?" Ishaan asked.

"Several storm systems, lined up one after another. We could be facing some flooding on the river. The boats can handle it, but anybody still living near the river may get washed out. The other thing is this; I'm not from Earth."

"Huh?" Clare's eyes went round. I was worried most about her reaction, although the others in the room I also was concerned about.

"You know the Krelk are from somewhere else." I said those words flatly. "Actually, the Krelk have overpopulated their own world and at least eleven others. Earth is the twelfth one they've taken for themselves, when they had no right to any part of it. Now, since you understand the Krelk are from somewhere else, there are many others from elsewhere, too—who aren't Krelk."

"Where are you from, then, and why are you here?" Clare asked, crossing arms over her chest. I wanted to wince at the gesture; I didn't.

"I'm from Revalus. Nyarr is originally from Karathia, and Cle-Anne was born on a private planet. I'm here as part of a scouting crew sent by the Reth Alliance, to submit information on the takeover of the planet. The Alliance is considering whether it should intervene with the Krelk's thirst for new planets."

"Why haven't they intervened already?" Ishaan asked.

"Because the Krelk are non-Alliance, and every world they've taken so far is also non-Alliance. The Alliances have to determine that the Krelk present a big enough threat to them that they should intervene. They generally don't have anything to do with non-Alliance worlds—you have to understand that."

"Not our problem, in other words," Clare said. She wouldn't meet my eyes, and I worried about damaging our relationship past the point of no return.

"Had the Krelk not taken over, would you want somebody else coming in to do just that? Earth had a lot of rules and regulations, and a bunch of individual countries, all who saw things differently. If you belong to one of the Alliances, the rules are generally uniform across the planet."

"So we weren't a good candidate," Clare lifted an eyebrow. People always felt insulted when they heard their planet wasn't acceptable to the Alliances.

"You'd need better cohesion, that's true," I agreed. "You'd also need to invest in a space port, funded by the entire planet. Tell me that was possible."

"It wasn't." Clare ducked her head.

"Besides the weather comin' in, what else did you need us to do?" Jessie asked.

"I'm glad you asked," I told him. "It seems that the commander of the scout ship has gone AWOL on the surface and took five others with him. The ship lost communication with him last night. Now that could mean one of three things. They're either dead, captured, or they're no longer on the planet. I don't know which is the truth. I do know where they set down, though. We need to try to track them before the rain gets here and wipes away their scent. If they're dead, we have to find who killed them and stole their communicators and their weapons."

"What weapons?" Cle-Anne asked.

"Laser pistols is what I was told. I wouldn't put it past Forneel to conceal a ranos pistol on him, somewhere. If he did, then we better pray it was touch activated."

"Touch activated?" Ishaan frowned.

"It means it will only work for Forneel. It requires his DNA to operate."

"Somebody is way, way ahead of us Earthlings," Clare muttered.

"If it wasn't touch activated, and some of the older models aren't, then we would be in big trouble," I went on. "Those things are solar-powered and don't need bullets of any kind. You can blast a house apart with three, well-aimed shots."

"Where did they set down?" Nyarr asked.

"I have the coordinates. It wasn't far from the Blackhearts, unless I miss my guess."

Clare

"I'll give you the option of coming with us," Rajeon told me as he threw on a leather vest minutes later.

"You said yourself to never take a gun to a vampire fight," I pointed out. "Although I really want to go." I still wasn't sure how I felt about him being an alien, but I tabled that for the moment.

"I have a laser pistol," he said. "It's touch activated, but I can program it to work for you, too. That means only you or I can use the thing. Anybody else will get a nasty surprise if they try."

"Will a laser pistol kill a vamp?"

"This one will," he took my face in his hands and leaned in to kiss my forehead. "A ranos pistol will blow a vamp to bits, but this laser pistol will put a nice hole in his head or his heart. Cle-Anne says you're a really good shot. I'll have my own method of protection, but just in case you see anybody threatening me, you have my permission to shoot their ass off."

"All right."

"After we do this and find out what we can tonight, we'll talk if you want to. Okay?"

"Yeah. I have questions."

"I bet you do. Let's get the pistol calibrated for you to use and we'll go."

Rajeon

Nyarr landed us far south of our position on the river. He could scry coordinates, and I appreciated that. Dan and Ishaan had turned to wolf before we left; it was easier to sniff the ground that way.

Far to the west, I saw lightning. Ginter was right about the weather coming in, and it could be severe, according to the weather-bot aboard the ship. Flooding and tornadoes possible, it said. The area was prone to both.

Ishaan yipped, telling us he'd found something. Dan was right beside Ishaan, gathering the scent. Jessie walked in their direction and nodded. Clare and I followed, keeping eyes and ears open for any sign of watchers and enemies.

We traveled into a wooded area, and I could smell the river nearby. That's where the trail was leading us. Silently I cursed Forneel as I kept my footsteps light on the ground; no need to alert the Blackhearts to our presence earlier than necessary.

Following behind me were Nyarr and Cle-Anne. They'd handle anything that came on us from behind. I'd be forced to act quickly if Ishaan, Jessie and Dan were threatened.

Clare had good military training; she strode silently through the trees, her hand on the pistol in its holster. Somewhere, not far away, an owl hooted.

I hoped it wasn't a signal of some kind.

All of us froze when the shadow passed between us and the river.

Vampire, Cle-Anne informed me. At least it had no bone dust to hide from her *Looking* skills. That didn't prevent any friends he might bring with him from having some, however.

A fish leapt and splashed in the river, making all of us jump. Clare carefully drew the pistol from its holster. Before Nyarr could toss up a perimeter shield, three vampires attacked us at once. Dan went down with a yelp and didn't get up. Moving swiftly, Cle-Anne sliced the head off the vamp who'd attacked Dan while Clare fired her pistol at another, hitting him in the head and blasting his skull apart.

The last vampire was torn apart by my thorns.

"Scouting party," Jessie breathed as he kicked through vampire ash afterward. He was carefully skirting what I'd become. Not many could survive a whirling vine of diamond thorns. It was a special trick I'd developed early on, and one of the reasons I'd been asked to join this mission; I could slice through Krelk armor plates like a hot knife through butter.

"What about Dan?" Clare struggled to keep her voice even. He'd died quickly when the vamps attacked.

"Grave or river?" Jessie asked.

"I can send him back to Fairlawn Point," Nyarr offered. "He can rest there with the others."

"I think he'd appreciate that," Jessie sighed. Ishaan, still in wolf form, yipped his agreement.

"It's done," Nyarr said after Dan's body disappeared. I was angry; we'd lost good help, and it was all because Forneel wanted to bag Je'Dik himself, when he didn't have any business being on the surface.

Thunder sounded in the distance; the storm was getting closer. Once the rain started, we could lose our trail to find Forneel. I nodded to Ishaan to go on, hoping the three vamps we'd killed weren't expected to report in soon.

Once again, we were lined up and traveling through the trees, watchful and a bit more jumpy than we were before.

The first raindrops fell when we came across Forneel's body and those of his party.

What was left of them after animal scavengers had their feast.

Taking my communicator from a vest pocket, I recorded the images to send to Mirlund. "Vampire work?" I asked Jessie and Ishaan.

Ishaan yipped.

"There's Krelk scent here, too," Jessie reported. Ishaan yipped twice, this time.

"Two Krelk?" I blinked at Ishaan's wolf.

Another yip.

If Je'Dik were here, he had a friend with him, and I reported that for Mirlund, too.

"Send the remains if you can," Mirlund's voice sounded amid heavier raindrops.

"Sending coordinates," I reported and tapped my communicator. Moments later, the remains disappeared, along with some of the dirt and detritus they rested on.

Forneel had gotten himself and five officers killed for a stupid bounty. Even I could still smell the amount of blood that had poured out of all of them.

"Ready to go back?" I turned to Nyarr.

He didn't reply; he transported us instead.

Clare

"Rain's coming," I told Mom when I slipped inside our cabin.

"What did you find out there?" Mom asked, watching while I toweled my wet hair.

"Dan was killed by a vamp. Three attacked us out of nowhere, and he went down before we could kill them. Then, we found the six Rajeon was looking for," I went on with a sigh. "Torn apart by vamps, then eaten by scavengers." I wasn't willing to go into detail about the first three vamps we'd killed—or how Rajeon had killed one of them. That would be discussed in the talk he promised me, though.

I shivered as the image of the vampire being ground to bits by sharp, glittering thorns resurfaced.

How could he do that? I didn't mean killing a vampire; I didn't mind that. How did anyone become something that didn't live and breathe? Questions crowded my mind, and one of those was how could we ever fit together, Rajeon and I?

Stories of the fish and bird came to mind. We had a lot to talk about, he and I. The pistol was given back to him the moment we'd landed on the boat. I'd barely said anything before stalking away.

He probably thought I was mad. He was partly right.

I was also scared.

What the hell was he?

Rajeon

"Here." Nyarr set a glass of amber liquid in front of me.

"Bourbon?" I asked.

"Whiskey," he replied. "Drink it. Cle-Anne went to talk to Clare," he added.

"What?"

"Drink that," he nodded toward the glass. "There's more where that came from."

Clare

When someone tapped on the cabin door, I thought it was Rajeon. It was Cle-Anne instead. "Can we talk?" she asked. "In private?"

"Sure," I said, partially relieved that Rajeon wasn't the one asking that question. I followed her to the back of the boat, where a small table and two chairs were placed. "Raje is having a drink with Nyarr on our boat," she said. "So we can talk."

"About what?" I asked, pulling out one of the chairs and sitting.

"About what he is, and why you shouldn't be afraid of him."

"You know what he—it—is?"

"He," she said forcefully, "is a pod'l-morph. Some people say they're the shapeshifter of all shapeshifters. They can become pretty much anything, including a razor-sharp vine of diamond thorns. There aren't a lot of his kind anymore, so he's special. Also, two scouts died before he came here; they didn't have his talents, and it's more than dangerous here, if you haven't noticed."

"I've noticed." My arms were crossed tightly over my chest again. I wasn't sure how to accept any of this news, and the truth was, it disturbed me.

"Do they know how the other two died?"

"Probably like those six we found earlier tonight. I figure that any weapons and communicators with them are now in the hands of the Blackhearts. If those two Krelk who are with them send that information to the Krelk government they've put in place, here, all hell could break loose."

"What are you talking about?"

"Krelk don't like interference. Oh, it's all right for them to do it, but they sure don't want any information on what they're doing to reach the Alliances. That's why they'll turn the weapons they have on this buffer zone, if they find out the Alliance is investigating."

"You're kidding?"

"No. The ones who asked me to come here with Nyarr to help Rajeon, well, they have suspicions about the Krelk. That means we need information and evidence to take back with us, to prove our theory."

"What theory is that?"

"That the Krelk want to keep expanding, until they're ready to take over the Alliances. You know yourself they're almost impossible to kill, and they just keep multiplying and taking over more worlds. Why is that, do you think? They say it's because of their religious beliefs. They're hiding behind that, I think."

I was now hugging myself. Was this true? In the short term, they could focus on killing everybody in the zone. In the long term, they could be aiming for the universe.

"What can we do?" I blew out a trembling breath.

"For now, hope those two Krelk are merely poachers and outside the Krelk law, and that they keep what they found for themselves, instead of handing it to Krelk authorities."

"Right." I shivered in the night air. Above our heads, raindrops began to drum on the houseboat canopy. Then as if a tap had been turned, rain began falling in heavy sheets, followed shortly by thunder and lightning.

"Don't worry, Nyarr has us spelled against lightning strikes," Cle-

Anne sighed. "My friends call me Le. It's easier," she said. "It started out as Le-Le with my parents, but it got shortened later."

"Are you and Nyarr together?" I asked.

"No, although I wouldn't mind if he offered," she smiled. "Rajeon loves you, I think. He's risking his life for you and everybody else in the zone. Don't forget that. Want a glass of wine? We have some on our boat."

"I haven't had wine in years," I confessed.

"Follow me, then. We'll fix you up."

Nyarr and Rajeon were drinking whiskey when Le led me onto their boat.

"Baby?" Rajeon sounded slightly drunk as he stared at me.

"I came to have a glass of wine," I said, taking an empty chair at the table.

"Same here," Le said, opening a refrigerator and pulling out a bottle of white wine. "Clare hasn't had wine in years, so we're about to fix that."

"Really?" Rajeon frowned at me.

"Hardly anybody makes it, it's usually bitter and it costs too much. Beer is more common, but I really don't like it, either."

"Sure you don't want whiskey?" Nyarr smiled slyly at me.

"I'd like some wine, thanks," I told him.

"How rare are pod'l-morphs?" I turned to Rajeon.

He drew back in surprise for a moment. "Hmmph. Rare enough, I guess. Everybody thought we were extinct or nearly so, there for a while. Somebody found a bunch of us, in tree form, standing in a grove. We were liberated, I suppose, from that existence. As a result, here I am."

"Somebody liberated you? What does that mean?" I made a face at Rajeon.

"Zaria did that," Le set a glass of wine in front of me. "She was the one who figured out what happened to the pod'l-morphs and went to rescue them."

"I think I want to meet this Zaria," I said. "Sounds like she knows everything."

"If she doesn't, then she's thinking about it," Nyarr said cryptically.

"Is it true that the Krelk could come in here and kill us all, if they find out the Alliance is investigating them?"

"I wanted to keep that from you, but it's true," Rajeon sighed. "That means we have to track the Blackhearts now, not only to save the shifters they may have, but to take back what they took from Forneel and his bunch. A lot is riding on this, as you may imagine."

"The Alliance doesn't know that Nyarr and I are here to help," Le said, sitting next to Nyarr. "They didn't send us; Zaria did."

"Is Zaria a member of the Alliance?" I asked.

"Larentii belong to themselves," Nyarr said and emptied his glass.

"Larentii?"

"You'd have to see one to believe it," Rajeon said. "Maybe Zaria will introduce herself sometime. She asked me to sign up for this investigation after the first two scouts were killed."

"Does she know about the latest ah, deaths?" I asked.

"She knows," Le nodded. "She wasn't particularly happy about it and called Forneel a difik."

"It means idiot, in High Demon," Rajeon sipped his whiskey.

"High Demon? Did I hear you right?"

"Relax, they're not the kind of demons you're thinking about," Nyarr soothed. Thunder boomed loudly overhead, making me jump. I was hearing too many things about too many aliens, I think, and wondered if I were going to have nightmares when I went to sleep.

"If they meant you harm, you'd be harmed already," Rajeon told me and patted my hand. "You see how you were invaded by the Krelk instead, eh? The High Demons are members of the Reth Alliance. They follow the rules like any other civilized society."

"I've met the Queen, the Prince-Regent and the Crown Princess," Le said. "You'd like them."

"So everybody has space travel, then?"

"They do, but the ones powerful enough can fold space. That's how Le and I get around," Nyarr explained.

"Pod'l-morphs can't fold space," Rajeon said. "Or mindspeak. Nyarr and Le can."

"Well, it sucks to be you, then," I sipped my wine. "I'd settle for grinding rogue vamps into powder with—whatever that was."

"Diamond thorns," Rajeon nodded.

"Right." I hiccupped, then. Le hid a smile. "Can you turn into an otter?"

"If I wanted to, I suppose."

"Wow. It *really* sucks to be you."

"I think that's sarcasm," Nyarr told Rajeon.

"It's definitely sarcasm," Le agreed.

"Take it any way you want," I sipped more wine. I was getting drunk fast, and I knew it.

"The autopilot is going off," Le said, when a series of pings sounded.

"I'll check it," Nyarr rose from his seat.

"I'll come with you," Le told him.

I drank more wine as they disappeared through an inside door.

"We're on autopilot?" The meaning of those words finally soaked into my brain.

"It's reliable and lets us know if there's a bend or a fork coming up, so we can choose which path to take. If we don't give it an answer, it makes the best choice it can, given the data available."

"What data?"

"Depth of the river, whether any sort of blockage is present, other traffic on the river, storm conditions and so on."

"That must be handy."

"It keeps me from having to drive the boat all the time. Mine has it and Nyarr's has it, too. Right now, his boat is steering, but its autopilot is talking to mine and the four new boats at the same time, so they can react together."

"Sucks to be you."

"Would you stop saying that?"

"We've got bad weather south of here; the boats have dropped anchor," Nyarr and Le were back.

"Bad weather?" I hiccupped again.

"Tornado went through. A lot of trees are down. The computers are talking with those aboard the scout ship before moving forward," Le replied. "We don't need to be running into a log jam in the dark."

"They're sensing blockage?" I frowned at Le.

"Yes. We're stopped in the safest part of the river for now. If bad weather comes our way, we'll get another signal. We may have to move northward; the worst of the weather system is coming from the south right now."

"Spring on the Mississippi," I said and emptied my glass. "Warm air from the gulf, cold air from the north. Mix well and you have a tornado."

"Why are we stopped?" Ishaan poked his head inside the galley door.

"Bad weather down south," Rajeon responded. "We may have to backtrack to get out of the way."

"I'll let the others know," Ishaan said and loped away. As if to punctuate the weather situation, more thunder rumbled overhead.

"Rain will wash away the vamp ash," Nyarr said, taking his seat again and pouring himself another shot of whiskey. "I got rid of the clothes, at least. Unless the Blackhearts were in a hurry to look, they may be wondering what happened to their scouts."

"To confusing Robert L. Williams," Rajeon raised his glass. Nyarr clinked his against Rajeon's.

"Robert L. Williams? Who's that?"

"Blackheart Bob," Rajeon shrugged, as if I should have known it already.

I went still. "The confederate bushwhacker?" I squeaked.

"That would be the one. Ask Jessie how bad Blackheart was—and still is. They came from the same era."

"Jessie was a?" I couldn't bring myself to say the word.

"Yep. He says becoming vampire freed him in more ways than one, although he still misses good cooking."

"Wow. Poor Jessie."

"Here." Le poured more wine for me. "You probably need this."

I sniffled and accepted the glass. "Don't let this upset you; Jessie counts you and your mother among his true friends," Rajeon scooted closer and put an arm around me.

"I'm sorry," I sobbed and hiccupped against Rajeon's shoulder. "I just didn't know how awful things really were."

"It's a lot to take in, baby," Rajeon rubbed my back. "Come on, I'll take you to your cabin."

We were almost halfway through the convoy to reach my cabin on the opposite end of our floating town when the boats came to life, anchor lines whined as anchors were swiftly pulled up and the convoy began pushing northward at top speed.

The winds picked up at the same time; even in my inebriated state I understood what was happening. Autopilot was taking us out of the path of a tornado.

"Come on, baby, we have to hurry."

Everyone else on the decks was now scurrying for cover—rain was lashing us as we ran for Rajeon's boat, now at the end of our convoy, rather than the beginning.

"Come on," Rajeon's arms clamped about me and suddenly grew—tentacles. Like an octopus or giant squid, he held onto me while wrapping multiple arms around this boat or that, forcing his way through the maw of the vicious wind to reach the last boat.

On the shore southward, I saw trees being uprooted and spun around before splashing into the river behind us. We were almost to the cabin when the hail started, and it wasn't small.

Rajeon's tentacle that held me widened to protect me from those blows, but he was taking a beating from the hailstones, some of which were larger than my fist.

Lightning came, striking the river behind us and illuminating the monster tornado that followed in our wake.

If I screamed, the sound was swallowed by the roar of the storm. Debris, in the form of trees, branches and anything else the tornado could lift into its whirling vortex was aimed at us.

Rajeon pulled in the tentacle holding me, before turning into something I didn't think possible.

Granite.

I was encased in granite, with only a small amount of space open for me to breath. I couldn't move; my cave was Clare-shaped, tight and unyielding.

*Was Mom safe? What about the others? Why didn't Nyarr—*suddenly we were moving on calm waters and the noise was shut off like a faucet. Thunder rumbled far in the distance. Rajeon pulled me into his arms and squeezed me so tight I worried I'd suffocate.

"Nyarr says we're north of St. Louis," Rajeon whispered against my ear. "The weather is now far to the south. You okay?"

"I may have peed my pants," I mumbled.

"I may have inked while octopus."

"I guess we both need to clean up, then."

"I reckon we do." He leaned down to kiss me. I could taste the flavor of the whiskey on his tongue. It wasn't bad.

"Storm systems north and south of us. I had to figure out where to set us down between them before moving us," Nyarr explained at breakfast the following morning. "The tornado came up fast and we didn't have much time."

"Then you're forgiven for scaring the crap out of us," Mom shook her head at him before setting a plate of food down.

Rajeon was still out checking the boats for hail damage and assessing the five boats without power, to determine the best way to install the solar panels. Ishaan and Paul were helping him.

"That was some weather we had last night," John said when he and Ray stepped into the dining room.

"There's more expected tonight," Mom said. "Food's on the counter; help yourselves."

She'd wait on Nyarr; he'd saved us last night. She wouldn't waste effort on John or Ray; they hid in the cabin the whole time, and only showed up at mealtimes so far.

I wondered whether Rajeon had considered giving them their boat and cutting them loose. *They'd be dead in a day*, my conscience reminded me.

"We'll do the breakfast dishes," Julie offered when she and Aaron wandered in.

"I'd appreciate that," Mom told her. "I'm going to bake yeast rolls for supper, so I need to set the dough to rise."

"Hey, Jeffie," I said when he and Barbara came in. "We have pancakes," I told him.

"With syrup?" he asked, his eyes widening with hope.

"You bet. Come on, I'll help you with your plate, so your mom can fix hers."

"I saw Rajeon crawling on top of the boats," he said as we put pancakes on a plate, with two link sausages.

"He's checking hail damage and looking for places to mount solar panels. If you're good, he may do your boat first."

"What will solar panels do?"

"Well, for one thing, it'll make the engine on your boat work, and maybe run a fan in your bedroom. How's that?"

"That sounds great." He carried his plate to a table and sat across from Barbara.

"Make the engines run, huh?" John asked.

"That's the idea," Nyarr grunted. "We could have used more power last night. Next time, I don't want to be that pressed for time."

"I hope there isn't a next time," Mom patted Nyarr's shoulder.

"Me, too. I hate scrying on the fly."

"How did you come by that, anyway. That magic you do," John asked.

"It isn't magic. It's native to my race, actually," Nyarr's words were cool, bordering on frosty. "There are a few other places where people are born with talents that only they or a few others possess. On Karathia, only a handful are born without power. It's similar to an albino deer being born, except more rare than that."

"So, you're not from here?"

"No."

"How did you get here?" Ray now joined the inquisition.

"Third star to the left, and right on until evening," Nyarr snapped. "I have work to do. Enjoy your breakfast." He shoved his chair back, stood and stalked out of the dining room.

"Could you be a little more rude?" Mom slapped a dishtowel against the table where John and Ray sat.

"We don't know if he's from the devil, and neither do you, Doreen," John huffed.

"John, right now, I think you're more of the devil than that man could ever be." She turned her back on them, then, and went to the kitchen to make bread.

"What Mom said," I told him, and went to help her.

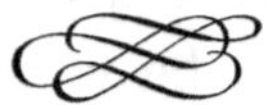

CHAPTER 8

*C*lare

"You don't have to change on the full moon, do you?" I asked Rajeon while we ate lunch.

"No. There are only a handful of shifter types who aren't tied to that event," he said. "My kind are one of those."

"Do you know any of the others?"

"Ask Le," he grinned. "They only change when they want to, and that's usually before going into battle."

"She wasn't changed when she was fighting the Northern gang's minions," I pointed out.

"Hmmph. She could take care of that with her blades. Her father is the best swordsman ever born on Falchan. He'd be embarrassed to hear she changed just to dispatch those louts. Besides, my baby got four of 'em."

"Good for her."

"I appreciated it," he grinned at me.

"I can't remember the last time I had a tuna salad sandwich," I bit off a corner with a happy sigh.

"You think we can go out again tonight—hunting?" he asked.

"If you don't mind getting wet."

"I don't mind. We really need to find those pistols and communicators."

"I guess it's too much to hope that the Blackhearts died in the tornado, huh?"

"I'd say so," Rajeon sighed this time. "They can dig deep when they're forced to."

"Too bad."

"We're starting from scratch, too, since the rain washed away any tracks last night. We no longer have a starting point."

"I refuse to lose my appetite in the face of insurmountable odds."

"That's the spirit." I watched as his eyes lit with humor and a smile tugged a corner of his mouth. He was handsome, no doubt about that. A lock of dark hair threatened to fall into his eyes; I wanted to brush it back. Instead, I gripped my sandwich and took another bite.

"Did you get your curly brown hair from your father?" he teased. Mom didn't have curly hair. I did.

"My dad was killed before I was born. I saw wavy hair in old pictures," I nodded.

"How was he killed?"

"Fishermen on the river during a full moon. Drunk and with a rifle on the boat. Mom found my dad on the bank the next morning, when he didn't come back to the den."

"I'm sorry."

"I never got to meet him. Sometimes what's fun to some turns into the worst tragedy for others."

"Taking pot shots at animals on a fishing trip. Damn," Rajeon swore.

"Drunk and bored. Dangerous when lumped together," I admitted.

"Brothers or sisters?"

"Older brother who moved to California. Prime real estate for the Krelk. He never made it here, so we figured," I shrugged. *Captured or killed*, I meant, but didn't reveal the obvious. "What about you?" I asked.

"After waking, I never found my parents or my sister," he admitted. "I figure they're gone, too."

"You'll have to explain that whole waking thing to me."

"I will—when we have time and aren't worried about the destruction of the zone."

"Promise?"

"I promise."

Rajeon

"Sanjay wants to come with us," Ishaan told me later. "When we go out tonight."

"I was hoping to leave him, Doreen and Barbara in charge of the boats," I said. "We still don't know enough about some of our group to trust them completely."

"I understand what you're saying, but he really needs this, I think."

"All right," I conceded. "He can come. I'll make sure Barbara and Doreen have access to the rifle, just in case."

"Surely it wouldn't come to that," Ishaan's forehead wrinkled in a deep frown.

"I've learned not to count on things like that. It's why we're going out again, and we will keep going out until we find what my former commander lost, in addition to his life. Besides, I can't say what they may find on the river while we're gone."

"True." Ishaan shook his head. "We're a floating town, and even if we are invisible, any shifter in the water will know something's passing through."

"Exactly."

"Where do you think we ought to go—to start looking?" he asked.

"Both sides are set to clash around Fairlawn Point, still. Unless Blackheart stops to search for his missing vamp scouts, I say we work our way southward from a mile south of town."

"You think the Northern gang is holed up in Fairlawn Point?"

"It's reasonable, I think. We killed all their minions and took their shifters. They'll want to replace both those things before meeting up with Blackheart—or the Krelk who'll show up to buy."

"I worry about how the Krelk are paying them," Ishaan said. "They got those rifles from somewhere."

"I agree. There were plenty of gun and ammunition factories in the territories the Krelk claimed. If they didn't destroy everything, it makes sense that some of it could be taken by the slavers."

"If Krelk politicians are as corrupt as humans can be at times, then they may have offered those weapons to the slavers and cage fight operators. Especially if they're fans of the cage fights."

"I think you just nailed it, man," I pointed a finger at Ishaan. "Having something to trade that the gangs would certainly want is the best way to ensure that the cage fights go on without a hitch."

"Once they trade guns, then ammunition becomes the coin for trade," Ishaan nodded. "Maybe food, too, for the minions."

"Could be. None of those killed in Fairlawn Point looked starved to me."

"And they all had rifles and more bullets on them."

"You think we ought to have a talk with John about where those other rifles went?" I asked.

"I figure we should."

"Come on, then. We'll have a short talk with him and Ray before supper."

"We ran out of bullets," John snarled when we asked about the rifles. He refused to admit that we'd been right—guns don't work well against vampires.

"So all those rifles got left in Fairlawn Point?" Ishaan asked the obvious question.

"Yes. Without ammunition, there was no point in keeping them. Are we done, now?" John wanted us off his boat.

"The vamps have them back, now," I turned to Ishaan.

"Yeah. And who knows whether they have more ammunition stashed somewhere, so they can load them up again."

"Where the hell would they get more bullets?" John waved his arms, as if that would convince us to leave him alone.

"From the Krelk," I snapped at him. "Come on, Ishaan. We're done, here."

Clare

"Coffee," Mom poured a cup for me, Ishaan and Rajeon. Nyarr had taken a cup with him; he'd refused to let John's glare ruin his meal, but he and Le left shortly after they finished, telling Rajeon they'd be ready to go whenever he was.

"None for me," Sanjay waved a hand. He'd only been awake since nightfall, so he was fresh. The rest of us had been awake most of the day, so we needed something to keep us alert while on the hunt.

"Sanj, are you sure you want to come?" I reached out to pat his hand.

"I'm sure." I watched his mouth tighten into a straight line; he wanted revenge for his capture and the death of his friend, Frank.

"We may not find anything tonight," Rajeon spoke softly. "Rain washed everything away last night, and we'll probably get wet again tonight, if those clouds to the west are any indication."

"I know. I just don't want to stay behind, when another nose could make a difference."

"I'll give you that," Rajeon nodded. "Let me round up Jessie and the others, and we'll go. Thanks for the coffee, Doreen. Supper was wonderful."

"Barbara and I will keep an eye on everything," Mom told him.

"Good. We'll be back by daybreak at the latest."

"I hope there won't be tornadoes tonight," Ishaan grumped as he drank the last of his coffee.

"You and me, both," I agreed.

Rajeon

Clare had my pistol back as Nyarr scried for a place to set us down. Once that was done, he nodded to the rest of us and folded space.

He did well; we landed in a small clearing not far from the river, with farmland to the east and trees between us and the water. Heavy clouds moved over our heads, promising rain soon.

"Sanjay, Jessie and I will take the lead," Ishaan told us. They had the best noses, although Clare could probably scent vampires, too, if they'd been in the area recently. I nodded to her; we took the middle like the night before, with Nyarr and Le not far behind.

Ishaan and Sanjay were large, black wolves, while the other two left on the boats were gray. Ishaan told me that he and Sanjay were second generation American citizens—before the Krelk came, anyway. Their grandparents had emigrated from India nearly a century earlier, bringing their father, who was a small child, with them.

This was the only home they'd known, although many looked at them the same way they did me; slightly darker-skinned, and therefore subject to suspicion.

Pod'l-morphs came in all colors, and nobody paid attention to that. Humans also came in many colors. We were normal—and equal. It had become an annoying side job, however, convincing some humans of that.

The one we hunted tonight certainly needed convincing; I wasn't willing to waste the time. If we found Bob Blackheart, I'd do my best to kill him. He belonged to an era long dead, although prejudices, like pernicious weeds, had a way of burying their seeds and then sprouting up at the worst imaginable times.

We froze when a twig snapped somewhere in front of us, and my thoughts were jerked into the business at hand. Something was coming toward us. Clare drew her pistol; Jessie crouched, preparing to leap, as did both werewolves.

Humans, Nyarr sent to me. *Le says so. She says they have a similar feel as those from the Northern gang. If there are others with them, they could be blocked by bone dust. I can't tell anything, and neither can Le.*

I held up a hand, letting him know to stand ready. If we were outmanned, he could move us quickly.

They looked almost like ghosts in the darkness; two of the five were dressed in lighter clothing. Probably all they had; I couldn't imagine the Blackhearts paying attention to human slaves other than feeding from them.

Their path would lead them between us and the river, unless they turned abruptly. We barely breathed as they walked past. Whatever shield Nyarr had put up, it was effective as they never saw us, even though they looked in our direction several times.

Rain began dropping onto trees and plants as the last of the five disappeared into denser trees to the north. Again, I held up a hand, letting Nyarr know to hold steady.

I had a feeling that something else would be along shortly.

Doreen

"Jeffie has nightmares, sometimes," Barbara took a seat at the table while I poured coffee for her. She'd come back from checking on her son.

"After those poachers grabbed him, I don't doubt it," I said. "Sick bastards, taking children."

I pulled out a chair on the opposite side of the table to sit and have coffee with her. I leaned the rifle against the chair beside mine; so far, the night was uneventful.

In the extreme.

The shifters were all awake and looking human; the alligator brothers were fishing off the side of their boat with the boar brothers. The horse was reading a book he'd found somewhere. The bear was sitting with the two werewolves on the back of the same boat, talking and watching the western bank of the river slide by.

Paul, John and Ray were asleep; at least they were locked inside their cabins and snoring noises were coming from Paul's when I checked half an hour earlier.

It was a good time to take a break.

"I've noticed something," Barbara said, lifting her coffee cup to drink.

"What's that?"

"That the ground coffee level doesn't go down. It's like it's bottomless or something."

"I've noticed the same thing about the cabinets, refrigerator and freezer," I leaned forward to whisper. "Sometimes, the same thing we cooked reappears; other times, something new takes its place."

"You think the warlock is doing that? If he is, every cook ought to have one."

"I don't know. Nobody said anything about it, and I was afraid to ask."

"I'm sure as hell not about to complain," Barbara huffed. "Jeffie hasn't had fresh, cold milk in forever, and he loves having a glass with breakfast."

"I don't want to complain, either," I admitted. "We haven't eaten this good since the Krelk showed up."

"Mama?" Barbara and I both rose from our seats when Jeffie's voice sounded outside the kitchen. He sounded terrified.

With good reason.

The boy was shoved through the door by John, who held a knife to Jeffie's throat. Ray was right behind John, holding a large butcher knife in his hands.

"You're going to stay quiet while we unhook this boat from the others and float away," John hissed. "You can stay here with Satan's spawn if you want to, but we're leaving."

"And taking our food with you? John, look at yourself," I snapped at him. I was almost as terrified as Jeffie was, and Barbara was frozen where she stood. Jeffie was all she had left, and the idiot who used to be sheriff was threatening his life.

Cautiously I moved a hand toward the rifle, but John was watching. A thin trickle of blood ran down Jeffie's neck.

"Do whatever you want, just let my boy go," Barbara's voice trembled.

"Ray, go get that rifle," John nodded to the weapon. "We may need it."

Keeping the large knife pointed at Barbara and me, Ray made his way into the kitchen to retrieve the rifle.

"I hope you rot in hell," I hissed at Ray as he lifted the gun by its strap and hefted it over a shoulder.

"You, first," he said, backing away and keeping his eyes on both Barbara and me. We were afraid to move past that point; Jeffie could die and John could kill both of us with the rifle, once Ray reached his side.

Ray was almost there when John's head snapped back, his knife hand jerked downward and he gurgled. Jeffie fell at his feet; Ray dropped the weapon in his hands, just as one of the alligator brothers hit him so hard in the face it knocked him out.

The boar brother behind John let John's body drop, pulling back the fishing line he'd used to strangle him.

"We don't take kindly to betrayals," the alligator brother rumbled.

"One-fifty test line—my compliments to Rajeon," the boar brother grunted.

"We'll get rid of these two," the other alligator brothers appeared. "We checked on your boat, Miss Barbara. Those two killed Paul, Aaron and Julie; looks like they were murdered earlier to keep them from interfering with the kidnapping."

"Oh, no," Barbara wept.

"Mom," Jeffie ran toward her and buried his head against her shoulder.

"We didn't think much of it when we heard them go in and out of their cabin a time or two, shortly after you two checked on them," the werewolves appeared. "We should have done a better job of helping watch. From now on, that's just what we'll do." He pulled the rifle away from Ray and brought it back to me. "I'm sorry about your friends. They were good people."

"Is Ray still alive?" I asked.

"He is, just unconscious. We can take care of that for you, if you want," the boar offered.

"I think I do want that," I said. "He became dead weight the minute he picked up that knife to kill Aaron, Julie and Paul."

"Good enough. I'll help," one of the werewolves volunteered. "We'll put them in the river afterward. I figure we'll wait and have a service for your friends."

"Thank you."

Rajeon

I wasn't wrong, except about who I was expecting. The Krelk—four of them—arrived first.

They had a meeting scheduled with the Blackhearts, no doubt, and there we were, in danger of having that meeting take place right next to us or possibly invading our space, forcing Nyarr to relocate us.

The others were afraid to move as the Krelk passed around a bottle of the foul-smelling liquor they preferred, and laughed about who they were meeting, in their own language, of course.

Le would understand what they said; her race understood all languages. I knew it too; I'd studied it long enough. What I heard wasn't easy to hear, either. They wanted the vampires who won the zone to raise shifters for them. They hadn't had success at it themselves, so the vamps were the next best thing. Place shifters under compulsion and they'd reproduce as humans.

It was the vilest of plans, but not unexpected. They didn't care which gang won the zone, either; they had dealings with both and either would do.

Too bad Blackheart didn't realize he was being played.

Two vampires walked through the trees; they'd been waiting for the Krelk to arrive. As I suspected, one of them carried a Krelki communicator in his hand.

"Greetings," the vampire said.

"Do you have something for us?" One of the Krelk asked in guttural English.

"Several. Do you have anything to trade?"

"We do." The Krelk lifted his communicator and told someone to bring the cases.

Those are too big to hold rifles, Nyarr sent as several Krelk brought cases from the river on anti-grav loaders.

"Just as requested," the Krelk opened the first, large case. I closed my eyes. Rocket launchers. They were handing rocket launchers to the Blackhearts.

This wasn't going to be a gang fight for the zone; it would be a war. I had a terrible feeling about this.

Another case held the rockets for the launchers, and still more cases were being offloaded and hauled up the bank.

"Tell Je'Dik we await his communication," the lead Krelk told the two vamps. "We hoped he would be here himself, along with the Blackheart."

"They are elsewhere, scouting for a suitable location," one of the vampires dipped his head to the Krelk. "At your request."

"Very good. Extend my greetings to them."

Fuck me, Nyarr sent.

"Shall we show you how to operate this weapon?" another Krelk asked.

"Please."

The Krelk lifted a rocket launcher from its case and loaded it, while the vampires watched. When he pointed it in our direction, preparing to fire, Nyarr hauled us away in a blink.

Clare

Mom and Barbara were waiting for us when we got back. We needed to have a talk about the scene we'd witnessed, but there was bad news waiting on the boats.

"They figured out we'd be by every twenty minutes or so," Barbara explained. "They got Paul, first, then they used the down time between our rounds to kill Aaron and Julie. They left them in their cabin, then came back later to grab Jeffie, right after I checked on him."

Rajeon listened, his face like stone. Nyarr was furious; it was in the set of his shoulders as he stood nearby, listening.

Le sat beside me at a table in the dining room, rubbing my back as we were told of Paul, Aaron and Julie's deaths.

"Aaron was a good friend of John's right?" Rajeon broke his silence.

"Yes. Or I thought so," Mom said.

"Then John approached him with this idea, and Aaron refused to cooperate," Rajeon growled.

"I wish Aaron had come to us, if that's the case," Mom whispered.

"Loyal to the friendship. John may have pretended that it was a bad idea when Aaron refused to help. Then he turned on Aaron and his wife."

"Is the boy all right?" Nyarr asked.

"He's asleep now. He was already having nightmares, though. This will make it worse."

Nyarr cursed in a language I didn't understand.

"The werewolves wrapped Paul, Aaron and Julie in their blankets; they were already soaked with their blood," Mom said. "In case we wanted to have a service for them."

"We'll do something," Rajeon sighed. "I think Nyarr and I will have a talk with the shifters who helped you tonight. They did well."

"Jeffie could be dead without them," Barbara nodded.

"Then they deserve our thanks." Rajeon and Nyarr stalked out of the dining room and headed for the shifters' boat.

"What about you? Did you find anything tonight?" Mom turned to me.

"You won't believe half of what we found," I said. "This night has been a nightmare in itself, all the way around."

"I don't know what happened," Sanjay said as he sat beside Ishaan at lunch the following day. I hadn't been awake long and was more than hungry.

"The others—are they awake, too?"

"Yeah. It's like whatever it was just—dropped off."

"I figure the Northern gang got a visit last night, too," Rajeon slid onto the chair next to mine. "Which means there was a time limit on the compulsion. Wouldn't do to let it stay once the shifters were placed in Krelk hands, now would it?"

"You think they got a batch of the same weapons last night?" I asked.

"I do. Now, what could vampire fights have in common with shifter slavery?" he asked.

"No idea," I said as Mom set a plate of food in front of me. "They can't put tags on vampires—those things would probably just piss them off."

"Very true."

"They can't place compulsion on vampires, either," Mom pointed out. "As far as I know, Krelk don't have any talent in that area."

"They don't have a drop of talent in that area," Rajeon agreed. "They also don't have mindspeech; I figure their skulls are too thick for anything like that to get through to them."

"So, they're manipulating the vamps in another way?" I had no idea where Rajeon could be going with this.

"Yes."

"By giving them weapons and ammunition?" Mom asked.

"Yes." Rajeon tapped his nose.

"I still don't understand; they have to trade something to the vamps in exchange for the shifters they're selling for the cage fights."

"Well, we know how much the Krelk love their cage fights, don't we?" Rajeon nodded to my mother when she set coffee in front of him.

"Bloodthirsty bastards," Mom grumped.

"Exactly. Now, what if they've become bored with pitting alligators against mountain lions and bears against rhinos?"

"Will you just say what you think?" I demanded.

"I think they're spoiling for the biggest cage fight possible," Rajeon sighed. "Only there won't be a cage, per se. You heard the Krelk and those vamps last night. The vamps said Blackheart and Je'Dik were looking for a suitable location."

"I didn't understand that at all," I shook my head.

"What do the words *fight of the century* mean to you?" Rajeon asked.

"They want to see the war between the Blackhearts and the Northern gang," I breathed as I finally saw the light.

"Yep. With Je'Dik involved, I'm not surprised by any of this. This could be his ticket into the good graces of the Krelk government, not just here, but everywhere."

"Who is this Je'Dik?" Mom asked.

"The Alliances have a price on his head. A big one. Why do you think my former idiot boss came down here to pick him up? The bounty on Je'Dik is in the millions, from the Alliances alone. There are some criminal factions who aren't thrilled with him, either, and they've probably upped the ante."

"Who or what exactly is he?" I asked.

"His lowest crimes are assassinations. For the right price, he'd kill his own mother. He's been involved in destroying governments and planets, in and out of the Alliances. Krelk aren't easy to kill, as you know."

"It's why we're stuck in the zone," Mom complained.

"Exactly. Some believe that Je'Dik was the one who stole the technology for the Krelk to begin with; technology that his world shouldn't have had for another two centuries, at least. Once they got their hands on that, they decided it was time to spread out. They've taken over too many worlds, in my opinion, and didn't mind murdering along the way to do it."

"How long do they live?" Mom asked.

"Too long. A lot longer than they used to, before the tech fell into their hands. Nowadays, they can live more than a thousand years, although the average is about eight hundred or so."

"How old is Je'Dik?" I asked.

"We figure he's around five hundred, so you see what we could be dealing with."

"Three more centuries of the same?"

"If not more. And if I'm right about this, he's selling tickets to the fight he's arranging, and getting whatever he wants for them."

"You're leaving out the part about the vamps killing each other," Mom said. "We won't miss any of those, I don't think."

"But there will be a winner," Rajeon pointed out. "Who will have the ability to make more vamps in his image. That means they could turn to breeding humans for vamps, along with breeding shifters for cage fights. Do you see where I'm going with this?"

"Slavery," I whispered.

"Yep. Blackheart has plenty of experience in that area already."

"What are we going to do?" Mom asked.

"I don't know. We still have communicators and weapons out there. I hope they weren't passed to the Krelk last night. If they find the Alliance has sent someone, they'll come hunting, and in huge numbers. That spells massacre to me."

"You were right to call your boss an idiot," I sighed. "This is a mess."

"There's something else," Rajeon said.

"Oh, there's more," I waved a hand in helpless surrender.

"The Sirenali bone dust," Rajeon said. "Where did Je'Dik get it? We know he had to either steal it or buy it; it's illegal in both Alliances, and there's a lot riding on where—and when—he got it."

"What exactly is this bone dust? It isn't actually bones, is it?"

"It is," Rajeon confirmed. "Powdered bones from a race once thought extinct. It is powerful enough to hide the bearer from the most talented warlock, wizard, all the powerful races—and even from the Mighty."

"The Mighty?"

"I'll explain that at the same time we talk about the waking," Rajeon held up a hand. "Without the Mighty, I'd be dead. The only good thing to come out of last night, I guess, is that our shifters are no longer under compulsion to sleep during the day. That could prove to be a big help. We can send out a day crew and a night crew, to search for our quarry."

"Won't we need another warlock?" Mom asked.

"I figure we will. Nyarr is asking one of his brothers to come. We'll see if that happens."

"Nyarr has brothers?"

"He has four brothers, and all of them are as powerful as he is."

"Is that common?" I asked.

"No. Generally, there are power level differences in even the most powerful families. The Blackmantle brothers were all blessed with the best talent."

"Loor is coming," Nyarr appeared as if called and settled on the chair beside Rajeon's. "Actually, they all wanted to come, but we're holding off on that," Nyarr grinned.

"Lure?" I asked.

"Loor. There's a slight difference, and if you spoke Alliance common, it would be easier to understand," Rajeon told me.

"Gotcha."

"Good." He offered a grin, to tell me he was teasing.

"Actually, Uncle Wellend wanted to come, but a man with red wings might stand out," Nyarr said, still grinning.

"I think the story you owe me just got bigger," I pointed a finger at Rajeon.

CHAPTER 9

*C*lare

Loor arrived shortly after Nyarr told us he was coming. Rajeon, Nyarr and Le met with him on Nyarr's boat.

I wanted to be in that meeting, too, but was left out, as was Ishaan. If Jessie hadn't been asleep, he may have been just as miffed as we were about being excluded.

"There are two voices I don't recognize coming from that galley," Sanjay walked into the kitchen, where Ishaan and I were working out our frustration by punching down bread dough for Mom.

"He didn't say two were coming. He only said Loor."

"Maybe we need another one. Who knows?" Mom said. "I figure we'll hear soon enough what they're talking about; Rajeon is good about sharing the information we need."

She was politely telling me that my snit hadn't gone unnoticed.

"We need all shifters on Nyarr's boat," Rajeon poked his head in the door. "Do you have a stopping place, Doreen?"

"I do if Clare and Ishaan will stop punching the dough for a minute." She frowned at me to get her point across.

"Be there in five." He winked at me, the slime, and walked away to inform the others.

"Everybody, this is my brother, Loor," Nyarr introduced the newest member of our crew. Like Nyarr, he had dark hair and eyes, and bore a definite family resemblance.

Loor was the only new one there, too. Had Sanjay been wrong about the second voice?

"I was brought here by someone else, who stayed to chat for a while," Loor nodded to all of us. "He gave us information we needed, and some things that the rest of you should have—some of you, anyway." He held out his hands and a shoe-box-sized chest appeared there. "Zaria sent these for everyone who doesn't have one already. Sanjay?" He lifted a much smaller box from the chest. I knew what it held—a medallion like the one I wore.

"Zaria is placing her trust in all of you," Nyarr explained as Loor passed out the other medallions. Even Jeffie had one, and his eyes grew round as his mother draped it around his neck.

"This is not only protection for you, but if you grip the medallion in your hand, you'll be able to send mindspeech to someone else who wears a medallion. That is a tremendous gift, all by itself. Since we need all of you to help track the vamps and the Krelk, you'll need these."

"We also have this," Le held up a small container. "Tamp and Ilya thought it only right that you get a sniff of actual bone dust, so you'll know if somebody carries it with them, or has sewn it into their clothing. If you find any of this, send mindspeech to Nyarr, Loor, Rajeon or me. We'll do our best to help you relieve them of the dust and anything else they shouldn't have."

"It's time for Sam to tell you what happened on their farm, too, when the attackers came through," Rajeon said, inviting one of the alligator brothers forward.

"I'm Sam, for those of you who don't know," Sam ducked his head shyly. "That's Boyd," he pointed to a second brother, "and that's Steve," he indicated the third. "We owned a big farm south of West Helena, Arkansas, and we figure somebody sold us out to the Krelk. The Krelk probably alerted the vampire gang to come take us. If it was the Blackhearts, they may have turned back from their northward journey just to get to us. That spells betrayal to me. Now, in all the chaos when the vamps and their bunch attacked us, there was only one of us missing and unaccounted for. That one was our fourth brother, Mick."

"We don't know if Mick survived after his betrayal, but it could be that he's either wondering how to put the farm back together or traveling with the Blackhearts or whoever it was who took us down," Boyd took up the story.

"Was there trouble between you and Mick beforehand?" Mom asked.

"Some. He wanted things his way, and his way included cheating the human and shifter workers out of their due. I guess he started plotting after the rest of us voted him down," Sam replied. "I know some of you are hearing this for the first time," he nodded to the other shifters. I understood, then, that they'd worked for the alligator brothers on their farm, and all of them were sold out by Mick.

"Easy pickings," Barbara nodded. "An entire farm full of shifters for the taking."

"I don't hold any of this against you, Sam," one of the werewolves spoke up. "You stood by us, even after the Krelk almost destroyed everything. We knew Mick didn't really care about the farm or anybody besides himself. We never said anything, because you three were so good to us."

The others were nodding at the werewolf's words.

"What we want to say is this," Steve spoke now. "We lost good people in the attack, and those of us who survived were kidnapped and destined for slavery and death. If any of you come across Mick, we won't mind hearing that he ah, died."

"Sam, I want to thank you for saving Jeffie," Barbara said. "You and your brothers."

"Like I said, we've had enough of betrayal," Sam told her. "And you and Jeffie are more than welcome."

"Sam, we didn't rescue you from the Blackhearts, we found you with the Northern gang," Rajeon pointed out. "That means the Northern gang was poaching in Blackheart territory, or what they considered their territory."

"Damn," Sam swore and shook his head. "We didn't know who showed up, just that it was a bunch of vamps and their slaves."

"There's something else," Le said. "And this message is for Barbara and Jeffie. Aunt Zaria says that you can both go to a safe place while this gets sorted out."

"Safe place?" Barbara asked. "Where would that be?"

"Jeffie, would you like to see people with wings?" Rajeon asked.

"People with wings?"

"Yes. The Queen of the Avii is Zaria's daughter. She's inviting you to stay with her until this is over."

"I don't know these people," Barbara began.

"If you want, we're allowed to bring Clare and Doreen with us to drop you off," Nyarr said. "So you can see for yourselves that you'll be safe and looked after. Jeffie can take classes while he's there—in English."

"Will they see to his health?" I asked.

Rajeon understood what I meant; Jeffie was having nightmares before John tried to kill him. He needed someone to help him with that.

"Queen Quin will see to it," Nyarr said. "She's a healer of the highest order."

"She has wings?" Jeffie asked.

"She has red wings, which show she's royalty," Le told him. "You'll see all colors of wings if you go."

"Are you sure of this place?" Barbara asked.

"Very sure," Le smiled at her. "I've stayed in Avii Castle with Aunt Zaria. It's beautiful, there."

"Jeffie?" Barbara turned to her son.

"Will they have cookies?"

"They'll have any dessert you want," Le said.

"I think I want to go," Jeffie said.

"When?" Barbara asked.

"Now," Nyarr shrugged. "Le will send the message, and we'll go."

I may have shrieked when we were pulled through a short tunnel of sorts, but the sound was swallowed by the wind rushing past my ears.

"Baby, you okay?" Rajeon's hand was on my elbow as I stumbled; my feet had left solid flooring for a moment, before finding other solid flooring.

When I lifted my eyes, I blinked.

The massive room where we landed was made of glass, which swirled with dark blues, greens and a few other colors. Standing in that room, waiting for us, was a beautiful, winged woman.

"These are my feathers," Queen Quin held out a wing for Jeffie to see. "We do fly—whenever we want. If you'd like to fly with us, sometime, just ask."

As they said, her feathers were red—like a cardinal's. Her hair was almost to her waist, and was blonde with strands of gold, silver and copper. Those three colors were also reflected on the edges of her feathers, which were beautiful.

"Where are we?" I mumbled to Rajeon, who stood between Mom and me.

"Le-Ath Veronis," he replied. "Come with me; I'll show you the water."

"Water?"

He pulled me toward a nearby balcony, where the sun shone brightly. I gasped when we looked over the glass rail; we were high up, and far below, a sea washed around the base of the glass castle.

"Le-Ath Veronis means *Heart of the Vampire,* he explained. I turned to him in alarm.

"It's nothing to be afraid of. Here, Queen Lissa rules the vampires, and she doesn't treat anyone kindly who mistreats children. Barbara and Jeffie are guests of the Avii Queen and King, and as such will have guards and special privileges. They'll probably get to meet Lissa, too, if they're here long enough. Plus, with one of Zaria's medallions around their necks, I'd really hate to be the one trying to attack either of them."

"What does that mean?" I asked.

"It means that anyone attempting to harm you may end up dead." Someone else appeared next to Rajeon.

"Clare, this is Ilya Ironsmith," Rajeon introduced the tall, dark-haired man dressed in black leather.

"I have a gift for you," Ilya said as a long, black case appeared before him. It floated toward me and the lid opened, revealing a rifle of sorts.

"This one will only fire for you, once you touch it," Ilya said. "I was told you'd be more comfortable carrying a rifle. A word of caution, however; whatever you aim at may be blown to small particles when you shoot."

"I'm sure he was told *blown to smithereens*," Rajeon grinned.

"I was told that. I wasn't sure of the context in this case."

"Go with what you know," Rajeon nodded, although he smiled when he said it. "Go ahead, lift the rifle," he coaxed.

I stared at the weapon for a few seconds before tentatively reaching out and lifting it. It was lighter than I expected it to be.

"Solar-powered, so leave it in sunlight after you use it, to recharge," Ilya explained. "Here's the power gauge," he pointed it out. "Always check to ensure you have a full charge before heading into a fight."

"Ilya. On Earth, that's a Russian name," I said while handling the rifle gingerly and checking the charge—it was fully loaded.

"I know." Now, Ilya was smiling. "I was named after someone from Earth, years ago."

"Time to go back." Nyarr, Le and Mom joined us on the balcony. A part of me wanted to stay; I hadn't seen nearly enough of Avii Castle.

"Did—somebody jump off that boat down there?" Mom pointed at several boats in the water.

I turned to look, just in time to see men flying toward a speck in the water, while one of them lifted a flailing man from the sea.

"Boat duty," Le shrugged. "People jump all the time, just so they can be saved by the Avii guards."

"They're thinking about increasing the fines for doing it," Ilya said. "It's gotten to be such a routine occurrence. It was good to meet you," he told Mom and me. "Good luck and good hunting."

With that, we went through the wind tunnel again. Sam and the others stared at us in amazement when we reappeared on Nyarr's boat.

The rifle was still gripped in my hands; Rajeon had thought to grab the case for me. He held it open while I set the rifle in its place and shut it.

"This rifle will only work for Clare; it's DNA activated," Nyarr said. "It will self-destruct if anyone else attempts to use it, and will probably destroy them with it. Since Clare has a new weapon, that leaves the other rifle available for someone else. Who has the most experience with this sort of thing?"

The alligator brothers and the boar brothers turned toward Clyde, the horse shifter. "He has a silver star and several marksman's medals," Sam said. "From the military."

"The other rifle is yours when we go hunting," Rajeon told him. "Remember, you're limited on bullets, unless we can find more."

"Understood," Clyde said.

"Great. Is there anything else? If not, those of us going out tonight need to rest up before we go. Sam, you and Clyde are in charge while we're gone."

"We'll make sure everything goes smoothly," Sam said. "And Freddie, here, is a good cook. He can help Doreen, if she wants." Sam pointed out one of the boar brothers.

"Good," Mom smiled. "I was worried, since Barbara wasn't here to help."

"I used to run Sam's kitchen at the farm," Freddie grinned. "It'll be my pleasure to help."

"Your medallion has a new ability," Rajeon informed Jessie after he woke for the evening. "If you want to talk mind to mind, just touch it with your hand and think your message at someone else with a medallion. How is the blood substitute working for you?"

"Tastes good—like it ought to," Jessie touched the medallion beneath his shirt. *The blood substitute works, too—I don't feel weak, like I was afraid I would.*

"I heard you," I smiled at Jessie. *Can you hear me?* I asked him.

I can hear you fine, he replied. "Never thought I'd see the day," he said aloud and grinned at Rajeon and me.

I understood, then. Not only did we have a way to communicate silently between us, the vampire planet we'd visited had supplied Jessie with a food source—one they also depended upon, I figured. They didn't need to bite anyone to survive.

"We're going to start where we left off last time," Nyarr told Jessie. "If you, Ishaan and Sanjay will do the sniffing for us, I hope we can pick up a trail and find where they're heading. This whole gladiator set-up isn't sitting well with the other folks we've talked to."

"It does sound like that, doesn't it? Only the gladiators are vampires, this time," I surmised. "Did they learn this after they came here, or have they always been bloodthirsty?"

"They've had leanings in that direction, and the farther they get from the original homeworld, the more bloodthirsty they seem to get," Le told me. "It's one of the reasons the Alliances are interested in their doings, although they're not quite frightened enough of the Krelk, yet."

"Only because the Krelk have stayed away from the Alliances, with the exception of Je'Dik," Loor said.

"Is it always somebody else's problem, until it becomes your problem?" I asked.

"That's it in a nutshell," Rajeon agreed. "Is everybody ready? We have vampires and Krelk to hunt tonight."

"I think we're ready," I clutched my new rifle and readied myself for transport. Nyarr took us in.

Rajeon

"I knew we should have stayed here," Ishaan grumbled as he, Sanjay and Jessie sniffed the area from the night before.

"I smell six shifters, all in Krelk hands, now," Jessie confirmed Ishaan's findings. "The scent goes to the riverbank before it disappears."

"We can't worry about that for now," Rajeon reminded them. "We're looking for the poachers, so this won't happen again."

"Poachers first, cage fights afterward," Sanjay turned to his brother, who nodded. Somehow, they were planning to shut down the Krelk cage fights. I wanted in on that, too, but we needed Je'Dik and Blackheart, first.

And we needed to shut down the gladiator event the Krelk had planned.

"They headed east from here," Ishaan pointed before dropping his clothing and becoming wolf. Sanjay followed his lead; Jessie stuffed their clothing in a pack and slung it over a shoulder before following the wolves.

"I think they're headed toward Ste. Genevieve," Jessie said after we'd gone several miles. "Plenty of humans still live there, so it would be a good place for vamps to fill up, if you know what I mean."

"I can mark this place and move us there," Loor offered. "If we don't find anything, we can come back to this point."

"I'm good with that," I said.

Loor moved us this time, setting us down on the outskirts of the town. We still weren't far from the river. Here, a light rain was falling, with the possibility of heavier rain to follow.

If I were the Blackhearts, I'd be looking for shelter about now.

What do we do if we find them? Clare's voice whispered in my mind. I jerked my head toward her; she gripped her medallion in her hand.

I fumbled for my medallion for a moment so I could answer. *Kill as many as we can, although I want to question one or two of them,* I replied. *Blackheart is at the top of that list, as is Je'Dik, if he's with them. We also need the weapons and communicators back, and any bone dust they carry with them.*

What happens if they fail to report in? she asked a follow-up.

That could turn into a problem, I conceded. *I really need to know if the Krelk are aware that the Alliance is watching them.*

If we kill the Blackhearts, we may be giving them confirmation.

Stop being so logical, I complained. *If we do any of this, we'll have to point toward a reasonable cause—like the locals rising up, or an act of the gods or something.*

Right.

Is that sarcasm? It sounded like sarcasm.

Maybe.

Look, Nyarr's voice sounded in both our heads.

Jessie stiffened ahead of us, while both werewolves growled. Jessie gripped his medallion. *There are vampires walking this way,* he informed us.

I've got shields up, Nyarr said. *They won't see or smell us.*

Good, because they're not stopping, Clare squeaked.

Three minutes passed, and those minutes lasted forever. Two vampires walked right past us while talking.

"Do we have enough to fight off the Blackhearts?" One of the vamps asked his companion.

"We have seventeen, and the word is the Blackhearts get here tonight. I hope we have enough."

I know one of those vamps, Jessie sent.

I can move us back and send Jessie in to talk with them, Nyarr suggested.

Do it, I agreed.

Nyarr set us down half a mile away, and allowed Jessie to walk past the shield perimeter. At the last minute, I became a finch and flew toward Jessie, settling on his shoulder.

If anyone looked close enough, they'd see the tiny medallion hanging around my bird's neck. Jessie didn't increase his pace; he traveled at the same gait he always used when he wasn't in a hurry. He didn't want the vamps to think he was an enemy and try to kill him before he could explain that we could help.

"Caleb?" Jessie called out the moment the vamps came into view.

"Jessie?" The vamps stopped walking, although the one who spoke took a step forward. Like Jessie, he was dark-skinned; the other vamp wasn't.

"It's me," Jessie said.

"I thought you got killed in the attack on Fairlawn Point," Caleb called out.

"Most people died. The fool of a sheriff told everybody to stay where they were when the Northern gang came along. Some of us left, and it's a good thing we did."

"You picked a bad night for a visit," Caleb's companion volunteered. "The Blackhearts may be coming here tonight."

"Then I hope you let me help you," Jessie said. "I have some old scores to settle with those bastards."

"Huh. We'd take all the help we can get," Caleb snorted. "Another vamp would be welcome."

"Some of my friends are behind me," Jessie said. "One of 'em is here with me." He lifted me off his shoulder; I gripped his finger with tiny claws to hang on.

"Is that a bird?" the second vamp asked.

"At times," Jessie chuckled. "Wanna come out, Rajeon?"

I materialized beside Jessie. "Can't be too careful," I said, taking clothes from Jessie and putting them on. Wouldn't do for the vamps to see me fully dressed after a turn; I didn't need suspicious vamps.

"How many others you got?" Caleb asked.

"Six," Jessie shrugged. "All good in a fight, if it comes to that."

"We'll be checking for tattoos," the other vamp said.

"I'd expect you to," Jessie replied.

"Rajeon?" Clare's voice called out behind us. Nyarr had wisely moved them forward.

"Come on in; we have friends here who want to check us for tattoos," I replied.

The two vamps waited patiently while both werewolves appeared, leading the rest of our gang. Clare had slung her rifle over a shoulder, so as not to appear threatening.

"They have two wolves," the second vamp high-fived Caleb.

"Your wolves are the best indication that you're not in league with either gang," Caleb grinned. "Those two would be in a cage with a tag on their necks."

"Clothes?" Sanjay turned first, just to show he could.

"Here," Nyarr handed clothing to Sanjay; that meant I was wearing what Sanjay wore earlier.

"I have yours," Jessie told Ishaan when he transformed. Ishaan stepped forward to take the bag Jessie carried. "Shoes in there, too."

"We don't have tattoos," Ishaan came forward once he had his pants on. "Check for yourself," he held out his hands, with his shirt hanging from his fingers. His neck and arms were clean.

"Come on, then. I don't suppose you passed the Blackhearts on your way in?" Caleb asked, leading us back toward Ste. Genevieve.

"No, but we caught scent of them, heading in this direction," Jessie confirmed. "It's why we came this way; I was hoping to warn folks."

"It may be a long night. I'm Ethan," the other vamp introduced himself. "We may be in a fight for our lives before it's over."

"Then we'll help," Jessie said. "It's time Blackheart got what's comin' to him. Does he know you're here?"

"He doesn't have a clue," Ethan replied.

"Even better."

"They burned Fairlawn Point," I said. "Jessie, Ishaan and I went back to check after the gang was gone. Most of the bodies were in the burned homes. With no way to protect themselves, they died where they lived."

I didn't want to bring up the sheriff and the judge; those were still sore points, and we should have left them behind to begin with.

We stood inside what used to be City Hall in Ste. Genevieve, where ten of the vamps and several humans had gathered to talk. The other vamps were patrolling the perimeter, watching for the Blackhearts to appear.

"Fairlawn Point was smaller than Ste. Genevieve," Clare pointed out. "We couldn't convince the people there they were in danger, so they died. I don't want that to happen to anyone else."

"We figure the Northern gang started all this, poaching in Blackheart territory," Caleb said. "They're the ones who took that farm down south and either killed or kidnapped everybody there. It was run by four alligator shifters, so they're all gone, now."

"They thought it was the Blackhearts attacking at first," Jessie said. "But they figured out eventually that it was another gang. Actually, one of the four brothers sold out the other three—and the rest of the hands," Jessie continued. "We rescued the other three brothers from the Northern gang, so what you're saying makes sense."

"Where are they now?" Caleb demanded.

"Floating down the river on a houseboat," I shrugged. "We found them, two werewolves, a horse, a bear and two boar brothers. They're guarding the houseboat flotilla while we hunt Blackheart."

"Too bad you didn't bring them with you; we could use the extra help."

"We can go get them. I'm sure they wouldn't mind getting in on this."

"How long will that take?" Caleb asked.

Nyarr turned toward me.

"This may require some suspension of disbelief," I quipped. "Just remember, we're here to help."

"I'm the Mayor, or I used to be," a man held up his hand. "I'm in favor of anything that will help us through this mess."

"I agree with Jack," Caleb pointed to the Mayor.

"Go get 'em," I nodded at Nyarr. He and Le disappeared together, making Caleb and several others gasp.

"They're good in a fight, too," Jessie grinned. Five minutes later, we had everyone from the boats except for Doreen and Freddie.

"Sam?" Caleb walked forward and grasped Sam's hand. "We

thought you were dead or taken. It convinced the rest of us to get together and try to stop this nonsense."

"We were taken, and I don't want to relive that experience. As for taking down the gangs, we want the same," Sam agreed. "We only have one rifle and a limited number of bullets, but Clyde may be able to distract a few of Blackheart's bunch."

"Doreen sends these with her regards," Nyarr unloaded a case that held silver-dipped hammers, tire irons and several other useful tools-turned-weapons.

"Now those are definitely useful," Mayor Jack lifted a tire iron.

"Strike fast. You only get one blow before a vamp turns on you," Caleb warned him.

"Yeah. I'll remember that," Jack hefted the tool in his hand.

"If the Blackhearts send in humans and shifters ahead of their attack, don't hesitate to make them dead," Loor said. "They may have instructions to burn the town ahead of Blackheart's arrival, and capture as many humans as they can. Because of that, my brother and I won't be holding back when any of them show up."

"They won't expect to meet a vampire resistance?" Caleb asked.

"I doubt they think it's possible," I said. "In fact, the reluctance for vamps or werewolves to band together may have left the door open for both the Blackhearts and the Northern gang. Now, one of them wants supremacy, and I have a feeling the Krelk are urging them on—separately, of course, because they want that battle to be epic."

"Why?" Mayor Jack asked.

"We think they want to make it the biggest cage fight ever, and say it's the gangs' choice, rather than have Krelk influence stamped all over it," Sam explained.

"In other words, they're using us, like they have been all along?" Caleb asked.

"Yes. Too bad Blackheart and the Northern bunch haven't figured it out, yet. The Krelk are arming them, too. That's how we got the rifle Clyde holds," I said. "Their human and shifter slaves all had rifles when they attacked Fairlawn Point. We got away with one and some bullets for it. The rest were depleted of ammunition."

"They have communicators, to determine meeting places to sell their shifters to the Krelk," Clare broke in. "Along with the weapons and whatever else the Krelk are trading for the shifters the gangs are poaching."

"Scumbags," Mayor Jack snorted.

"I'd say worse than that," Jessie told him. "It's time somebody took a stand."

"Let's hope it ends here for the Blackhearts, then," Caleb agreed.

"There's movement to the south," a vampire rushed into the meeting room. "Looks like they'll be here in less than half an hour."

"Get ready," Mayor Jack said, cradling his tire iron in his arms. "If we go down, we'll let them know they had a tiger by the tail before we fall."

I've sent mindspeech to Ironsmith and Tampirus, Nyarr's words echoed in my mind. *So they're aware.*

Thanks, I returned, gripping my medallion. *I hope you work,* I thought at the gold disc in my hand.

Wait and see, a voice—*her* voice—replied. Zaria was aware of our predicament, too.

"Let's go," Caleb nodded toward the door. We followed him into the night, waiting for Blackheart and his slaves to arrive.

Caleb and Jessie stood between Nyarr and Loor at the front, not far from where the approaching army was spotted. Less than a quarter mile in front of us, a grove of trees stood. I figured they'd burst from them at a run. If the vamps joined the vanguard, we'd be hit like a storm.

The rest of Ste. Genevieve's vampires were sprinkled among us; the humans had to be armed in some way, or Mayor Jack sent them to protect the others inside the town. The shifters had either turned or held a weapon of their own. The alligator brothers had changed and now waited to snap legs and other vital parts from attackers.

Clare stood at my side, her ranos rifle held steady, pointing it toward the approaching enemy.

I was ready, too, although my response in this battle would be determined by who attacked us, first. No sense pulling out diamond thorns until the vamps were within easy reach. Best to surprise them with my most effective weapon, or they could turn and run.

I didn't want that. I wanted to eliminate this threat, once and for all. Blackheart, after all, had the deaths of two fellow scouts to answer for.

I could include my former boss in that, but he'd walked straight into his own death with his eyes open. His associates, perhaps, had been clueless, but they should have known better, too.

Their eyes were on the reward, no doubt, and they'd forgotten how dangerous coming to the surface could be.

They're coming; I can hear them, Jessie reported. Clare lifted her rifle, preparing to fire at the first attacker she sighted.

I love you, I told her, gripping my medallion. Her eyes closed for a moment as she digested what I'd said, then nodded.

That's when I turned and became the giant owl. Nearby, Ishaan dipped his head in agreement; I could fly behind the enemy and take them from there, if possible.

Good luck, Nyarr sent as my owl lifted silently into the night sky. *I have you shielded from sight*, he added.

All the better.

Clare

I suppose it made sense for Blackheart to send his expendable force ahead of the rest; if they were met with resistance, he could better gauge what he was dealing with. I watched as the human and shifter line running toward us was cut down by combined efforts of the vampires, shifters and armed humans.

Something held me back from firing my rifle; no need to announce its presence to Blackheart, especially when the vanguard was being obliterated by our forces. I worried that Blackheart's vamps would come in with the force of a hurricane, and I wasn't wrong.

The moment the last human slave fell, the vampire gang came running—so swiftly I almost couldn't get them sighted quickly enough.

When I did fire after getting a clear view of a running vamp, he exploded in a rain of flesh that turned to powdered ash.

Ilya had been right; this weapon was prone to blast targets to smithereens. I sighted another vamp and fired again.

Rajeon

I heard the pop, pop, pop of vampires exploding; Clare was having some success at killing Blackheart's minions.

As for Blackheart himself, I worried he wasn't with this group after all; that he'd sit this one out while his army did the dirty work. My owl flew more than half a mile southward, and I was ready to give up and turn back when I spotted movement in the trees below.

Three vamps walked casually through the woods, while one of them held a communicator to his ear.

They were talking to the army ahead; I had no doubt about that. Would Blackheart turn and run?

No.

Instead, he was joined by six other vampires, who materialized from nothing. He had misters with him, and that infuriated me. What made it worse was what each of them carried; the rocket launchers that the Krelk had provided during their last meeting.

They were about to turn the tide of this fight in their favor.

I wasn't willing to let that happen. All I needed was a clear enough space around them, but they didn't oblige; instead, they walked beneath denser trees, obscuring themselves from my sight.

I had to keep them in my line of vision; if they started running, they could move faster than my owl could fly.

I couldn't grip my medallion, either, to let Nyarr know what I'd found, and he must be too busy fighting to keep me updated himself.

On top of all that, a light rain began to fall, which meant another heavier rain was likely on the way, if all the dark clouds massing overhead told me anything.

Wait—were they walking into a clearing?

Time to attack.

Clare

Like me, Nyarr and Loor waited until the vamps attacked to pull out their best weapons, and those were eye-popping. Lightning poured from their hands and struck running vampires, who screamed as they burned, some of them still speeding toward us.

A few shrieks sounded at first, when it looked as if burning vamps would be running among us, but just before they reached us, they became ash and crumbled to the ground. Thunder rumbled to the west of us, announcing another spring rain, as drops began to fall.

The weather couldn't stop us—not now, when we were in the middle of a fight for our lives. Yes, we were killing plenty of them; they'd taken a toll on our side as well. Most of our human helpers were wounded or dead already. Jessie and Caleb, fighting in tandem, were still standing, as were a few of the other vamps.

Twice, too, Ishaan and Sanjay had been saved from certain death by a bloom of light around them; I figured it was their medallions, saving them from harm, as promised.

The same went for the alligators and the others; I was more than glad that they'd been given that gift, too.

My rifle, however, had been the best gift, perhaps; no other weapon I'd ever held could take down a vamp with a single shot.

Not only was I protected by the medallion; I was able to protect others with the weapon I carried.

That's when I saw the vamp knock down Mayor Jack, and, with claws fully extended, he prepared to remove Jack's head.

My shot hit him square in the forehead, causing him to explode.

Mayor Jack rolled away, came to his feet, somehow and brandished his tire iron at the next attacker who came against him.

A hailstone bounced on the ground ahead of me, then it looked as if thousands more were bouncing around me, while I hadn't been hit once.

That didn't hold true for the others from Ste. Genevieve; they were getting pounded, just like the enemy vamps were.

I'm sending the others back to city hall, Nyarr shouted into our minds, so we'd hear him over the pounding of hailstones, which had increased from dime-sized to that of a quarter and larger.

Not even vamps needed to be out in a hailstorm of this size and intensity. They had their orders from Blackheart, however, and kept fighting, although a few were down after being hit in the head by hail that was now the size of golf balls.

Jessie, Caleb and the five remaining vamps relieved unconscious vamps of their heads; Nyarr and Loor were back after transporting our vulnerable fighters to safety. I lowered my rifle; the weather was taking down the last of our attackers for us. I wondered if they'd considered the weather when they planned their attack.

Look out, Nyarr shouted.

I went still in alarm, as something terrifying appeared in the night sky over our heads.

A tangle of diamond thorns, with the wings of an eagle, was bearing down on us. Like us, the hailstones never hit any part of it.

It's Rajeon, I shouted to everyone while clutching my medallion, although how he'd shifted into two different things at once defied everything I'd ever learned about shifters. When that conglomeration landed, it changed. Most of it became Rajeon.

The same one who said he loved me.

Except one arm remained a lengthy tangle of diamond thorns, and within that tangle a single vampire was held.

I wouldn't have recognized him, perhaps, except for the confederate frock coat and gray hat he wore. Bob Blackheart was now Rajeon's prisoner, but how were we going to get information out of him?

CHAPTER 10

*R*ajeon Blackheart wasn't a mister. That made a difference to both of us. If he could, he'd have misted away from my tight nest of thorns already. He couldn't, and that meant he'd slice himself to death if he attempted to escape.

Too bad, too, that his misters had materialized and then walked into an open space. They'd died before they could become mist again. Most vamps took a few minutes to change. I'd caught them before they could do anything.

Behind me, too, I'd stashed their weapons and communicators where I could find them again—high in a tall tree, cradled among thick, sturdy limbs. The hail hadn't been as severe there, so they'd probably be undamaged. What I hadn't found was Forneel's laser pistols and communicators. That was a subject to be broached later. For now, we had Blackheart and a whole lot of questions that needed answers.

Blackheart hissed whenever his skin raked against one of my sharp thorns; he knew he was caught and that infuriated him. Nyarr and Loor, with arms crossed over their chests, watched my prize with interest, while Jessie and Caleb glared at their nemesis.

Across the City Hall meeting room, Clare was helping someone bandage the mayor's arm; he'd taken a slice from a vamp. I hoped the wound didn't get infected; Mayor Jack was a good man and we needed more like him.

Touch your medallion and ask your questions, her voice came to me again. *I will tell you if he's lying.*

"Well, Blackheart," I began after gripping my medallion, "Were you aware that you were being played by the Krelk?"

"I don't know what you're talking about," he hissed at me. "I don't deal with the Krelk."

"That's a lie," I stated, even as Zaria's voice informed me of the same. "You got those rocket launchers from the Krelk. Didn't you?"

"We found them."

"Right. Because those things are just lying around, waiting for someone to discover them," I snapped. "Start telling the truth, or your death may be a slow one." To demonstrate, I tightened the thorns around his throat for a moment.

"Maybe I got those weapons from the Krelk. So what? We have to defend ourselves in the zone, just like anyone else."

"I doubt there's anyone else like you in the zone," I pointed out. "Most of the folks in the zone need protection from you and your bunch. Your people are all dead, by the way. In case you didn't figure that out already."

"I'll kill you for that."

"Let's table that for now. What I really want to know is this; what's your relationship with Je'Dik, and where is he at the moment?"

"Je'Dik's schedule is none of my business."

Partly true—Je'Dik doesn't tell Blackheart anything, and that irks him.

So Je'Dik doesn't tell you anything, and that pisses you off, doesn't it?"

"Hmmph."

"Did you know that you not only got in bed with the Krelk, but you managed to get in bed with the worst one ever? Were you aware that he's wanted by both Alliances and on at least sixteen other, non-Alliance worlds?"

"Alliances? What the hell are you talking about?"

"He didn't tell you anything, did he?"

"No." Blackheart sounded sour about it, too.

True, Zaria informed me. *I'm not surprised*, she added.

"Did Je'Dik promise you a victory against the Northern gang?"

The anger in Blackheart's eyes told me everything; that's exactly what he'd been promised. "Would it interest you to know that he probably promised the same thing to the Northern gang? Or that he probably set up that raid on the southern farm to put you on that path —to a fight to the death for one gang or the other?"

"What would that accomplish?" Blackheart's words were bitter.

"It would be the cage fight of the millennia," I pointed out. "He won't care who ends up on top; he's set to make money off this, I'd bet my life on it. Yours, too, as it turns out."

"Who are you?" Blackheart demanded. The truth of what I'd said was finally sinking into his brain, and he couldn't decide whether to be angrier at me or at Je'Dik.

"Somebody who was sent by the Reth Alliance to investigate the deaths of two scouts who were looking for Je'Dik, hoping to keep him from harming more than he has already. Word is that you're responsible for both those deaths. This time, you met me instead of two humanoids."

"Je'Dik said they were spies, sent by Adolf," Blackheart grumbled.

"Adolf—the leader of the Northern gang?" I was guessing, now, but it made sense, in a sick kind of way. No wonder Je'Dik had to intervene and turn them against each other. In most cases, they were cut from the same cloth.

"It's not his real name."

"Just as Blackheart isn't yours, *Robert*."

"Hmmph. Those scouts of yours weren't the only ones we killed." He wanted to make sure I knew he'd killed Forneel and the rest of his party. "I hope they weren't your friends." He forced a grin as I tightened the thorns around his face and throat.

"Is there anything else you'd like to tell me before we end you?" I asked, watching as a trickle of blood ran down his right cheek.

"If I don't check in, the Krelk will come."

True.

"Ah. Now that's worthwhile information," I said. "When do you have to check in?"

"You think I'll tell you that?"

In three days, Zaria informed me.

"Three days, eh?" I crossed arms over my chest, then.

"I have to meet with them personally this time," Blackheart claimed. "With Je'Dik beside me."

True.

"Then I suppose it's too bad that we have someone here who can make themselves an exact duplicate of you," Nyarr stepped forward. In moments, he'd transformed his image to become Blackheart's twin.

"I'll kill you for this," Blackheart struggled against my thorns again, causing his neck to bleed. "You still don't know what Je'Dik looks like," he added. "You need to keep me alive to deal with him and the Krelk."

"Too bad you're not the only one who knows what Je'Dik looks like, then," I pointed out while transforming everything except the thorns holding Blackheart. His indrawn breath let me know how convincing my disguise was, including the dark goggles that Je'Dik never removed. "Now, I think we have everything we need from you, and you've become redundant. Jessie, would you or Caleb like this execution?" I became myself again and turned to the two vamps.

"I'd rather watch him die from here," Jessie said. "It will be justice that's been a long time comin'."

"Same here," Caleb agreed with Jessie's words.

"I have something to say, first," Loor stepped forward, surprising me.

"To him or to me?" I asked.

"To him, for sure," Loor nodded at Blackheart.

"Have at it," I tossed out a hand. "He's not going anywhere, and he can't move his hands to cover his ears."

Loor cleared his throat while he studied Blackheart. "Your time was over, long ago," he began. "You thought you were important. Powerful, even, because you could convince others to follow you and help you commit your crimes. What I have to tell you is this; you're no different from a thousand other petty murderers on a thousand other worlds. I've seen too many of your kind, and you know what? They always lose. If not now, then a day comes when they fall—and they always fall hard. You should have died when recorded history says you did. You're nothing but a cadaver that has kept hate, bigotry and racism alive. I wouldn't want to be you when you see the other side."

"You think I believe that shit?" Blackheart rasped. My thorns had tightened again around his neck.

"It doesn't matter whether you do or not. I'm done," Loor nodded to me.

Blackheart started to say something; I suppose we'll never know what it was. I clenched my thorns and he exploded in a mass of flesh, bone and blood-turned-ash. By the time I allowed my thorns to disappear and become a normal arm again, only a dusting of black powder streaked the floor to mark the passing of Bob Blackheart.

"What do you mean, we have to replace Blackheart's bunch?" Sam asked during our subsequent meeting.

"You don't have to act like them, just stand in for them. As long as the Krelk believe that there's a fight at the end of this, they'll keep their bargain and the people in the zone will be safe—or as safe as they can be in these times," Nyarr explained. "Rajeon has their communicator and the weapons given to them. Our job, now, is to stalk the Northern gang and eliminate them if we can. If we accomplish that, I think we can find stand-ins for that bunch, too."

"What will that achieve?" Clyde asked.

"Let's just say that the Krelk don't like being embarrassed," I said. "They also don't like being caught at something they swear they don't do. Trust me; track that gang and do your best. After that, well, we'll hope for better things to come."

"It makes sense," Mayor Jack said with a nod. "If we get rid of both gangs, maybe we can put a government together in the zone and work our way out of local or martial law everywhere."

"That's a good start," I agreed. "But first, we have to follow the script Je'Dik has laid out for the Blackhearts. I know where Blackheart is supposed to meet with Je'Dik and the Krelk who are coming. We have work to do before then."

"What's that? Other than looking for Adolf and the Northern gang?"

"We have to find a suitable location for the fight of the century," I shrugged. "That will make the Krelk happy."

"What about Je'Dik?" Jessie asked.

"Oh, I think he needs a vacation from his criminal doings," Loor studied his fingernails. "I believe I can help with that."

"Once the real Je'Dik is out of the picture, then Nyarr and I will stand in for Blackheart and Je'Dik. We'll give the location for the fight and everybody's happy."

"Are we going to really fight?" Clare asked.

"I hope we can find the Northern gang before it comes to that," I told her. "If we find them, we need to pick them off—one at a time if necessary. They'll think it's Blackheart, when it's us."

Clare's eyes locked on her rifle; she'd done well enough killing vampires with it; Nyarr had already told me that. The weapon gave Clare an edge she wouldn't have otherwise. Raising her head, her eyes locked with mine and she nodded. We had deaths to avenge, and she was prepared to help.

Frankly, I was happy we were still in one piece; many of the townspeople hadn't made it.

"I'm willing to join the new Blackheart gang," Mayor Jack offered. "As one of the humans."

"We'll be needing more volunteers, although I'd like to keep some here to protect Ste. Genevieve," Caleb agreed.

"Then let's sort that out before daylight comes, and we'll discuss feeding the group and providing necessities."

"We can handle the food detail, for vamps and the others," Nyarr said. "Loor and I can transport food and blood substitute."

"Blood substitute?" a vamp asked.

"Tastes like blood, feeds the body," Jessie shrugged. "I've been living off it for days, now."

"You have enough?" Caleb asked.

"Don't worry, I think we have you covered," Loor grinned.

"We can handle the hunt in shifts; that's what we've been doing with the Blackhearts," I said. "That gives each group a break for meals and rest on the houseboats before going out again."

"Then let's work that out," the Mayor said. "Before the vamps have to go to ground for the day."

Clare

"All the bodies are gone, along with any other evidence." Nyarr explained to Mom when she asked. "I hope the northern bunch doesn't go near Ste. Genevieve. There's still a sizable human population there, and they had the daylights scared out of them last night."

"They're lucky to be alive," Mom sighed.

I knew what she was thinking—only six of us; Barbara, Jeffie, Sanjay, Ishaan, Mom and I, had survived Fairlawn Point and the aftermath.

Again, I wanted to curse John and the Mayor, but shoved those thoughts aside. Nyarr had brought most of us back to the boats; Loor and Rajeon stayed in Ste. Genevieve to work out volunteers for the hunts. We planned enough to schedule three full shifts.

"Raje intends to ask for human volunteers to help cook," Nyarr told Mom. "You can't cook for more than one shift—it's not fair."

"Thank goodness. I was worried," Mom let her shoulders droop and released a sigh.

"Whoever cooks on graveyard shift won't have to cook much—it'll be mostly vamps on that one," I pointed out.

"True," Mom hid a smile at my accidental irony. "If I supervise the day shift, Freddie does the evening shift, and we find one more to supervise at night, then we can sleep better, I think."

"Outside of Ste. Genevieve, where do you think we ought to start looking for Hitler and the Northern gang?" Sam walked in, followed by his brothers.

"The Northern gang needs to eat, same as anybody else," Mom huffed. "And they have to feed their humans. It wouldn't hurt to start with Fairlawn Point. A lot of gardens got left behind, and those should be producing something for the humans about now. They can fish in the river, too, for protein. As for the vamps, they'll either feed off their humans or be forced to find a fresh source somewhere. Fairlawn Point isn't far from a few other towns to the west. They could be hitting those."

"A good place to start sniffing, for sure," Sanjay came in. "Is there anything to eat?"

"I can make a turkey sandwich for you," Mom offered.

"I'd take it. Their humans can only provide so much blood, and usually not more than two or three times a week, according to Jessie, unless they're draining them and finding new ones. Still means the surrounding towns could be hit, one way or the other."

"Then why did they kill everybody in Fairlawn Point?" I glared at Sanjay. "It makes no sense."

"They were angry." Jessie walked into the kitchen and nodded at us. "We killed their best soldiers and took their weapons. They had a score to settle with us. John thought the town could survive. It couldn't—not after nightfall. Rajeon was right to ask everyone to come to the river."

"Bad decisions, all the way around," Mom started slicing turkey for Sanjay's sandwich. "Want mayo or mustard, hon?"

Ste. Genevieve

Rajeon

"We'll start looking north of here," I said. "I think we can stop them before they reach the area."

"That would ease our minds," Mayor Jack said. "We want to keep them as far away as possible. We lost too many tonight; I'm not sure we can withstand a similar attack."

"Understood. Is everybody on board with their shifts?" I looked around; daylight would arrive in half an hour, and the vamps either needed to come with me or find a place to dig in.

"I think we have it," Jack said.

"Where are my cooks?" I looked around.

"Here," three women and two men stepped forward. They figured they'd be cooking a lot of fish. They were in for a pleasant surprise.

"We have some vegetables coming in," someone offered in the back.

"We can trade for those," I said.

"Trade what?" Jack asked.

"We're stocked on staples. I think we can make it a fair trade. Especially if you have salad greens or tomatoes."

"Sounds good. Everybody going with Rajeon, gather around," Jack ordered. We'd be taking a small party of volunteers back with us, so they could shower and sleep during the day. Loor would be back for the vamps who weren't coming with us now.

Le would stay in Ste. Genevieve to protect the people; she could send mindspeech to any of us if they were attacked.

You'll be okay? I sent to her while gripping my medallion.

You'll know it if I'm not, she replied.

I'll get your replacement here in about eight and a half hours. Can you stay awake that long?

I will.

Good. See you in a few. I turned to Loor and nodded; he transported our party to the boats.

Clare

Mom and I had gone to our cabin shortly after Rajeon and Loor arrived with a small party from Ste. Genevieve. They coordinated with Ishaan to find sleeping bunks and arrange for showers and such. I left them to it; they didn't need me and I was exhausted.

Standing in the shower, I let warm water wash over me while the night played on an endless loop in my head. I hoped I could sleep, though; images kept invading my mind of the battle earlier.

Once or twice, I'd barely gotten shots off before a vamp reached one of the residents of Ste. Genevieve. More than once, I'd been too late to save someone because I couldn't move fast enough to hit two enemy vamps fighting in tandem.

In the end, I couldn't savor the victory; I only counted the smaller defeats and failures.

My failures.

People had died because of them.

Stepping out of the shower, I toweled off and stared at my reflection in the mirror. There were no marks on my face—none on my skin anywhere. I'd been protected well enough by my medallion.

Others around me weren't, and I was glad I couldn't see the scars left on my soul as I gazed in the mirror. Pulling my pajamas off the peg on the bathroom door, I dressed, turned off the light and walked into the bedroom. Mom was already in bed, but the lamp between our beds was still on.

Mom stared at the ceiling.

"You okay?" I asked her.

"I haven't been okay since the Krelk showed up. None of us have."

"We could ask Rajeon to take you where Barbara and Jeffie are," I began.

"No, hon. I have to see this through. If the planet goes down, it won't be because I deserted, you know."

"Yeah. I kinda feel the same." I pulled the covers back on my bed and sat down on the side. A tapping on the door interrupted our conversation.

"I'll see who it is," I said, standing and walking toward the door. When I opened it, I found Rajeon standing outside.

"Clare, can I see you for a few minutes?" he asked.

"Sure. Mom, I'll be back," I told her before shutting the door behind me.

"Rubber duckies?" Rajeon fingered the collar on my pajama top, which depicted dozens of the old, standard tub toy.

"I love rubber duckies," I sighed. "They're so—yellow."

"Clare?" Rajeon said softly.

"Huh?" I stopped watching his fingers as they stroked the duckie on my collar and looked up at him.

"This." He leaned in and kissed me—hard. Before I knew it, I was lifted in his arms and my legs were wrapped around his waist as he kept kissing me, and I started kissing him right back.

Was it the night, and all that had happened? I can't say, but if he'd asked me, then and there, to go to his cabin, I would have. Instead, he kissed me one last time, then drew back to lock eyes with mine.

"Someday, we won't be stopping," he breathed before leaning in and kissing my forehead. "Not for a long time."

"Uh, okay," I whispered. Honestly, his kisses had scrambled my brain, I think, they were so intense. I watched as his mouth curved in a smile.

"Go to bed, baby," he said, setting me down on the deck.

"You should, too," I pointed out.

"I'm going. After a cold shower, I think."

"Your choice," I called out softly as he walked away. He lifted a hand in a backward wave and disappeared toward the opposite end of the boat.

That night, I went to sleep with the memory of late-night kisses, which blocked out anything else that troubled me.

"The day shift belongs to the group with the most humans in it," Nyarr explained at breakfast the following morning.

"That makes sense," I said. "The most they'll have to deal with is human slaves and shifters, if they find the Northern gang."

"Le will be with them after today; we'll find somebody else to do guard duty for Ste. Genevieve."

"Is she sleeping?" I asked.

"Yeah. Dead tired," Nyarr shook his head. He didn't like it, I could tell, but I think we all were there or nearly so. "Loor is with them right now. He'll trade places with the graveyard shift starting tomorrow. You, Rajeon, Ishaan and I are on the evening shift. That's when the vamps will start to rise, and we have to bring in our special ops."

"Special ops, huh?"

"That's what Raje says."

"Which shift is Sanjay on?"

"Day. Sam, Le and Sanjay are taking that one."

"Good. Thank you." I tried to hide my relief, but Nyarr tended to notice those things.

"He's still a bit new to this," Nyarr stuffed half a biscuit in his mouth and chewed for a few moments.

"And you don't send out the newbies on the worst shifts," I finished for him. "Like John did."

"Mm-hmm. I set them down not far from your mother's garden this morning," Nyarr said. "Looked to be some evidence of pilfering, but the scents are up to Sanjay and a few others to find."

"Could be animals—could be nearby towns coming to scavenge," I said.

"True enough."

"Anything left for me?" Rajeon walked in and took the chair beside mine.

"I'll get you a plate," I said, rising from my seat.

"Thanks," Rajeon sighed. "I'll get yours next time."

I had to hold myself back from leaning down to hug and kiss him. Well, nobody needed that kind of embarrassment at breakfast, I guess.

Rajeon

"Mayor Jack suggested Magnolia Hollow," Le said as we pored over a holographic map of the area later. Nyarr supplied the map while the rest of us studied the portion of the former conservation area Jack described.

"See, here is the flat part, between the rise and the river," she pointed at Nyarr's images, which he automatically enlarged for her. "Trees have come up in the clearing since the Krelk took over, but what's there is relatively scattered and won't get in the way like the heavily-forested area to the west."

"It has a high lookout," Sam said. "I was there roughly fifteen years ago, and it was a great place to take pictures. If the Krelk want a good vantage point, that would be it."

"We can't disappoint their audience, now can we?" Ishaan growled.

"They'll probably have micro-cameras flying around during the fight; it's how they transmit the cage fights to their viewers," Le said. "Once they have a single base of operations set up, the cameras will transmit to the main transmitter, then a vid-bot editor will choose the best shots and they'll see all the action, all the time, on multiple screens."

"They'll bet on outcomes, and even individual battles if some of the fights last long enough," Nyarr huffed. "It's a big business—under the table, of course—with the Krelk."

"With plenty of the money going to Je'Dik, no doubt," I said. "Otherwise, he wouldn't be here. Not if there isn't a big payday in it for him. And, since he's probably covered to his chin in bone dust, we can't find him beforehand unless we do it by more conventional and much slower methods."

"We really, really need to find him before that meeting with the Krelk tomorrow night," Le said.

"Don't I know it," I grumbled. "We're monitoring the communication device twenty-four-seven, but there hasn't been a squeak of air from that asshole."

"Did you find the items taken from your supervisor and his party?" Sam asked.

"No. That means they either tossed them because they didn't know how they worked, or Je'Dik has them now, and that could be a really bad thing."

"I have a question," Clare spoke for the first time during the meeting.

"What's that?" I turned toward her. She sat between Le and Ishaan, so we weren't close together. I found it less distracting that way.

"How did the Northern gang get to Sam's farm so far south, and then back to Fairlawn Point so fast? Those things happened within days, and humans don't walk that fast. Plus, they had the cages to deal with."

My eyes dropped to the table as a terrible fear gripped me; one I hadn't considered before. "Sam?" I turned to the eldest alligator brother. "Tell me as much as you remember about the attack on your farm."

"We thought it was the Blackhearts at first, you know that," Sam blinked at me. He was beginning to worry, too—I saw it in the creases of his forehead and the way his hands gripped the table.

"Why did you think it was the Blackhearts?" Nyarr asked.

"Several of them were dressed in confederate garb—you know—but the regular uniforms, not the hat and coat we found the real Blackheart wearing."

"Blackheart wasn't with the ones attacking us," his brother, Boyd, said with a sigh. "We didn't know much of anything until we woke the following evening. The weapons they had were Krelk weapons—the same kind that freeze us so they can tag us and throw us in cages," he shook his head. "We went down fast, there were so many firing at us. Our human friends died right away; they couldn't handle the force of those weapons—their lungs froze and they couldn't draw breath."

"The smallest shifters died, too," Sam sighed. "Two cardinals and three rabbits."

"The following evening, we woke to find one of the northern vamps grinning at us through our cage bars," Steve took up the story. "They had meat from somewhere. I worried it was our friends, but we were ordered to eat it, so we did."

"That's horrible," Le breathed.

"Did they tell you they were the Northern gang?" Clare asked.

"They didn't, but some of their slaves said they'd come from up north. They were talking about passing the outskirts of St. Louis and doing some killing while they were there."

"One of the vamps—the one who never talked in front of us—he had a swastika tattooed on his neck, here," Clyde pointed to the right side of his own neck. "Shaved head, mean look, I'd have kicked him if he'd come close enough."

"I'd say that's probably Adolf," I tapped fingers on the table while digesting what the shifters told us. "Now, back to Clare's question— how did they get from Sam's farm to north of Fairlawn Point so fast— with humans and big cages to transport?"

"I'd say they had help," Nyarr suggested. "Although the Krelk don't have any transport facilities close to the zone—not that I'm aware of, anyway."

"Transport facilities?" Clare asked.

"It's technology they shouldn't have, along with a lot of other things they shouldn't have. Little more than a century ago, they were still riding gahks and using bows and arrows to hunt their food. The weapons and technology they now use to take over worlds shouldn't have been possible," I explained. "Transport facilities can do mostly what Nyarr and Loor can do when they take us from place to place. Our method is much more comfortable than what the Krelk can do, though."

"Do they have somebody like Nyarr, then?" Sam asked.

"It's possible. I can't help saying that I hope they don't. This would really screw up everything." I didn't add that if Je'Dik was involved, anything was possible, and that was terrifying. If he had a witch, warlock, or a wizard, even, plus evidence that I was here, investigating for the Alliances, we could be in more trouble than I previously feared.

"The full moon is a week away," Doreen warned. "Most of the folks here will be forced to change—there's no way past that. I'd say that the biggest danger to all of us will come then."

"That's when they want the fight to happen," Clare's eyes were wide. "When some of us won't be able to ah, fight back properly."

That's what I was afraid of, too.

CHAPTER 11

*R*ajeon

"Who do you want with you tonight, for the meeting with the Krelk?" Nyarr asked.

"Since we don't have Je'Dik right now, and we have no idea whether he'll show up." He gave me a concerned look.

I shook my head, telling him I hadn't made plans.

"Then it's you and me for sure," Nyarr said. "Plus a couple of vamps —but they have to be ah, of the lighter variety. It's a dead giveaway if we have black vamps when we're trying to be Blackheart and company."

"I'll take Clare and Clyde, to act as our human slaves," I said. We need the vamps to be our guards—just make sure they can hold their anger in check while we have our discussion with the Krelk."

"I can make ah, Caleb and Jessie look somewhat lighter—just for a little while. Do you think they'll be upset?"

"I sure hope not. I trust those two with my life."

"I'll ask them, then. I can also hide the rifles from sight; only Clare and Clyde will be able to see them."

"Sounds great."

"You're really worried about this meeting, aren't you?"

"It's not just this meeting. We should have heard something from Je'Dik by now, and we haven't. That tells me he knows more than we want him to. I'm not sure what it will mean for the long term, but I have a very bad feeling about this."

"Then we'll hope he doesn't crash the party tonight," Nyarr grimaced. "That could cause all sorts of grief, and have the zone razed by tomorrow morning."

"I need to check in with the ship, too, before they get antsy," I admitted.

"To tell them all is well, just before all goes to hell? In a handbasket, I believe is the term?"

"Oh, yeah."

"Have fun with that. I hope you have your dancing shoes on, bro. All this will require some moves, I think."

"Hmmph."

"I don't have complete confirmation; all I have is word that someone claiming to be Je'Dik is here. It could be some random Krelk trying to push his way onto a bigger stage by pulling others into his wake," I explained.

"Damn. If you had solid evidence, we could pull out of here now and let the ASD know," Keela Mirlund huffed. I watched her carefully in the vid-screen while keeping my face as impassive as usual.

She wanted to get out of here and let the ASD handle things, which would require a long chain of command and meetings out the ass before they decided to do anything about it. Besides, they had other battles to fight. This one was mine, but I wasn't going to tell Mirlund that. Let her keep thinking that things weren't on the edge of a knife in the buffer zone, even though they were. And, if I pulled rank on her now, I couldn't prevent her from communicating with Headquarters and telling them I'd gone 'round the twist or the bend or whatever idiom was appropriate in this case.

They'd order us out of here anyway, and I'd have to respectfully decline. I had a mission and higher orders, and it could take a while to get a message to the Reth Alliance Founder, Ildevar Wyyld, to change the hive mind at Headquarters with a direct order.

While I considered that, and Mirlund went on a journey of speculation regarding Je'Dik's presence or lack thereof, I fingered my medallion.

I'll tell the ship to report back and leave you there, by my orders, Ildevar's voice rattled my nerves, making me jump. *Where they are, they could become a target. I trust you'll let me know how things go?*

I will, sir, you can count on it, I replied swiftly.

Good. I'll send the message now. The ship's commander will let you know when they're leaving.

Yes, sir.

Zaria has faith in you. That means I do, too. Don't fail us, all right?

I'll do my best, sir.

"We have an incoming message," Mirlund interrupted her train of thought on Je'Dik. "It's from Headquarters. Rajeon, they're recalling the ship," she began, then gasped. "They're telling me to leave you on the surface."

"I'll be fine," I told her as she turned a worried gaze on my image in her screen. "I'll follow along eventually, I think. Plus, I still have my communicator."

"Are you sure?" She was already waving at Ginter and a few others, to get the ship ready for travel.

"I'm sure."

"All right, then. We'll let you know when we get under way."

"I'd appreciate that."

She ended the call in the middle of shouting at Ginter. Mirlund wanted away from this place, and I couldn't blame her. Earth had claimed eight of our crew already, and that wasn't normal.

Nothing about this situation was normal, actually. When she reached Headquarters, there would be a long interview session about Forneel and the five who died with him, in addition to the two scouts killed by Blackheart. I was glad I wouldn't be a part of it, frankly, and hoped they'd only request personal notes from me when I got back.

If I got back.

Je'Dik's silence in all this troubled me a great deal, and that was never a good thing.

"Are you ready for this?" I asked Clare, who arrived on Nyarr's boat, her mother right behind her.

Nyarr had provided clothing for her—black leather pants and boots, with a deep-red, long-sleeved shirt. He'd also used power to create a temporary black heart tattoo on her neck.

The others wore one, too, on their arms, although Nyarr promised to remove them the moment the Krelk left. Jessie didn't like it at all, I could tell. Who could blame him? That black heart tattoo represented hatred and violence.

As for the paler skin, Jessie and Caleb shook their heads about the temporary change. I was accustomed to disguising myself as whatever would be most useful, but to them, it probably felt like a massive disservice.

"Don't worry about it," Jessie turned and patted my shoulder. "I could've turned it down and stayed behind, but I'd rather be there with you, you understand? Caleb, too."

"Thank you, Jessie. I trust you both with my life," I nodded to him. "That's why we asked you and Caleb, first."

"I wouldn't let Jessie have all the fun," Caleb grinned. "We're good."

"Thanks, Jessie," Clare put an arm around his waist for a hug.

"Any time," Jessie smiled and patted her back.

"If you're handin' out hugs, I'd take one," Caleb said. He got one, too.

"Let's get this mess over with," Nyarr breathed, turning himself into a replica of Blackheart.

"Right there with you, bro," I told him, while become Je'Dik's twin. "Time to go see the Krelk."

Nyarr transported us to a place not far from where we were

supposed to meet. I lifted Blackheart's communication device and signaled the Krelk, who answered right away.

They were already there and waiting for us.

"Shield up," Nyarr breathed. Jessie and Caleb dipped their head to me, letting me know they were ready.

"Let's go," Clare breathed, allowing her rifle to drop into the crook of her elbow. I was glad Nyarr hid it and Clyde's rifle from the Krelk; we could be in big trouble, otherwise.

Clare

Clyde and I took the lead, as the usual, expendable shifters in front of Rajeon and Nyarr, while Jessie and Caleb came behind, to protect them from anything coming from that angle.

To anyone else, I'm sure we looked very much like Blackheart and his entourage, although it almost made me ill to see Rajeon's skin look like Krelk armor-plating, and over that, he was dressed in leather, as Krelk males were accustomed to doing.

Nyarr wore a confederate hat, pinned up on one side, and the gray, double-breasted frock coat that I'd seen Blackheart wearing before he died. Nyarr even placed a look of normal wear and tear about it, to make it appear natural.

Six Krelk waited for us when we reached the designated meeting place. One's cheekbone plates moved into what might be taken as a smile, I suppose, when he saw Rajeon and Nyarr approaching.

"I hope you have a suitable answer for us," another Krelk stepped forward.

"I believe we do," Nyarr grunted, sounding so much like Blackheart it sent a shiver down my spine.

"Where is that?"

"Roughly nine miles north of Ste. Genevieve, in what was known as Magnolia Hollow. There's a large, bare space there that will be suitable, I think." Nyarr pulled a worn paper map from a coat pocket.

The map had been marked. He offered it to the Krelk who'd smiled at us.

"Yes," the Krelk agreed after studying the map for a moment. "I will examine this area myself, but I believe this would be more than suitable. The river is very close, too, and that is quite fortuitous." He handed the map to two other Krelk. Well, they were subordinates to the boss Krelk we spoke with, unless I missed my guess. The other four were guards.

As for the fortuitous part of his comment, were they planning on taking shifters after the battle, or would they have boatloads of spectators?

Something about that bothered me, especially if they planned to bring spectators. This bore thinking about, and I really wanted to have a discussion with Rajeon about it. Another worry I had, was that the real Je'Dik could arrive and throw us into another fight with actual Krelk.

Consequently, I kept my nose and my ears open for anything that was out of the ordinary. I figured Jessie and Caleb were doing the same thing.

Clyde stood beside me, with hardly a muscle moving—definitely ex-military. I almost jumped when boss Krelk spoke again.

"Meet us at this designated place on the full moon," he directed. "Bring as many shifters as you can capture. We will pay you well."

"I'll see to it," Nyarr agreed.

"Je'Dik," boss Krelk nodded at Rajeon.

"Ar'Kon," Rajeon nodded back.

Ar'Kon released a pent-up breath; I think this was the last test to be passed, and somehow, Rajeon had managed it. I'd ask him about that, too—when we were far away from here.

"Large shifters are preferred," a subordinate Krelk said as Ar'Kon turned to leave. He and the guards fell in behind Ar'Kon and walked toward the river.

"Let's go," Nyarr jerked his head in the direction we'd come. He took the lead, with Rajeon right behind, while the rest of us followed.

There are micro-cameras following us right now, Rajeon pretended to scratch the armor-plating around his throat. *Nyarr and I are hoping they'll leave after we get far enough away.*

We walked for more than a mile before Nyarr called the all-clear.

"Thank the Lord," Caleb muttered when Nyarr transported us to Ste. Genevieve and returned Caleb and Jessie's appearances to normal. Clyde's and my black heart tattoos disappeared, too. Rajeon was already himself again as we walked past a vampire guard into Ste. Genevieve.

How did you know Ar'Kon's name? I sent to Rajeon.

Zaria. She saw his eyes through mine.

I really, really, wanted to meet her in person, because I had no idea anyone had talents like that.

"How did it go?" Mayor Jack walked out of City Hall to meet us.

"As well as can be expected, and about the way I figured. They want us to rendezvous at the Magnolia Hollow location on the full moon and bring shifters with us," Rajeon replied.

"We have six days to find the Northern gang, don't we?" Jack asked.

"That's right."

"We found some evidence of their presence, and, as you may have guessed, they've hit some of the nearby towns to replenish their human slaves and shifters," Jack reported. "As for where they go to ground, it's still a mystery. Sanjay and the bear, Monty, couldn't get any kind of scent on that."

"They have to be out of the light somewhere," Caleb grumbled. "All of us do."

"We'll be looking again tomorrow," Jack shrugged. "If you don't find anything tonight."

"Yeah. We're headed that way after we get a drink of water," Rajeon said.

"Come on in," Jack waved toward City Hall. "We got the containers of cooked turkey you sent. Folks around here haven't had that in a while."

"No problem," Rajeon said. We trooped into City Hall for a short water break before heading toward Fairlawn Point. We stood the chance of running into the northern vampires there, and after a tense meeting with the Krelk, we needed a breather.

"Where do you want to start looking?" Nyarr asked as we held cups of water and discussed our next mission.

"How about the nearest town?" Rajeon suggested. "If there's anybody there to talk to, I want to ask questions or sniff around to see if there's fresh vamp scent."

"I'll go get Ishaan and the others, then," Nyarr said before disappearing. They'd been waiting on the boat for the meeting to be over and for Nyarr to come for them. I was happy to have Ishaan and a few others helping; the Krelk had made me uncomfortable and I felt on edge because of it.

"What's wrong?" Rajeon came to me and settled a hand on my shoulder.

"I don't know," I told him. "I just got the willies, seeing those Krelk."

"Don't let it bother you," he patted my shoulder and took his hand away. "It's over and we didn't even get a scratch from it."

I didn't tell him that something felt off to me about the whole thing. He seemed satisfied with the way things had gone, so we were heading northward to track the Northern gang.

Nyarr arrived with Ishaan, Sam and the others, then, and we were on our way.

Rajeon

I couldn't help feeling that the Krelk knew something, and in all likelihood, they had the weapons and communicators belonging to Forneel and his party. I hoped we'd passed inspection, standing in as Blackheart and Je'Dik, although Je'Dik's absence and silence troubled me a great deal.

Like Clare, I was getting the willies, too, but I didn't want to ramp up her fears by adding mine.

"This is Bernet," Jessie whispered as we approached the small town closest to Fairlawn Point, where Nyarr set us down.

"How many live here?" I asked him softly.

"Last I knew, about sixty or so. Can't say for sure, now."

I nodded at Jessie's words; who knew whether the Northern gang had taken or killed the residents?

The main street was paved at one time, but now the road was deteriorating with continued use and neglect. Empty store fronts faced the streets; only a few looked as if they were still in use.

I knew when we passed the butcher shop—the smell of fish guts and offal reached my nose, while Jessie grimaced at the stench.

Clare carried her rifle, barrel down, as we carefully made our way through Bernet. So far, there were no lights or sounds anywhere.

Were there shifters in Bernet? I grasped my medallion and sent to Jessie and Ishaan.

A few, Jessie replied. *The stench hasn't ever been that bad from the butcher shop, either. They usually carry that stuff away or use it for fuel.*

Has to be at least two days old to smell that bad, Ishaan informed me.

Let's check the houses, I sent to the entire party. *Ishaan, you and Jessie take the lead and let me know if you pick up human, shifter or vamp scent.*

Bernet was a typical small town; a main street of businesses, with houses populating smaller streets on either side. A gibbous moon hung overhead as we took the nearest side street, heading toward the homes on the north side. Still, there were no lights visible anywhere, and there should be candlelight, at the very least, if not an oil lamp or two burning.

I don't hear anything except bugs, Ishaan told me.

Nothin' but the usual, Jessie sent. *Normal town scents, although some of it is wearin' thin, if you know what I mean.*

I do. You don't smell human deaths, do you? Can you tell that? I sent to him and Ishaan.

I'm not getting that from here—human decomposition can be overwhelming, Ishaan replied.

Keep looking.

I'll check this house, Ishaan offered, as we approached a small, frame home along the street. I watched as his wolf cautiously broke away from the group and stepped onto the concrete front porch.

It's open, he sent as he carefully pushed the wooden front door open with his nose. The subsequent explosion could have killed all of us; medallions protected those of us wearing them. Nyarr's shield covered the ones among us who weren't wearing Zaria's medallions. Without those things, we'd have perished.

Instead, all of us were flattened on the ground in a heap from the outward blast. When I was able to lift my head afterward, I found Ishaan's wolf still standing where the house had been only moments before. Zaria's medallion had somehow kept him from being blown to bits.

"Damn," Caleb swore aloud, startling several of us. "You think they're all set to blow?"

"I'm not taking that chance," I said, struggling to stand. "Come on. I don't think there's anybody here. They've either been taken or killed elsewhere."

Leaning down, I offered Clare a hand to help her up. The others were rising and helping their companions to do the same. Ishaan finally turned and made his way back to our group.

You okay? I sent to him.

I watched as he nosed his medallion. *Close call,* he growled mentally. *Too close.*

I hear that, I agreed. "Nyarr, take us to the Coquina farm. We need to regroup."

Clare

I was glad Mom couldn't see her garden. There was evidence of trampling, and potato and carrot plants had been pulled up when they weren't even close to yielding anything yet.

"Where do you suppose the people of Bernet are now?" Rajeon asked as I surveyed the wreck of all our hard work.

"Depends on whether they're alive," I shook my head. "Alive, they'll need food. Dead, doesn't matter, does it?" I turned and lifted my eyes to his.

"Yeah. I'm sorry they damaged all this," he nodded to the garden before us. The soil was soft and dark beneath our feet, the rain had been bountiful but not too much, and that made conditions perfect for growing vegetables this time of year. The garden would have been a good one, had we not had to leave it behind for scavengers to ruin.

"You think all those houses were rigged to explode?" I asked Rajeon.

"Baby, I'm worried about just that," he replied. "I'm also concerned about the fact that not only were there explosives there, but somebody is pretty adept at putting things together so the house would explode as it did."

"You mean a tripwire or something?"

"Yes, and all that requires knowledge, the proper equipment, and the explosives. That wasn't a small bomb, sweetheart. It blew that house into matchsticks."

"I uh, noticed."

"Somebody was hoping we'd show up there," Rajeon went on. "Somebody was either expecting us or the Blackhearts."

"What difference would it make?" I asked.

"If they're looking for Blackheart, then that explosion would warn that they were in the area. Blackheart would have sent his expendables in to check a house, and they probably understand that. If they're looking for us, then it's almost a sure bet that Je'Dik is behind that, and he's gunning for us, now."

"You think he may be in communication with those Krelk we met earlier, don't you?" I frowned at him.

"I'm concerned, yes."

"Rajeon, you're not making me feel better about any of this."

"I know, and I'm sorry. After this latest blow-up, things may have taken a far more sinister turn."

"We still need to find the Northern gang, don't we?"

"More than ever."

"Yeah. Where the hell could they be going to ground? It has to be in this area somewhere. Doesn't it?"

"It could be within a twenty-mile radius or so," he said. "They have to feed not long after they rise, and it's either their slaves or another town that provides their meals. Nyarr, Loor and Le can't get anything on any of them, and that means bone dust is involved."

"I'm beginning to hate whoever is behind spreading that filth around," I hissed.

"You're in a long line of people who feel the same," he informed me. "Come on, let's go to the river and follow it northward. I don't think Sanjay's bunch went that way."

In a few minutes, we had everybody gathered, and Nyarr transported us to the river bank. Again, Jessie and Ishaan were in the lead, searching for scents of vampires and their slaves.

How are they getting those cages around, if they have captives? I sent to Rajeon.

That's been troubling me, too, he replied. *There could be a lot of methods employed, and most of them I don't like.*

Yeah. I didn't elaborate, but if the Northern gang had access to someone with Nyarr's capabilities, we could be in worse trouble than we already were.

We walked perhaps four miles before Ishaan yipped and Jessie stopped in his tracks. They'd found vampire scent, either going to or coming from the river.

Rajeon

Ishaan now led our group westward, with Jessie right behind him. I had no idea which way the vamps had been walking to lay that trail. Jessie said at least three vamps had come that way, and Ishaan agreed. They also said the trail was relatively fresh, perhaps a day old.

Therefore, we followed their scent, and hoped we'd find something useful at the end of it. Clare walked in front of me, her rifle in her hands, her shoulders tight with tension as Ishaan and Jessie led us toward a stand of trees.

If the Northern gang wanted to ambush us, this would present a good opportunity. *My strongest shields are up,* Nyarr informed me. *We have medallions scattered throughout our group, so I'm hoping those two things together will be enough if a clutch of vamps attack—especially if they have bombs or ranos weaponry.*

He was worried that Je'Dik was now fully aware of our presence, just as I was. If any Krelk could buy or steal ranos weapons, it would be him. The other thing that worried me was this; how did he get here in the first place? Was he smuggled in by the Krelk currently in charge of Earth, or did he find a ride elsewhere?

I think we're on the same wavelength, Nyarr replied after I'd accidentally sent those thoughts to him while still holding my medallion. *Le and I had a long discussion about that already, along with what the other half of him actually is. He looks mostly Krelk, with only a few, minor differences. They've welcomed him here with open arms, apparently, so those differences don't matter.*

If there's ground to be gained or money to be made or cage fights to watch, the Krelk are all over that shit, I grumbled. *Wait, Jessie's signaling.*

Dead body, Jessie sent back as I strode forward, leaving Clare and the others behind me.

It's nobody I know, Ishaan nosed his medallion.

Me, either, Jessie agreed. *Human, though. Not shifter.*

Anything else around it? Is it a trap? I asked as I approached the still form lying amid spring weeds and grasses.

Don't know, Jessie said. *Not long dead—maybe a couple hours. Not much blood around it.*

Human male, Ishaan added.

You think he was killed here, or moved from somewhere else? I asked.

I'm gonna turn him over slow, Jessie leaned down to grip the man's arm while I watched. If there were a bomb lying beneath the body, I had no idea whether we'd be knocked down while our medallions saved our skins.

When Jessie turned the body over, there was no bomb, much to our relief. We did find the cause of death, however. At least five sets of vampire bites were on his neck; he'd served as their dinner, and they'd left him where he dropped.

Two more vamp scents joined these three here, Ishaan sniffed around while Jessie and I studied the body. *Those two came from north of here, and they brought the human with them. Like they invited the other three for dinner.*

That makes me think they were going this way from the river, rather than going toward it; all five vamps went west from here, Jessie joined Ishaan as they circled the dead man.

They had to go into the river somewhere, and then come out where we picked up their trail, I pointed out. *Probably to hide their tracks.*

I reckon that's right, Jessie agreed. *No vamp wants to stay in the river longer'n he has to.*

Ready to go on? I asked.

Yeah, Ishaan growled.

Let's go, then. Keep your guard up when we get to those trees. I don't feel anybody watching, but you never know.

I dropped back to walk near Clare, who lifted her rifle again. With cautious trepidation, we crept forward behind Ishaan and Jessie. No scents other than the vamps we tracked had reached our sniffers so far, and we'd almost reached the darker shadows beneath the first trees.

Crossing beneath the overhanging limbs and new leaves of elm and cottonwood, I suddenly felt as if I'd entered a tunnel, where normal sound had been sucked away. No night insects made noise; no animals or night birds scuffled away or called out.

Spooky, Clare sent.

The sound, when it came, reminded me of a snake slithering through grass, only amplified. We froze; the sound stopped. Ahead, I could barely see Jessie's shoulders in the gloom. He took a cautious step forward.

The sound came again.

Le, we need you, I heard Nyarr's sending.

Why would we need her? My eyes widened in sudden understanding. Le appeared ahead of me, and between Jessie and Ishaan.

Nyarr, she sent, *can you remove these trees when I say the word?*

I can. I'll move the others back at the same time.

Thank you.

She screamed the word of challenge, the trees disappeared and the world turned upside down as the huge, serpent-like Ra'Ak struck at Le's giant jaguar.

With a snarl she leapt out of his way before attacking from her new position. Huge claws raked across the Ra'Ak's scales, leaving trails of greenish goo behind.

Every part of that was poisonous—not only to Le but to almost anyone else. I was prepared to step in if Le wasn't successful; I had no binding laws with the creature she faced.

The Ra'Ak roared and struck at Le again, almost hitting her shoulder as she jumped high to avoid the fangs and horned tail he whipped about himself. Already he was tearing up grass and soil with his tail in an effort to blind Le's jaguar.

Right after his forward attack, which Le barely avoided, she dug in her back claws to strike at him again, leaving another raking down a quarter of the Ra'Ak's thirty-foot length.

The older they are, the longer and deadlier, or so said the information I'd read on the copper-scaled monsters. A thirty-footer had to be at least two centuries old, and age meant nothing to the creatures.

All I could do was grasp my medallion and send up a prayer that Le wouldn't be poisoned; we had no healer to deal with it.

Are you ready to go if she falls? We can't interfere with their fight, Nyarr sent. He sounded afraid, and Nyarr never sounded like that.

Stupid rules, I replied. *And yes, I'll go if she falls.*

Stupid rules, indeed.

Le yowled, making Nyarr and me jump, but she'd sunk her claws into the Ra'Ak's eyes, making him scream in agony.

"Harder, love, pierce his brain," Nyarr shouted aloud at Le. The serpent's tail thumped and flailed behind him, although the monster was too afraid to move his head—if Le did pierce his brain with her claws, he'd die. Moving his head could bring about his demise even faster.

The scream from Le terrified me, until I realized it was a scream of victory. The second she pierced the Ra'Ak's brain, he exploded in a massive dusting, sending larger-than-fist-size chunks hurling outward at a frightening rate of speed.

Nyarr, thinking swiftly, dumped all of us flat on the ground as those chunks whizzed over our heads with deadly velocity. Had we not been shielded and on the ground, we'd have died.

CHAPTER 12

*C*lare
 "My people were created to fight those things," Le turned a small glass of bourbon in her hands as Nyarr and I sat with her.

Jessie, Rajeon and Caleb had gone back out with Loor and the graveyard shift after Le killed the monster. It wasn't a long battle, thank goodness, and I wondered at first why Nyarr had moved us so far away while they fought.

I learned the reason when the monster exploded into huge chunks when it died. Those chunks could have killed any of us if Nyarr hadn't dumped us on the ground and thrown an extra shield over us. Anyone standing closer than a quarter mile would have died quickly, and farther than that they'd still have been seriously injured by even one of those chunks.

"Drink that, you need it," Nyarr placed a hand over Le's to stop her from toying with the glass. She looked up at him. I don't know what passed between them, but I felt it was time to excuse myself.

"I'm going to bed," I told them and rose from my chair. "See you in the morning."

"Good-night," Nyarr said while keeping his eyes on Le.

I hoped Mom was asleep as I made my way to our cabin; I had to digest what I'd just learned about giant, poisonous serpents called Ra'Ak, who could transport themselves and others, just like Nyarr did.

Is that how the Northern gang had gone to take Sam's farm, and then made it back to Fairlawn Point so quickly? Rajeon was probably considering the same thing.

I hoped there were no more Ra'Ak to contend with, but I'd seen Rajeon's eyes after this one died; he was worried there could be more.

Rajeon, Loor and Nyarr had a short, intense conversation after Nyarr brought us back to the boats, before going out again with the late shift. Neither I nor anyone else had been invited to join those three on Nyarr's boat.

I figured the terms *Ra'Ak* and *Je'Dik* came up regularly in that conversation, because I had questions about both those things now, and how they could be connected.

I opened the door to the cabin as quietly as I could so I wouldn't wake Mom. I should have known better. "What happened?" were the first words out of her mouth.

Rajeon

Chunks of the Ra'Ak's dusting were everywhere as we struggled to relocate the scent of five vampires where the stand of trees used to be. With two werewolves and six vampires, it should have been easy.

It wasn't, and I knew why.

Those vamps had been transported away after reaching the trees, and were then replaced by the Ra'Ak, who may or may not have transported the vamps in the first place.

We're back where we started, Jessie informed me.

I know. My words held defeat. I'm sure Je'Dik sent his Ra'Ak to destroy us. Would he realize we had a Saa Thalarr working with us, now that the Ra'Ak was dead? Only a few were powerful enough and talented enough to kill the giant serpents. Le was one of them.

There's something we can do that may prove useful, Loor said.

What's that?

I should destroy the houses in Bernet. Think of what may happen if innocents wander in looking for food or such?

Good idea. "Everybody, we're about to move," I said aloud. "Bernet is a trap for anyone coming across it, so it needs to be destroyed."

Clare

Rajeon was tired, dirty and discouraged when he and the others returned from the night shift.

"All we accomplished was blowing up the rest of Bernet. The whole thing was a trap waiting to explode," he sighed, taking a seat at the table where I nursed a cup of coffee. I hadn't been able to sleep and neither had Mom, so we talked most of the night and then got up to set bread to rise.

"I hope you're going to sleep after you eat," I told him as Mom put a plate of breakfast in front of him.

"I plan to. You need sleep, too," he frowned at me before lifting his fork and cutting into his eggs.

"Yeah, well," I shrugged.

"Have you had breakfast?"

"Yes."

"Didn't find any scent of those vamps when we went back. They were transported out of there," he bit into a biscuit and chewed.

"Do they have a warlock, or did the Ra'Ak do that?" I asked.

"Could be either. We don't know."

I watched him eat after that; he was exhausted and my questions could wait. What I didn't expect was for him to take my arm when he finished and rose from the table. "Come on," he said.

I blinked and opened my mouth to argue, before snapping it shut. He pulled me from my chair and stalked toward his cabin.

Apparently, I was going with him.

"Here," he sorted through a drawer before pulling a clean T-shirt out and tossing it toward me. "Put that on; it's not comfortable sleeping in jeans. I need a shower."

Before I could argue, he walked into the tiny bathroom and shut the door. After a minute or two, I heard shower spray hitting tile.

Was I really doing this? My mind wanted to balk as I kicked off my shoes and unsnapped my jeans. With shaking fingers, I pulled off my shirt and bra before diving into Rajeon's T-shirt.

Now what? Should I lie on the bed? Sit on the bed? Stand there like a dolt who couldn't decide?

Finally, I folded my clothes and set them on top of his dresser, then put my shoes beside it. His cabin was roughly the size of the one Mom and I shared, but with a single, larger bed instead of two smaller ones.

The water cut off in the bathroom; he'd be out soon. I sat on his bed and leaned back against the headboard, while pulling the quilt over my legs.

Some women might have struck a pose to look sexy. Others might have gone for a demure look. I figured I was the deer-in-the-headlights girl.

"Damn, I'm tired," Rajeon opened the bathroom door and stepped out, wearing black sleep pants and drying his dark hair with a towel. I think his muscles had muscles as I watched him move; his chest, ribs and abs mesmerized me.

He tossed the towel into the bathroom, raked fingers through his hair and turned toward me. "Ready to sleep, baby? Because that's all I have strength for."

"Yeah."

"All right, then. You a side or back sleeper?"

"Uh, side, usually."

"Good. You like arms around you or not?"

"Around is okay."

"All right, then. Scoot over, you're on my side of the bed."

"Sorry." I scooted over quickly.

"Good. Great." He sat down where I'd just been, his weight making the bed creak softly. I hadn't heard that sound in a long, long time. "Turn on your side," he motioned for me to roll over.

I did. He moved in behind me and wrapped an arm around my waist. Ten seconds later, he was snoring softly. I closed my eyes, feeling protected for the first time in what seemed like forever.

Rajeon

When I woke, I was on my back and Clare was halfway sprawled across my chest, her cheek resting on my shoulder. The T-shirt was far too large for her, and the neck of it hung off a shoulder, leaving soft skin exposed.

If I moved to kiss it I might wake her, so I settled for watching her sleep instead. Moments later, she stirred and opened her eyes. I watched the clouds of confusion clear as she realized where she was.

"Hey, sleepyhead," I rumbled, lifting a hand to stroke her cheek.

"Rajeon?" she tried to move away, but I pulled her closer instead. "Come on, you don't have to worry while you're in bed with me," I breathed against her hair. "We won't do anything you don't feel comfortable doing."

"Will you be mad if we don't do anything?"

"Clare, look at me," I said. Raising her head slightly, she blinked worried eyes at me. "Never, ever, think I'll be mad because you didn't feel comfortable about something. Got that?"

She sighed, laid her head on my shoulder again and closed her eyes. "I like this. What we're doing right now," she whispered. "I want to do it for a few more minutes before we get dressed and go find food."

"All right, then," I lifted a hand and played with her brown curls before leaning in to kiss them. "You can have whatever you want, darlin'."

"I want things the way they used to be," she nuzzled my bare shoulder. That did things to me—woke things up that probably should have stayed asleep. "I'd take you to breakfast at Lena's, it was the best home-cooking restaurant in Fairlawn Point," she continued. Her stomach growled to punctuate her words, and then she planted a kiss on my shoulder.

"Then let's go find food before my body overrides my good intentions," I told her.

"Is that what this is? Good intentions?" She lifted her head and smiled.

"Yep. Come on, darlin', let's go find something to eat and some coffee to drink."

Clare

Nothing happened—we slept, I clutched my medallion and sent to Mom, whose eyebrows were lifted high when Rajeon and I walked into the kitchen. If we'd done anything, I wouldn't lie to her about that, either.

"Any word from the day shift?" Rajeon asked as Nyarr walked in.

"I just heard from Le; she says they haven't found anything, although they're about to head farther up the river bank. The Northern gang has more than five vamps, so the others had to go somewhere. She's trying to pick up more scents."

"I hope she doesn't find other—monsters," I said.

"That makes two of us," Rajeon nodded at me.

"Want ham and beans and cornbread, or roast chicken?" Mom asked.

"Beans and cornbread," I lifted a hand. Mom knew how much I loved that, so she'd probably made it with me in mind.

"I'll have what Clare's having," Rajeon grinned. "With lots of butter for the cornbread, please."

"I'll help," I walked toward the giant stove, where a huge pot of ham and beans waited. I pulled out bowls for Rajeon and me while Mom sliced generous squares of cornbread for us.

"Lots of ham, just the way you like it," Mom patted my back as I dipped into the pot with a huge ladle.

"Thank you. I love you," I said, leaning back to kiss her cheek.

"Is that beans and ham?" Clyde walked in with Sam right behind him.

"Yep. I'm dishing out if you want some."

In minutes, they were sitting and talking with Rajeon while I put bowls of food out and Mom took an entire plate of sliced cornbread and a dish of butter to them.

Rajeon got up to serve seconds to those who wanted them while I ate my serving with butter-slathered cornbread. Mom's cornbread was like heaven from an iron skillet, and I hadn't had any for a while.

"This is mighty good, Doreen," Sam grinned at Mom. I blinked—she turned pink at the compliment.

Alrighty, then.

"Sam and I have been discussing farming," Mom sniffed as I blinked at her.

"Doreen's been telling me how to do organic farming," Sam grinned. "She has plenty of good ideas we can use at our place."

"I hope we get back there soon," Clyde said while buttering another piece of cornbread. "We can save part of the crop if we make it back in less than a month."

"It'll be slim pickings for the winter if we can't save some of it," Sam agreed. "I know how much you like carrots," he teased.

"Goes with the territory," Clyde grinned. "Apples, too. Nothin' better on a full moon."

"Says the full-moon vegetarian," Ishaan walked in and slapped Clyde's shoulder.

"That's right, squirrel boy," Clyde grinned at Ishaan.

"Nah, raccoons and possums are easier to catch," Ishaan said. "Although deer is the best."

"Those have been hunted down to nothing," Sam sighed. "If you see one, it's a miracle, nowadays. Same goes for the wild pigs."

"The world is a different place," Mom sighed and set a cup of coffee down before taking the chair next to mine.

"That's for damn sure," Sam shook his head. "Too many friends and family gone. Our world squeezed to the size of a thin strip of land on either side of the river. Makes you wonder what the hell happened, and why we were singled out."

"You weren't singled out," Rajeon said. "There are plenty of other worlds in the same situation—some worse, some better, but only by a little, you understand. Planets taken over that shouldn't have been, and mostly those who had no way to fight what landed on them."

"Is somebody helping them?" Mom asked.

"As many as can be spared. Doreen, it isn't just anybody who can walk in and handle this sort of thing, for lots of reasons. You saw how easy my two predecessors went down. They were humanoid and didn't stand a chance. They might have lived longer if Forneel hadn't been such an asshole, but they were doomed the second they landed on Earth."

"Why were they sent, then?" Clyde asked.

"Because those who sent them are only now getting the idea of what they're up against in this. Maybe they'll understand soon that only a few can stand up to the demands made on the scouts in situations like this. Otherwise, these scouting trips will continue to be suicide missions."

"What he's saying is that we need more scouts who can turn into a mass of diamond thorns," Nyarr walked in and pulled up a chair. "And even then, they have to be properly trained and evaluated before they're sent."

"How many others like you?" I asked the pointed question. Rajeon's dark eyes met mine briefly before he went back to his food.

"Not enough," he breathed. "Not nearly enough. The sad truth? The same one who may be behind all these takeovers and destruction may also be the one responsible for destroying much of my race."

"Je'Dik? Is he the one?" Mom asked.

"Je'Dik is likely only a finger on a hand of the one responsible," Nyarr answered her question. "You've seen how difficult it is to track Je'Dik. Consider that there may be dozens of Je'Diks on dozens of worlds, and all of them bent on destruction. Toss in a few planetary wars, and you can see how those able to deal with these messes may be stretched past the limit."

"This is horrible," I whispered. Earth wasn't alone it its suffering. We were just another planet in a large group of suffering worlds, and help was either non-existent or difficult to come by.

There'd be no Marines landing here to save us; that hope had died years ago. What we had was a handful of people with unusual talents, helping a few of us stay alive against impossible odds. Whether we ultimately survived remained to be seen.

"Where are we heading tonight?" I asked Rajeon, who was now lost in thought.

"We have the coordinates of the northernmost trek made by the day crew," Nyarr said. "We'll arrive to relieve them and go farther north, searching for more signs of the Northern gang. If we don't find them soon," he shrugged.

I knew what he wasn't saying. The full moon was coming, as was the expected fight between vampire gangs. I had no doubts that Krelk would come; I merely didn't know how many.

Most of us were at the mercy of the moon, too, and would be forced to change. In several cases, that would hamper more than help, and I fell in that category. My otter couldn't lift or fire a rifle, no matter how much I wanted to.

Dear otter goddess, would the end come like this?

"Grab your gear, it's time to go," Rajeon pushed back his chair and stood. "We'll find them or die trying," he added before turning abruptly and heading toward our boat.

Rajeon

Clare's fears and emotions crossed her face while we'd talked at dinner; it was easy to see she was losing hope that we'd find our quarry before the full moon.

I was losing hope that we would avoid walking into a trap; the longer Je'Dik and this gang eluded us, the surer I was that a trap waited. If we were unsuccessful when the moon came full, I worried about the ones who weren't protected by medallions, and some of those who were.

If the entire buffer zone was destroyed, and Je'Dik was vindictive enough to do just that, where could Sam and the others live and survive?

Pushing that worry to the back of my mind, I cleaned my teeth, shoved the laser pistol in the back waistband of my jeans and stalked out of my cabin to meet with Nyarr and the others.

Rain fell as we landed next to the day party. They'd traveled to a location roughly fifteen miles north of Fairlawn Point.

"We found nothing," Le and Mayor Jack reported. "No scent, no prints, we may as well be hunting ghosts in this wet," Jack added.

"There's hot food and showers waiting on the boats," I told them; they looked weary in the early night, and all were drenched from the relentless rain. Sanjay's wolf chuffed his readiness; I nodded to Le, who transported her bunch back to the boats.

"I can provide a shield overhead to keep the rain off, but it won't help with tracks or scents the rain has already washed away," Nyarr told Ishaan, Jessie and Caleb.

"Then don't worry about it; we've been wet before," Jessie said.

"And we'll get wet again, count on it," Caleb agreed.

"Then let's go. Everybody, keep your eyes, ears and noses open to anything unusual on either side. With this rain coming down, they won't need the river to hide themselves."

I hope this rain doesn't last all night, Clare sent to me after we'd trudged through the muck for more than an hour, with no sign of the Northern gang anywhere.

It's a slow-moving system, I warned her. *Keep your hood and collar up, darlin'. Flooding is a possibility, because this is coming from the northwest and is just now reaching this section of the river.*

Great. Something to look forward to, came the sarcastic reply.

I thought you were a water creature, I responded.

If I were otter right now, I'd be holed up in my den, waiting for the rain to be over.

I stopped dead in my tracks and turned to blink at her while rain slapped against the slicker and hat I wore. "Say that again," I held up a hand to stop the others.

"I said I'd be holed up in my den if I were otter," Clare said, then sneezed. I motioned for Nyarr to join me as I watched Clare pull a soggy handkerchief from a pocket and wipe her nose.

"Nyarr, I think I know where those assholes have been hiding," I breathed as he stopped at my side.

"Where's that?"

"Clare, you didn't build your den, did you?" I asked gently.

"No. I think it was originally built by beavers, but they moved to a different arm of the river where it wasn't so active. Why?"

"You think they've been using dens with entrances below the water line?" Nyarr asked.

"Yes. Vamps can swim quite a distance, too, if they're motivated enough and don't mind getting wet."

"How are we gonna find them, then?" Sam came forward to ask.

"During daylight, when Miss Clare can swim up and down, looking for them."

"I can help with that—my brothers, too," Sam declared.

"We have otters and gators," I said, giving Nyarr a fist bump. "And I can become one or the other if I want. Let's pull everybody back to the boats; we have a day mission to plan."

"You'll be without us," Jessie and Caleb approached.

"I know, but they won't be able to fight us if we dig them out," I said. "Let's give this a try before we waste more time tracking what can't be tracked—especially in this mess."

"Show no mercy if you find 'em," Caleb said, slapping my shoulder.

"Let's go," I nodded to Nyarr. "This rain isn't doing any of us any good."

Clare

"I don't know what caused it," I told Mom as I accepted a clean handkerchief. I'd sneezed at least four more times after coming back to the boats, although it was easier to breathe there.

"I don't remember you being allergic to anything," Mom said as she felt my forehead. At least I was dry and in clean clothes, although I felt chilled from being in the rain for more than an hour.

"You still sneezing?" Rajeon walked into the kitchen where Mom and I were talking and having hot tea.

"Yeah. Still congested, although it's not as bad, now."

"You don't have allergies?"

"No." I wiped my nose, which insisted on a continuous run.

"You didn't feel this way when we came across the Ra'Ak, did you?"

"No." I shook my head and wiped my nose again.

"Nyarr," Rajeon gripped his medallion and spoke aloud at the same time.

"You have something?" Nyarr appeared, a mug of steaming tea held in his hands. He had the same idea I did—getting warmed up.

"I'd like to take a fast trip back to our last location on the river," Rajeon told him. "Give us the best shield you have; I may have missed something."

"Doreen," Nyarr handed his mug of tea to my mother.

"I'll keep it for you," she smiled at the warlock.

He and Rajeon disappeared.

Rajeon

If we hadn't gone back when we did, rather than waiting until morning, we wouldn't have seen them. If Clare, Sam and his brothers had gone into the water, they could've been killed quickly.

How was this possible? Je'Dik was certainly employing every trick he could to destroy us, and this one had almost worked. Could still work, actually, with the appearance of this new threat.

These creatures were definitely not local, and most definitely a problem. Three kapiri had crawled from the river, while a fourth kapirus was in the act of climbing from the water.

They were sniffing where we'd stood earlier to have our discussion before leaving. If we'd stayed, would they have attacked us? Water demons were dangerous to any human or humanoid; they found their blood to be a delicacy they couldn't get enough of.

Six more kapiri climbed the slippery bank while Nyarr and I watched from the invisible shield he'd placed about us.

Should we kill them? Nyarr asked.

They're bigger and just as hard to kill as the Krelk, I reminded him. *At least the Krelk don't want to drink your blood while you're fighting them. Plus, they may be waiting for you or Le to expend power again. If Je'Dik has a power sniffer, we could be in big trouble. If he has more Ra'Ak, we're certainly in trouble. They'll recognize Le's power from several light years away.*

I'll have to strengthen the shield around the boats on the underside, Nyarr pointed out. *If we leave these things alive, they could come hunting us.*

And if they come hunting us, then they could be bringing lots of friends with them.

Just what I was thinking.

This could be what made Clare sneeze, I said as the thought hit me.

You mean she's a walking barometer for these fuckers?

Looks that way. The rain may have obliterated their scent on the ground, but if one poked even part of his head above water for just a second, she may have scented it without realizing.

You think we'll find them holed up with the vamps?

They could be protecting the vamps, I suggested. *And they could be the ones to expand existing dens to hold several vamps at once.*

Then we don't need our shifters in the water, Nyarr said. *We need Clare on the banks, getting sneezy around the kapiri.*

I hear that. Take us back; we've seen enough for now. We have plans to make and they include a dozen kapiri or more.

Clare

"They're water demons," Rajeon explained as Nyarr created a two-dimensional image of the creatures, which hung in the air before him. "They like human blood. If they can't get human blood, they'll settle for shifter blood, or animal, even. I'm worried they're protecting the vamps during daylight, and at night, too, if we get too close."

"You didn't need to be fighting them and any vamps that were hidden tonight," Le pointed out. "We don't know how many vamps we're dealing with. That could turn into a massacre, and not one in our favor."

"Raje is worried Je'Dik has a power sniffer," Nyarr said, causing Le to go still. "Or more Ra'Ak, which is almost the same thing."

"Power sniffers?" Sam asked.

"Warlocks who can scry for power signatures. They're rare and expensive," Nyarr explained. "Sometimes they can feel it in the air around them and then tell who or what the power wielder is."

"Ra'Ak are tuned specifically to my race," Le mumbled, twisting her fingers together. "They know if we expend power, sometimes within a planet's orbit, if they're really sensitive to it."

"We won't worry about that right now," Nyarr said. I think something else passed between him and Le; her fingers relaxed, at least.

"We'll concentrate our efforts on vampires and kapiri tomorrow," Rajeon said. "Until then, nobody goes in the water. It's too dangerous."

"Are the kapiri amphibious?" Clyde asked.

"Yes. They can do just fine in or out of the water. That makes them extremely dangerous, and they can sniff blood from half a mile away if the wind is right."

"Why would these creatures protect vampires? Are they sentient?" Ishaan asked.

"If there has been some ah, manipulation with them, they could be ordered to protect vampires," Nyarr said. I could tell he wanted to grind his teeth over that information.

"In other words," Rajeon spoke up, "Kapiri are just sentient enough to be obsessed—by someone with that talent."

"This is sounding more and more like a well-planned,

concentrated attack," Le said. "One in which they know who, how many and what we are and are gearing up for that."

"I think so, too," Rajeon nodded. "But what else can we do, except see this through to the end?"

"It's not something we can walk away from," Le sighed and stared at her hands. "If we want people to live."

"I know you're here now, but where was everybody when the Krelk came in the first place?" Boyd spoke for the first time.

"Fighting a war," Nyarr's mouth tightened. "Trust me, it wasn't just a distraction so the Krelk could invade Earth and a dozen other planets, either. Some are still fighting the remnants of that war. That's why they send scout ships now, instead of sending the RAA and RCA at the beginning, to prevent the Krelk from landing on the planet in the first place."

"RAA? RCA?"

"Regular Alliance Army and Regular Campiaan Army," Rajeon explained. "They used to have a joint force that dealt with these kinds of things, but all of that was ended once the war started and those forces were pulled in to fight the planetary wars."

"How did those wars start?" Sam asked. "If you can tell us, that is."

"It's not a what, but a who," Nyarr shrugged.

"Who, then?"

"A dead god, to begin with," Le huffed. "Before his son took it over."

"What? Did you say a dead god?" I whispered, staring at Le.

"I did. He's been dead at least three times, and he just keeps coming back to cause more trouble, in ways you can't imagine."

CHAPTER 13

Clare

"He wants us there as the sun is rising," I told Mom, as she and I handed breakfast plates to those who'd arrived early to eat. Most of them would be going with us to search for the Northern gang and their guardian kapiri.

"I hope things go well," Mom dished up more pancakes with one hand and held out a small container of heated syrup with the other.

"That makes two of us. Full moon is in two days."

"It's like knowing when your heart attack is coming," Mom grimaced as she poured more pancake batter on the griddle. On any other day, I'd have stood there, watching as the cakes rose slightly and bubbles formed over the top surface of batter.

Not today. "Hey, Boyd," I handed a plate of bacon and eggs to him as he walked in. "Pancakes will be out in just a few seconds. I'll bring 'em to the table."

"Thanks," he grinned and turned toward a table where Sam and Clyde were already eating.

"Clare, go eat; I can help with this," Freddie arrived to lend assistance, with another kitchen helper from Ste. Genevieve behind him.

"These are for Boyd," Mom handed the plate of fresh pancakes to Freddie. "Get a plate, baby girl, I'll get your cakes out next."

"Thanks, Mom," I said, taking off the apron that I wore and handing it to the woman who'd arrived with Freddie. "Thanks, Mae," I told her, too.

"Not to worry," she smiled at me in a grandmotherly way.

Rajeon, Nyarr, Loor and Le walked in together; I got the idea that the meeting they'd just finished had only included the four of them. Releasing a sigh at being left out again, I took the plate of scrambled eggs and bacon Mae gave me and headed for the table where Ishaan and Sanjay ate.

Freddie arrived moments later with my pancakes and syrup.

Soon enough, Rajeon settled on the seat next to mine, while Nyarr, Le and Loor claimed the remaining chairs. Their meeting had gone on for quite a while; that's why they were late to breakfast.

"At least it's only fog this morning and not rain," Le mumbled, digging into her scrambled eggs.

"I hope it burns off fast," Nyarr grumped. "I'd like to see what I'm fireblasting, if it comes to that."

"Clare needs to see her targets, too," Rajeon reached over to rub my back gently.

"That would be nice," I agreed, cutting into syrup-laden pancakes. The sweetness hit my mouth shortly after, and I let it settle there with a sigh of pleasure.

"Fresh coffee," Mae set a tray of mugs on the table.

"Thank goodness," I said, lifting the nearest mug and sipping. "Wake-up juice," I then held my mug up in a salute to Mae, who laughed.

"I hear that and second it," Nyarr gripped his mug and drank.

Rajeon moved his hand from my back to take his coffee. I felt the absence of his warmth immediately.

Darlin, does your rifle have a full charge? I watched as he gripped his medallion.

Yeah. I didn't use it yesterday, so we're good, I replied. *I double-checked this morning, just to make sure.*

Good.

You're expecting a fight, aren't you?

I asked Nyarr to scry the river bank where he and I saw the kapiri last night. It's full of vampire dens. He couldn't scry for the vampires themselves because of bone dust, but he found the hollowed-out spaces where they've been hiding. Nyarr says there's some flooding, too, but the dens are high enough beneath the bank that the vamps can still use the space. My worry is that the kapiri we saw may have friends we didn't see last night. Those friends could be patrolling the river. Unless Nyarr can scry where they're hidden or focus on something specifically worn or held by individuals, scrying for moving entities is mostly useless.

"That's not good," I mumbled and went back to my pancakes. It wasn't good. The kapiri Nyarr showed us were all naked and covered in scales, much like the Krelk, although the male Krelk dressed in fur, linen and leather most of the time. It supported their macho, caveperson mentality.

The female Krelk went for fur and linen, or so I'd heard. Where they'd come from, there were no cotton plants. They weren't interested in cotton after they arrived, either. As for silk worms, well, those were just bugs to the Krelk. No bug threads for them, thanks.

I was surprised about the linen, actually, because it was plant-based. Everything else they wore involved an ultimate sacrifice.

Mayor Jack and the day crew wandered in for breakfast; they'd be coming with us. In fact, everybody was coming except for the cooks and our vamp contingent, for obvious reasons.

I hope this isn't a trap, Sanjay sent to me. He'd never used his medallion to speak directly to me before.

That makes two of us, I replied. *At least we won't be fighting vamps in daylight.*

That may be the only blessing we'll have in this.

Don't jinx us, Sanjay, I told him. *I'm worried enough as it is. What does Ishaan say?*

He's worried, too, but he'll follow Rajeon straight into hell, if that's where he's taking us.

That statement stopped my breath for a moment, because it

sounded envious and resentful. I wanted to remind Sanjay that Rajeon had saved his life and the lives of others, when they'd been pulled away from the Northern gang's captivity.

Was Sam feeling the same way? Clyde, too? I was too afraid to speak to them like this; their answers could be the same.

I'm sorry you see things this way, I told Sanjay. *Would you rather stay here with Mom and Freddie?*

And look like a coward? No, thanks.

It's not a matter of what it looks like. It's a matter of how you feel. If your heart's not in this and you don't think it's safe enough, then stay here. Nobody will say anything.

You said yourself that you're worried, he fired back. *Why don't you stay?*

I considered my answer carefully. It was close to the full moon, and werewolves felt it more than most shifters. They often became angry over next to nothing, and it was advisable to give them a wide berth and use discretion.

Because I'm thinking about the big picture, I guess, I said. *This may be the difference in whether the buffer zone lives or dies. Let's face it; the Krelk could kill us all if they want. I'd rather go out on my own terms. You know as well as I do that if they come in to destroy the zone, they'll kill or capture as many of us as they can. I have no desire to die in Krelk hands. Do you?*

No. Now he sounded sullen. I'd never seen him like this and wondered if his capture had done something to him that we didn't understand yet.

Did Ishaan know how his brother felt? My guess was Sanjay hadn't talked to him about it, but then he'd been reticent about sharing personal feelings with Ishaan before, mostly because he felt inadequate next to his older brother.

Ishaan had served in the military, like I did, although he'd served in army intelligence while I'd been toting rifles on the perimeters of army bases.

Was that why Sanjay had taken the job Sheriff John offered? Because he'd stayed home and gone to business school rather than choosing the military for a while? Had John shamed him into working as a deputy? Now I was more worried about Sanjay than the monsters we were about to hunt. The thought made me shiver.

"You cold?" Rajeon's hand was back, steadying me and calming my fears somewhat.

"Just a little," I lied. "I'll warm up when daylight hits."

"It's a cool spring; not too unusual," Sam said. He didn't sound worried or out of sorts like Sanjay did.

"Could be worse," Clyde agreed. "I remember snow on May first, a few years back."

"I remember that, too," I said. "I had pictures on my phone. I don't bother to look at those anymore or waste the generator's electricity to charge it up. There's no point."

"Too many memories," Boyd said. "I feel the same way."

"Hey, now, are we getting all sad and morose before we go out to destroy monsters? Is that any way to be?" Sam teased.

I snickered at his words and the world righted itself.

Rajeon

Sanjay and Clare had a private conversation at breakfast; one that upset her. I didn't want to pry, but if she was worried about what he'd said, then it worried me, too.

I considered leaving him behind on the boats as a precaution, but decided against it. I hoped Ishaan would keep an eye on his brother while we were out; our job was going to be difficult enough as it was.

"I've asked Freddie and Doreen to stay here, and asked the others to go back to Ste. Genevieve, like we talked about," Nyarr appeared beside me on the back of my boat while we waited for the sun to rise.

"What about Sanjay?"

"He didn't volunteer for either of those details. Most of the others were humans, and not armed well enough to take on kapiri. Le took them to Ste. Genevieve and is staying to protect them; it would be Je'Dik's sort of revenge to strike there while we're elsewhere. She's ready to join us if she's needed, though. All I have to do is send mindspeech."

"Does she know to call for us if she needs help?"

"I told her to."

"Then let's hope they don't attack in two places at once."

Nyarr was clearly worried about Le; she was probably worried about him, too. As the strong, fifth-level warlocks they were, he and Loor could defend against ranos weapons—for a while. Neither of us knew if their power could outlast a full charge on any ranos weapon. Nyarr and I worried that Je'Dik could have almost anything in his arsenal, including that deadly technology.

Our private meeting had been about many things, but we ended up discussing what might be thrown at us, and what to do with humans who didn't hold sufficient weaponry to fight back. Clare and the others felt left out, but information like that could make things worse for them in the long term.

"Sun's coming up," Nyarr breathed.

"Let's get the others and go."

Clare

"Ready?" Rajeon met us in the dining room, where we'd taken chairs to wait for transport. Nyarr and Loor walked in behind him; Le had taken Mayor Jack and the other humans to Ste. Genevieve. She planned to stay with them, in case there was a simultaneous attack there.

That's what the private meeting was about, I figured. After all, if Je'Dik knew Blackheart was dead, along with his gang, then he could take revenge against Ste. Genevieve, where it happened.

Le was set to call for help if it was needed; she'd told me that before she took her crew to defend their city.

I stood and slung my rifle over my shoulder; everyone else around me rose from their seats, too. Clyde only had a few bullets left for his gun and was determined to make them count.

What's wrong with Sanjay? Ishaan sent.

I wanted to sigh but didn't; Ishaan waited until now to ask that question?

Nerves, maybe? I replied. *He has some misgivings, I think.*

We all have misgivings. He's acting—weird.

I tried to get him to stay here, but he wouldn't, I said. *Maybe his captivity affected him more than we thought.*

Took a while for that to happen, then, Ishaan sounded skeptical.

Could it be the full moon coming?

Before now, I'd say he was one of the least affected by that.

Should we tell Rajeon?

Sanjay will know something's up if Rajeon makes him stay behind.

Yeah, you're right about that.

"We're going," Rajeon announced, and our subsequent relocation to the riverbank curtailed further conversation.

Rajeon

The sun wasn't quite above the trees on the east side of the river when we landed on the western bank. Still, more than bright enough for the vamps to have taken cover and gone into the rejuvenating sleep.

"I'll scry for kapiri, first," Nyarr said softly beside me. "Loor will keep watch and hold a shield around us."

Nearby, Clare held her rifle in her hands, its barrel pointed downward. Her posture was tense and watchful, in case anything came from the river that endangered any of us. How could I not feel responsible for what was about to happen, knowing that secrecy was required so reactions would be genuine?

"The kapiri are gone," Nyarr announced aloud. "I can't find any evidence that they're nearby."

"What about the vampires?" Sam began when the trap was sprung, pulling all of us into the capture sphere the Krelk had planted around us.

Clare's shriek almost broke my heart—and my resolve; we were all jerked upward and the force of power inside the sphere prevented any weapon from discharging. Her rifle was rendered useless as she and the rest of us were being tossed about like clothing in an old-fashioned dryer.

Only the medallions that most of us wore kept us from breaking bones or other injuries while we were spun around and flung against the interior walls of the invisible sphere.

Capture spheres were too expensive to create for just anyone to have one. My thoughts were fleeting and chaotic as I was tumbled about inside this one.

Je'Dik was either extremely wealthy or extremely larcenous. Either way, we were caught up in his snare.

For now.

Doreen

Barbara and Jeffie were far better off where they were, but I couldn't help admitting to myself that I missed her company when Clare and the others were off hunting monsters.

Freddie wasn't the talkative kind; not one for idle chat or to share my worries. He was talented in the kitchen, though, and I appreciated that.

"Do you worry about them—Sam and the others?" I hesitated before asking the question.

Freddie was busy cutting vegetables for the pot pies we were making. His knife stopped making the regular chop-chop-chop sound against the wood cutting board as his hands stilled. "Yeah, I guess I do, but what can I do about it? I'd be no help to them, even if they were in trouble." The chopping continued. "I wasn't much help when the vamps came for us," he shrugged. "My brother is much better at defense than I ever was."

"I suppose I feel the same—I never was good at shooting anything, but I was pretty handy with a garden hoe, the few times I found a snake in the garden."

"My grandmother was the same," Freddie grinned while he chopped. "She fended off snakes and gators with hers."

This was the most information I'd gotten from Freddie since we'd met. "How old was she when she passed?" I asked him.

"Nearly three hundred, I think. Nobody messed with grandma."

"I never met my grandmothers—either of them. Otters have a habit of getting captured or killed while in the river."

"Wild boars have to find safe places. We used to roam the forests, but the minute a human showed up, we had to skedaddle unless we wanted to be shot. Now, with bullets as rare as they are, we have to watch for traps or vampire gangs looking to sell to the Krelk."

"Same here. We got to the point where we had a big meal before going out, instead of waiting and catching fish. It was safer. Have you always enjoyed cooking?" I asked him.

"I have. I learned from Ma and Grandma. They taught me how to make everything from biscuits to steaks."

"What happened to your mother?"

He turned his head away—this was a fresher wound. "She moved to Kansas when she met my stepdad. You know what happened to anybody outside the zone."

"Yeah. My oldest died in California. Sometimes I like to imagine that he's living in the mountains in one of the freshwater rivers or lakes, but that's just a dream."

"I hear that," Freddie agreed and patted my shoulder. We both knew the Krelk had ways to track anybody or anything, and they'd have found him, whether in human or otter shape.

"He was in the military before—in fact, he was the one to convince Clare to enlist, because he went to college afterward with the benefits they offered. She did, too."

"That training sure helped us in Clare's case; she doesn't miss much with that rifle of hers."

Something big flopped in the river during the silence that followed

Freddie's words; both of us went still. I reached for the largest knife in the knife block on the counter; Freddie still held his knife in his hand.

Cautiously I walked toward the door, with the worst possible images going through my mind.

What we found was just as bad or worse; a ring of the monsters that Rajeon and Clare had gone to hunt now surrounded our flotilla of house boats. Somehow, they couldn't get past a certain point; something held them back. If it were Nyarr's shield, I'd give him a hug and a kiss when he returned.

"What are we supposed to do?" Freddie whispered in alarm as the huge monsters began to hammer against the shield around the boats with huge, scaled fists. When it didn't break after their initial assault, they roared their anger.

"I don't know." My voice trembled when I answered—would those creatures continue to attack our protection? If they did, could they eventually break through? Gripping my medallion, I sent a message to Clare.

Your monsters are here, surrounding the boats, I told her.

She didn't reply, and that made me shiver. *Le*, I sent next, *the kapiri are surrounding the boats, trying to break the shield.*

We have Krelk attacking, Le replied, her sending curt and frazzled.

"Heaven help us," I turned to Freddie, then. "I think we're being attacked in all three places."

Clare

Just go along; I think Nyarr and I will be questioned first, Rajeon sent. We'd stopped tumbling in an invisible sphere as a small army of Krelk began to walk toward us.

I was huddled against one side of the sphere; my rifle had gotten tangled around me and I was attempting to stand and pull it around.

You want them to question us? I sounded incredulous.

I want to see if Je'Dik is with them.

I went still. Many things went through my mind, and one of those things was this; could it be that Rajeon was just as foolish about that monster as his previous supervisor?

If I find out you planned this, I responded.

He didn't reply. I jerked my head toward him; he looked guilty.

I wanted to curse. At him, the Krelk, Nyarr and anyone else close enough. *Your medallion will only work for communication inside the sphere; it keeps everything inside and lets nothing else in*, Rajeon informed me.

If I survive this, I may kill you myself.

If we survive this, I hope I can explain.

There is no excuse for this, I hissed back at him. *No explanation is going to work.*

At that point, the Krelk had reached the sphere, where we hung inside it in various poses, none of them comfortable.

"When we release the sphere, you will drop your weapons or die," a Krelk informed us through a translator.

"What do you want?" I snarled back at him.

Clare, Rajeon warned.

"Why, to talk," the Krelk grinned. I hated Krelk smiles. They were hideous, revealing sharp, pointed teeth. The armor plates on cheeks and forehead wiggled in ways that defied normal expression, so I had no idea why they bothered.

"We have weapons aimed at each of you," he was now frowning directly at me. "Drop yours when I release the sphere or you'll die."

Please do what he says. You could get all of us killed, Ishaan sent.

Nearby, Sanjay stared at the Krelk outside the sphere. He didn't look frightened or angry, as the rest of us did. His stare was blank, and that troubled me more than anything. Sam, Boyd and Clyde didn't have the same blank stare, making me think that whatever was going on was solely contained within Sanjay.

What had they done to him?

The moment the sphere was released, we landed on the ground amid mud, weeds and grasses. I fell to the ground after failing to prepare myself for the drop.

"Drop your rifle," a Krelk lifted his weapon and pointed it directly at me.

"Clare," Rajeon barked.

I pulled the strap over my head and set the weapon in front of me before pulling my hands away and holding them in the air.

"Stand," the Krelk commanded.

I stood as quickly and as gracefully as I could, given the circumstances, before turning to glare at Rajeon. Not far away, Clyde's rifle was already on the ground at his feet.

We'd been caught like mice in a trap.

"We have orders to capture all of you, including your friends in Ste. Genevieve and those on the boats," the lead Krelk grinned again. "We won't chain you; if any of you think to escape or attack, you'll be shot and left where you fall."

We were lined up single file and ordered to walk westward, toward a stand of trees. I hoped there wasn't one of those Ra'Ak monsters waiting there to kill us. Le apparently had her own battle to fight; I wondered if she was giving up as easily as Rajeon did.

As for Mom and Freddie, if Nyarr's shield failed around the boats, they had no real weapons to protect themselves. Would they be taken captive, or killed outright? Hunching my shoulders and silently cursing Rajeon, I followed behind Boyd as we were marched along by our Krelk captors.

Rajeon

Not only was Clare furious with me, the unexpected news that her mother and Freddie were also in danger frightened her. I hadn't expected that when these plans were made earlier.

We'd only imagined that Ste. Genevieve might be attacked, and Le was prepared to get the humans out of there to keep them safe. The boats had to be under attack by kapiri; they weren't in the river nearby, Nyarr said so.

If this entire gamble went the least bit wrong, I may have ruined anything that existed between Clare and me. Boyd, Steve and Clyde passed under the canopy of trees first, followed by Monty, Sam, Clare, Ishaan and Sanjay. Chuck and Will, the gray werewolves, went next, then Nyarr and I came last, guarded by six armed Krelk.

Sanjay was reacting oddly, too, and I wondered why that was. The rest of us were wary and watchful; Sanjay acted as if we were out for a morning stroll.

That spelled trouble; I merely wondered what sort of trouble it was, and whether the medallion he wore would keep him out of danger or prevent him from causing the rest of us problems.

Perhaps I shouldn't have been surprised when I walked beneath the trees. At least fifty more Krelk waited there, with the human slaves of the Northern gang huddled on one side.

They'd been hiding them during the day, no doubt, so we couldn't eliminate them as we'd eliminated Blackheart's gang.

"So, our wanderer came back," a Krelk broke away from the larger group and approached Sanjay. "Tell me, what has rendered you invisible to us?"

A chill ran down my spine; they'd tagged Sanjay a different way, and he was either under a vampire's compulsion—or worse.

I hoped it wasn't worse, because that had happened *before* he received the medallion. It wouldn't protect him from what was already there.

"The only difference is this," Sanjay pulled his medallion from beneath his shirt and held it out. Ishaan growled softly as he watched his brother. Sanjay heard but didn't even twitch at Ishaan's anger.

Fuck me, Nyarr's sending echoed in my mind. Was I hoping for no trouble? Trouble had just arrived, and it could spell doom for the entire zone.

Doreen

I almost fell when the boats started moving on their own. This wasn't a storm to be steered away from, and I wondered why it was happening.

"Take a seat," Freddie caught my arm and led me to a table. We both sat while the boats picked up speed, heading northward. I could see the eastern bank of the river passing by in the distance.

Roaring sounded behind us; the kapiri didn't like this turn of events. Once we'd taken seats, however, the boats kicked into a higher gear; one I didn't know they had. Now the far bank was flying by, as if we were on a speed boat instead of houseboats tied together.

"How is this possible?" I asked Freddie over the whine of the engines.

"No idea," he replied. "I'm going to take a look behind us, to see if the kapiri are keeping up."

"Be careful," I warned him as he rose from his chair.

"I will," he made his way toward the door leading to the outside deck. He was only gone for a few seconds before he was back.

"There's no sign of them," he said. "It either means they're swimming after us, or they can't keep up."

"Maybe both," I said. "I don't know how this is happening, but I hope it doesn't stop. I think Clare's in trouble," I added.

"I get that idea, too," Freddie's expression was a grim as his words. "I don't think they'd leave us here under attack for any other reason."

"So the boats are our protectors, now?" I shook my head.

"Looks that way."

Ste. Genevieve

 Le

So far, my shields protected those of us remaining in Ste. Genevieve against the Krelk. When six Ra'Ak arrived to lend aid to their armored allies, I started to sweat.

All along, we'd imagined that the big battle would come on the full moon. That's why we'd made these plans, to force the enemy into the open early and to hopefully catch them before their plans were finalized.

How had we been so wrong?

"I want to send you and the others away from here," I told Mayor Jack. "There's no need to sacrifice more lives. Sam's farm is where I sent the others; you can make your way back here in a day or two, when this is over."

"I don't want to leave; this is our city to protect," Jack sounded determined.

"Jack, if those Ra'Ak break through my shields, you'll die in seconds. Every bit of them is poison, and there's no antidote. Only a healer who can neutralize poison and do it quickly can save you."

"You fought one of them," he pointed out.

"There are six here. I can't defeat that many at once." I wished I had Queen Lissa's talents right then, but I didn't. All I had was the power and ability inherent to my race, and a decent ability to wield blades.

And Aunt Zaria's medallion, I reminded myself.

"I'm sorry, Jack, but I have to send you and the others away," I turned to him. Before he could object, I employed power to send him and the few defenders left in Ste. Genevieve to Sam's farm, where the others waited.

If I died here, they'd have to make their own way back. That, in my mind, was far safer than being here at the moment.

Turning to my giant jaguar, I watched as the Krelk continued to fire at my shield, the hits blooming in clouds of green sparks. When the Ra'Ak joined in, hurling their giant serpent forms against my shields, I carefully watched their attack, searching for patterns. When I dropped the shield, I wanted to inflict the most damage possible.

Rajeon

"Don't touch it." A Krelk stalked forward as Sanjay held up the medallion for the other Krelk to take. Je'Dik had finally arrived.

"Of course, Je'Dik." The Krelk bowed to Je'Dik and moved swiftly out of the way. I figure he wanted to ask what the medallion was, but didn't; Je'Dik wasn't in the mood to suffer fools or their questions.

Yes, he was half Krelk. The armor certainly covered exposed flesh. His face, however, consisted of finer scales than those of his full Krelk counterparts. The part that confounded everybody, including the most powerful, were the dark goggles he wore.

When I'd disguised myself as him, I'd worn those goggles, too. He'd never been seen without them, and therein lay the problem. We needed to see his eyes, and that wasn't possible as long as the goggles covered them.

"Take off the medallion and drop it on the ground," Je'Dik ordered Sanjay. Clare stifled a protest, causing Je'Dik to look in her direction. My heart stopped beating for a moment, before it resumed at triple time.

Sanjay began to lift the chain over his head. Time slowed as he appeared to argue with himself over the removal. I understood that the young werewolf's sanity was completely gone the moment the chain dropped from his fingers.

All of us gasped and recoiled as the medallion disappeared immediately; shortly afterward, Sanjay, without a whimper, even, was reduced to winking sparks that dissipated before our eyes.

Je'Dik watched dispassionately as Sanjay died; Ishaan howled mournfully at his brother's passing. Clare's right hand covered her mouth and unshed tears shone in her eyes.

They had no idea what had just happened, although I did. I'd explain later—if there were a later in which to do it. Someone had understood that Sanjay was compromised, and until now, his medallion had kept him from acting on the compulsion or obsession that he'd borne.

Until Je'Dik arrived.

Terrible ideas began to form in my mind concerning Je'Dik, and they horrified me. The other thing that concerned me was this; were all our medallions programmed to disappear if we removed them?

Probably. An innocent could find one and die by picking it up, if it were left lying around.

"Well, well, now we see who is the stronger one, here," Je'Dik snorted a laugh. He'd overcome the power of Sanjay's medallion, proving that my worries held some truth. Je'Dik stepped in front of me, and I felt frozen.

Several Krelk who walked behind him wore Krelk army uniforms. Their government here on Earth was allied with Je'Dik; there was no longer any doubt in my mind. Je'Dik had either joined with the Krelk overlords, or he'd been with them the whole time, no matter how often they argued the opposite.

They are always liars, I reminded myself. No doubt Je'Dik had his finger on the button that could destroy the zone if any real threats came his way. My only hope was that he still valued his life—enough that he'd take time to get away before detonation, giving us a short amount of time to save ourselves.

"Now, then," Je'Dik sounded pleased with himself as he tilted his goggled head to study me, "Which of you belongs to the Alliance?"

CHAPTER 14

*C*lare

Je'Dik was far more dangerous than I thought. Did Rajeon know that, too, or was he only learning it now? Sanjay was dead—had Je'Dik done that? Could he turn people to sparks, killing them instantly, without even a whimper?

Je'Dik toyed with a small device in his right hand and studied Rajeon and the rest of us after asking who belonged to the Alliance.

None of us spoke.

"Come now. I have in my possession confiscated weapons and communicators made by the Reth Alliance. Surely one of you must be looking for them."

If Je'Dik hadn't murdered that hunting party, he'd learned of it shortly afterward, and that's what concerned Rajeon the most. How long had Je'Dik known, and why was the zone still in place—at least for now?

The cage fight of the century ran through my mind, although Je'Dik knew we'd offed the Blackheart gang. Who would oppose the Northern gang, now?

Us. He wanted them to fight us. I swallowed hard.

"Not talking, eh?" Je'Dik held the small device up. "Very well. This device controls the ranos weapons trained on the zone, and they'll fire the moment I activate them. Now, I assume you want the zone to survive," he went on. "With that in mind, I'll leave the zone alive and as it is, if you agree to one small stipulation."

Here it comes, I thought.

"We were planning a vampire cage fight, to occur on the full moon. Now, I know, as do you, that the Blackheart gang, one-half of that cage fight, has been killed. I have many, many people waiting to see a fight. If you volunteer to take on the gang from the other side, I'll grant freedom and control of the zone to the winner."

Je'Dik didn't expect us to survive; I could see that easily in the expressions of the Krelk around him.

"Is that your only stipulation?" Nyarr asked.

"Of course." Je'Dik shrugged.

Liar.

You'll be fed while you're ah, our guests," Je'Dik went on. "We don't want any of our participants fainting from weakness or dehydration. Our customers demand authenticity, without interference of any kind."

In other words, the bookies were demanding it be as fair as possible.

"As for what our shifters become," Je'Dik smiled, "We already have that information, do we not?" Clyde and the others stirred uncomfortably. That let me know that Je'Dik was indeed behind their capture.

What about Nyarr, Loor and Rajeon? Did he understand what they were?

"We're in the process of taking the boats and the vampires aboard," Je'Dik went on as if he were discussing what he had for breakfast. "The vampires will be allowed to fight beside you, if they want."

Or they'd be forced to do so if they wanted the zone to survive.

My rifle now lay where I'd dropped it on the riverbank; I suppose the Krelk understood that it wouldn't work for them and could prove dangerous if they touched it. My fingers itched to hold it again; I'd shoot Je'Dik first. I didn't care what happened to me afterward; he was threatening my mother, Jessie, Caleb and Freddie. My hands clenched into fists just thinking about it.

As for who I'd shoot second if given enough time, I considered Rajeon for a moment. He'd gotten us into this mess, and unless I was imagining things, his plans had gone wrong after the first few minutes. Rajeon wanted Je'Dik to be here. Well, he *was* here, and things were far worse because of it.

I, a river otter, would be fighting vampires in roughly thirty-six hours. I doubted any of our shifters had any sort of chance, especially if our medallions were rendered useless, as they'd been inside the capture sphere.

"We accept your terms," Rajeon hissed at Je'Dik.

Lifting a hand carefully to touch the medallion beneath my shirt, I sent a short, succinct message—*fuck you, Rajeon.*

Doreen

The moment Freddie and I imagined that we'd gotten away from the kapiri, some of them poked their heads above water behind us. My heart, which had begun to slow down, kicked into high gear again.

"Oh, no," Freddie whispered when the water on both sides of our speeding boats lifted as if large whales were passing by.

"What else have they got to destroy us?" I moaned.

"Look," Freddie pointed behind the boats. The water suddenly boiled with scaled creatures, as if giant piranha were attacking.

"Is that how kapiri eat their prey?" Freddie turned wide, terrified eyes in my direction.

"I hope not," I replied, hugging one of his arms with both of mine. *Would they crawl onto the boats, next, and devour us?*

More waves came as if more whales were joining the fight. *What was happening, and why were they fighting one another, instead of attacking us?*

Le

"It's all right, they're gone, now," I reassured the frightened crowd at Sam's farm.

"What happened to them?" Jack asked.

"They ah, learned the error of their ways." I couldn't tell them exactly what happened—not yet, anyway. Only time would tell whether the moment would come for that truth to be revealed.

Besides, they had learned the error of their ways, and in a fashion they'd likely never dreamed of. I felt as if every scrap of energy had been drained from me afterward, and all I wanted to do was find a place to rest.

That couldn't happen as long as Nyarr and the others were captives of Je'Dik. Plus, Doreen and Freddie were under siege until the cavalry showed up. I hoped they'd arrived by now or would do so soon. Kapiri weren't easily fooled or turned aside from their goals.

Perhaps they'd learn the error of their ways, too, but I couldn't guarantee it.

"I need to move you all again," I told Jack.

"Where? I'm not sure there's a safe place anywhere else."

"We'll find one," I told him. "I just have to catch my breath before taking you there."

Rajeon

Another capture sphere was where Je'Dik placed us, and we'd probably stay there until the following night, just before the fight was scheduled to begin. Unless I was very wrong, the fight itself could be held inside the largest capture sphere ever created.

There'd be no escape from it unless someone released us. The scripted plan had taken several crooked paths. I hoped it could right itself before this was over, because only a fool would believe Je'Dik merely had vampires waiting to kill us.

So far, there'd been no word regarding Le, Doreen and Freddie.

They hadn't been brought in to join us; therefore, they'd either escaped or were dead.

Nyarr didn't look happy; he couldn't communicate outside the sphere, leaving him in the dark about Le's status. Clare was tight with fury, her arms crossed as she refused to look in my direction.

Her last message to me left no doubt as to where we now stood. *Fuck you, Rajeon,* still echoed in my brain. I couldn't afford to listen to my shattered heart in this; I had to force myself to grieve later.

For now, the same mantra whispered through me as my eyes grazed over Sam, Boyd, Clyde and Clare; *don't let them die. Don't let them die.*

Clare

"They'll wait until we can't help but change," Sam growled. At least they'd placed the sphere so it encompassed a bit of ground within. If we weren't captives, the grass I was sitting on would be comfortable enough.

No cage was a comfortable one, even with benign captors. These were far from benign. These captors would cheer at our wounding and death, as it was entertainment for the bloodthirsty hell spawn they were.

"Every civilization has a dark past, except for the Larentii," Loor dropped to the grass beside me. "The Krelk are still in their infancy and should be killing themselves rather than other races. Technologically, they should be confined to their homeworld, and they aren't."

"So we're forced to pay for that ironic, universal injustice," I mumbled.

"We're not dead, yet," he pointed out.

"You're not a shapeshifting otter, either," I countered. "You won't be stuck on a leash when this is over—if you're still alive."

"Nyarr and I hope they won't put you in the fight," Loor said.

"You want them to put a collar on me early, and drag me off after my friends are dead?"

"We're not helpless," he reminded me.

"No? These capture spheres seem to indicate otherwise."

"What is it that he said—the one who wrote all those plays? Something about more things in heaven?"

"*There are more things in heaven and Earth, Horatio, than are dreamt of in your philosophy.* It's from Hamlet, where several characters die, including Hamlet. Surprisingly, Horatio is the one who survives."

"That is surprising. I could probably read it, although I hear it's difficult in your language. I suppose I'll search for a translation, sometime."

"What is your native language?" I'd only now thought to ask, because he and the others spoke excellent English.

"Alliance common," he shrugged. "I'm surprised Je'Dik didn't try talking to any of us using that language, just to see if we'd answer."

"I think he knows already who's who," I grumbled, turning my head away. "He had everything else pegged. I can't say how much of that Sanjay may be responsible for, but it could be most of it." I shivered as I recalled that Sanjay was dead.

"Sanjay can't help what happened to him. If they'd done the same to you, you wouldn't be able to stop it, either. I figure he was obsessed rather than having a vampire place compulsion. Obsessions are virtually impossible to be rid of, and they can lie dormant for centuries, until the time is right for them to manifest. The only sure way to kill an obsession is to kill the one who bears it."

"Are you saying that this is why Sanjay is now dead? Because we can't get rid of it?"

"I can't say that for certain. It goes back to your quote, of more things in heaven and Earth. Clare, I've seen the obsessed before. They are no longer themselves—they are an extension of their master; the one who laid the obsession. Would you want to live like that—no longer in control of your mind and body?"

"But Sanjay was normal until today." I felt like crying. Loor was telling me my friend since grade school had been gone before we rescued him, and a stranger had taken his place. He was also telling me there wasn't anything that we could have done about it.

"Some days, I wish I were a bigger, badder shifter," I grumbled.

"Those things we can't change," Loor said. "No matter how much we want to."

"Nobody can change anything; not with the Krelk. You have no idea how many people prayed for help after they showed up and started killing everybody. Nothing happened. Nobody came."

Loor took a deep breath, as if he wanted to say something, but didn't. Yes, I'd thought Rajeon, Nyarr, Loor and Le were our help. It turned out they weren't, and we'd probably die come the full moon the following evening.

"You should talk to Rajeon before the full moon comes," Loor told me before rising from his seat on the grass.

"That won't happen," I snorted. "We're going to die; it's as simple as that. He got us into this mess, and that doesn't deserve conversation from me."

Loor snorted this time, before striding away to sit beside Nyarr. I figured they were busy talking in mindspeech, since they didn't have to touch medallions to do it. I left them to it and stared through the transparent sides of our capture sphere.

In the distance, I could see tents and pavilions going up, no doubt to welcome Je'Dik's important guests and give them a space to have refreshments and place bets. We were going to be the spectacle of a lifetime, and it was our lives on the line.

This is Magnolia Hollow, where we suggested the battle be held, Ishaan sent to me. *I figure they'll set the capture sphere inside the tree line on all sides, and the spectators will line the outside of the sphere, for a front-row seat.*

Lucky us, I replied. *I'm worried about Mom, Freddie and the vamps,* I added. *He said the boats were being taken.*

Le, too, Ishaan pointed out. *She could be dead already, and we'd never know.* Ishaan's words let me know that he thought we were doomed. I looked around at those who'd come with Rajeon today; three werewolves, a bear shifter, a horse shifter, three alligator shifters, a boar shifter, two warlocks, an otter shifter and one pod'l-morph.

Most of us wouldn't survive the first attack of a vampire gang; not without weapons or vampire allies of our own. Something tickled my brain; something about our capabilities, but the thought melted like snow on a warm sidewalk.

Does a capture sphere dampen your ability to think? I sent to Nyarr. My mind wasn't as clear as it should be, and my thoughts had begun to drift away half-formed.

This is a relatively new and rare technology, so there's no way to tell what it can do to us, he replied. *I've never been inside one before.*

The longer I've been inside it, the worse it's ah, getting, I told him.

Clare, stop worrying. We're not helpless, Rajeon decided to join the conversation.

Fuck you, Rajeon, I told him for the second time that day.

Doreen

"What are those things?" I asked Freddie. The boats were still floating along, although the speed at which they traveled had slowed considerably. On all sides of our flotilla now swam what could have been a pod of whales, the creatures were so large.

These weren't whales, however. They looked like dinosaurs that had died out long ago, and they'd fought—and eaten—the kapiri that chased us. It didn't bode well for our future if they'd eat that filth; we probably looked ten times tastier than kapiri.

"I've never seen anything like it in my life," Freddie said. "While I'd like to think they're protecting us, I can't begin to speculate about that."

"Why would they protect us? We have no idea where they're from, what they are or whose side they're on. For all we know, they could be herding us toward capture."

"True. I guess we'll find out eventually. In the meantime, I can't argue or fight if I don't eat something. Come on, let's have a sandwich at least, and we'll watch what's happening while we eat."

"I can't stop thinking that just one of them could swallow a houseboat whole," I mumbled.

"Well, they haven't done that yet, and I'd say that works in our favor. At least for now."

"If they're protection, then I sure hope Clare and Rajeon have the same thing," I sniffed before turning to go back to the kitchen. "I've tried fifteen times to communicate with her and the others, and I haven't heard anything back."

"I'd just like to know where we're going," Freddie's voice faded behind me as I walked away.

Le

"Time to put all the participants in the same trap." The Ra'Ak had taken his human shape so we could speak to one another. This was the deal; I was allowed to take the humans to safety, then return to Ste. Genevieve to surrender myself and be delivered to Je'Dik by the Ra'Ak team.

Magnolia Hollow was our destination, where I'd be reunited with the others. There, we'd wait to fight in Je'Dik's cage fight the following evening, come the full moon.

I wondered how long it would take for Freddie, Doreen and the vamps to be forced to follow. The boats carried six vampires, including Jessie and Caleb. So many things could go wrong, and I was afraid someone would be killed before the cage fight began.

Shoving that worry aside, I nodded to the Ra'Ak, who transported me to Magnolia Hollow. I found the others sitting inside a capture sphere near where we landed. Soon enough, an opening was created and I was shoved inside.

Rajeon

Dinner was barely-cooked fish, provided by Krelk who likely hadn't cooked in years, if ever. There were no female Krelk here; their mate's attitudes toward them were medieval at best, and most were cloistered if not accompanied by their bonded males.

Night was falling, too, and it was only a matter of time before we'd see if our vampire allies had been forced to join us.

Le was already here, having been shoved inside the sphere at mid-afternoon. At least we'd been given water, although it was tepid and heat was building inside the sphere.

Nyarr and Loor didn't dare attempt to change the temperature; we couldn't draw attention to either of them, and spellcasting would certainly draw attention. Le had taken a seat between Nyarr and Loor, although they didn't touch and didn't appear to be communicating.

I knew better; Le was probably discussing her trials in Ste. Genevieve, and how she'd arrived here. It was judicious not to let the Krelk see any fondness or relationship between any of us; it could be used against us, if they chose to make threats or push the coming battle in one direction or another.

I had no doubts that every Krelk here now, and those coming to watch the battle, would be betting heavily on one outcome or another, as well as individual fighters.

We'd become fish in a bowl, as Krelk came to stare at us throughout the day and early evening, some of them recording information on comp-vids or other devices. Like bettors in a horse race, they were examining the participants, hoping to find insightful advantages before spending their credits.

I hoped the regular parade of gawkers would be gone when full darkness fell, although a near-full moon hung low on the horizon, promising better light in only an hour or two.

Clare wouldn't look at me. Wouldn't even glance in my direction. When Krelk came to stare at her, she studied her shoes or the grass she sat on, head bowed, refusing to meet their questioning gazes.

The weight of this entire debacle, in her opinion, rested solely on my shoulders. If it didn't twist my heart so much, I wouldn't be concerned. For now, Sam, Clyde and the others had taken things in stride, and I hoped that continued. Clare was the one who was furious, and that could destroy me.

Rajeon, Nyarr's voice hissed in my head. I jerked my head up to find Doreen, Freddie, Jessie and the other vamps from the boats were being herded in our direction by a company of kapiri.

They didn't like to stay out of the water long on a full moon; I wondered if they'd flee the moment their captives were placed inside the sphere.

Clare was on her feet, now, while fear and joy warred in her expressions. No doubt she was happy to see her mother alive, and fearful for her continued existence.

As expected, the kapiri were dismissed after our vampires and cooks joined us inside the sphere, and they immediately headed toward the safety of their normal habitat—the water.

Clare and Doreen wept as they embraced one another. Freddie joined his brother. The vampires made their way to open spots on the grass. Jessie and Caleb came to sit on either side of me.

"What happened?" I asked Jessie.

"Those monsters were waiting for us to wake," he replied. "They already held Doreen and Freddie hostage, saying they'd die if we didn't cooperate. We cooperated."

"We'll be fighting the Northern gang come tomorrow night, won't we?" Caleb asked.

"Yeah. That's the plan."

"I figure we'll be fightin' more'n vamps, too," Jessie huffed.

"I think the same thing."

"What are we supposed to do come daylight?" Caleb asked.

"This sphere extends below ground several feet. You'll have to dig in, I suppose. We'll help, if you need it."

"Just watch our spots during the day. That's all we ask," Jessie said.

"We'll do it," I promised, "Although I doubt they'll want to reduce the opposition by destroying any one of us. There's too much money riding on the outcome."

"Bastards," Caleb grunted.

"Agreed," I said. "At least you'll be rested when you wake after sundown tomorrow. I'm worried about the others, here."

"I'm worried we won't be able to feed when we rise," Caleb said.

"That is a concern," I agreed, "but Je'Dik did say we'd have food and water. I assume that meant for all of us and not just part of us."

"You think that lying piece of dung will keep his word?"

"No idea."

lare

Mom and I slept close together, if our restlessness and jerking at every night noise could be called sleep.

I should have sent Mom to sleep next to Sam, actually. I think his arms would have been around her and at least one of us may have felt safer. As for Rajeon, had he not led us into this trap, I'd have gone to sleep beside him gladly.

That would never happen again. The sad look on his face every time I glanced at him? That didn't faze me.

Much.

If I faced the truth, I'd admit I felt betrayed, abandoned and heartbroken. I had no idea where Mom and I would end up, but it wouldn't be anyplace good. No doubt the moment we turned, they'd put collars and tags on us and we'd spend the rest of our lives in otter shape, while the memory of our friends dying in the biggest Krelk cage fight ever would plague our memories until we died.

Maybe Rajeon believed he'd survive, but he could be the only one. Especially if the capture sphere negated Le, Nyarr and Loor's power.

The rest of the shapeshifters didn't stand a chance against who knew how many vampires in the Northern gang, and for Jessie, Caleb and our other vamps, it could be only a matter of time before they were overwhelmed by superior numbers.

"Exercise in the morning, rest in the afternoon," Loor said as he set food next to Mom and me. I'd been lost in thought and missed the Krelk delivery of breakfast. Chiding myself for not paying attention, I watched Mom tackle what looked to be tasteless mush before trying it myself.

It's protein, Loor informed me in mindspeech. I nodded and forced myself to eat.

Le, who'd slept near Nyarr, came to join us, carrying her bowl of mush. "If you want, I can work out with you after we eat." I watched as she gracefully lowered herself to the ground, no hands involved.

"I'd like to learn how you just did that," Mom said.

"It takes practice, and my dad wouldn't let me spar with steel blades until I learned that and a lot of other things."

"Tell us about your family," Mom invited. "It'll distract us from this awful food."

"Well, my dad is considered the greatest blademaster Falchan ever produced, although there are several others who can give him a run for his money. Plus, he once took on my great-aunt, and said he'd never try it again." She smiled as she told us that.

"Who's your great-aunt?" I asked.

"Queen Lissa of Le-Ath Veronis."

"She's that good?"

"She's that fast. Dad says if she's really into it, you can't even see the blades coming at you. Generally, she slows down enough to give her opponents a good workout."

"Maybe we should have invited her to this barbeque," Mom sighed.

"She has a planet to run," Le shrugged. "And she has to coordinate her vamp army; they're working with the RAA and CAA to quell takeover attempts on several worlds belonging to the Alliances. They're lucky to have a legion of vampires each to help."

"How many vampires are in a legion?" I asked.

"In this case, there are three thousand each, although it could go as high as six thousand. For now, they're rotating three thousand on and three thousand off, every half-year, so they're not fighting constantly. The off-half of the vamp troops are on call, though, if they're needed."

"Are they drafted or volunteers?"

"They're volunteers, actually, and there were so many who volunteered that they had to form a lottery system. Those who were qualified were all trained in weapons and hand-to-hand, and there's a list, in case they lose troops in a battle; the vamps next in line go in as replacements."

"Is it like that on every world?"

"No. Most worlds have conscriptions; a few have mandatory service of all able-bodied people within a certain age range."

"What is the age range?" Mom was curious.

"Between thirty and ninety-five. Those are prime years. People in the Alliances tend to live longer lives."

"They have to serve sixty-five years?" I whispered.

"No. Only ten years, usually, if it's wartime. Sometimes they can get a deferment, if they're enrolled in university or it would present a hardship on the family at that time. Regardless, they have to serve ten years within that sixty-five-year period, eventually."

"How long has it been wartime?" I asked.

"For more than thirty years." Le frowned, as if that troubled her greatly. "I've only been involved for the last two years; I wasn't old enough until then."

"So you studied blade work with your dad until then?"

"Yes. And I studied strategy with Uncle Dragon and Uncle Crane. I learned how to use my power from Aunt Zaria and Aunt Kiarra."

"What about your mom?" I thought to ask.

"Oh. Mom taught me to heal."

"That was handy," Mom nodded.

"More than handy. I learned plenty from Uncle Karzac, too, because he's a trained physician. I took classes in anatomy and other stuff from him."

"Sounds like you used your time wisely, then, before you joined the military."

"I'm not part of the military. I'm exempt, because of my race.

Nyarr, Loor and their brothers are also exempt, because they're part of a different program. They asked for my help, and here I am."

"What program is that?"

"They call themselves the *Formidables*. They're only a small part of a larger organization."

"What do the *Formidables* do?"

"I can't talk about that, it's forbidden."

"Like special ops or something?"

"It's as close as you can get to an explanation," Le said.

By that time, we'd finished our mush and a Krelk had arrived to collect our bowls and utensils, all of which were carefully examined and counted.

"Now, if you want, I can show you some limbering exercises, and a few self-defense moves, although Clare probably knows most of those already."

"I'd appreciate that," Mom said. "I'm not much without my garden hoe."

Rajeon

Le had the entire batch of shapeshifters in an impromptu class before long. They were all stretching, then learning defensive moves. She even showed Sam and his brothers how to defend from a lower position, since they'd be low to the ground when they turned.

Clare had no words or kind glances for me. Only the occasional, accusatory glare came my way.

Rolling my shoulders, I considered that stretching was probably a good idea for me, too. Not far away, Nyarr and Loor were engaged in a lengthy mental conversation, outlining what their plans were for the cage fight, no doubt.

My plan was already formed in my head, and both warlocks and Le had been apprised. I merely waited to see whether that plan would be foiled in some way, and if the situation we found ourselves in would gain us nothing.

As for the potential loss of life, I refused to consider that. For now, I was grateful that Le found something constructive for the others to do, to take their minds off the coming battle.

I had no respite from my fears, and everything, good or bad, rested on my shoulders. That wasn't comfortable; not even in the minutest sense. Especially since this involved my heart—and Clare's. This—all of it—hung on the thinnest thread; on words uttered that could turn to dust in the smallest of moments.

It's all we have, I reminded myself. *A few words of foresight and a minuscule chance for a miracle.*

Clare

While I closed my eyes during the afternoon and attempted to sleep, I couldn't stop the worries whirling through my mind. All kinds of scenarios played out, and none of them were good.

In the distance, when I opened my eyes and looked to the north, I could see the lookout area, where covered rows of seating had been placed. That was the VIP section, no doubt.

Not only were we getting a live audience, this massive cage fight would be transmitted to anyone who'd paid Je'Dik a sufficient amount of money to watch. Whether Mom and I would be outside the cage or left inside remained to be seen.

Being left inside was an immediate death sentence; outside could mean a fate worse than death; one that would last through the ends of our lives.

"We'll get through this, baby girl," Mom reached out to touch my shoulder. "They're bringing food. It won't be long, now."

Placing my hand over hers, I breathed a sigh. "No matter what happens, I hope we get to be together," I told her softly.

"Me, too."

"Moonrise in two hours," the Krelk who brought our food announced dispassionately through his communicator. "Eat and ready yourselves."

"We who are about to die salute thee." With an angry, mock salute, Clyde's heavy sarcasm filled our sphere as the Krelk stalked away. He was right; this was a battle of gladiators, and the odds were heavily stacked against most of us. *If they'd only let me have my rifle back*—but that wasn't to be.

Those of us from Earth had what we were born with and nothing more.

Rajeon

At least they'd provided bottles of blood substitute for Jessie and our other vamps. Those were handed out the moment they broke through the ground after nightfall.

Jessie brushed soil from his clothing meticulously before drinking. He offered me a nod and a half-grin as he finished with his clothes and pulled the cap from the bottle.

"How long, now?" Caleb walked toward me after draining his bottle.

"They said moonrise. Half an hour ago, we were told two hours. I suppose that means an hour and a half, now."

"Looks about right," Jessie joined us and looked up at the stars through the clear sphere around us. "Our friends should be feeling the change soon."

He was right, of course. The best barometer we had was our shifters. When they made the change, it meant the moon was in full force for shifters in this area.

"It won't be long," Sam confirmed as he walked toward us. "Most of us are starting to feel—itchy."

"Sam, I swear if there's any way to get us out of this alive," I said quietly.

"We won't hold it against you if it turns out otherwise. Our brother sold us out, first, and then Sanjay was compromised. We were doomed from the start; we just didn't realize it. Good luck, brother," he held out his hand. I shook. He then shook with Caleb, Jessie and our other vamps, before going to talk to the shifters while they were still human.

Clare

Sam made his way to Mom and me last of all. We felt the pull of the moon just as he did, and our time was short.

"Clare, it's been an honor," he held out his hand. I took it, then moved forward to give him a hug. He looked a little misty as he let me go and turned toward Mom. "Doreen, I wish we had more time," he told her before leaning in, framing her face with his hands and kissing her.

That's when I was forced to wipe tears from my cheeks. Mom only sobbed once when Sam pulled back. He nodded to her and moved away. By the time he reached his brothers on the other side of the sphere, he'd already removed his shirt for the change.

"Clare," Mom turned toward me and wrapped me in a hug.

"I love you," I whispered against her ear.

"Love you, too, baby girl."

That's when the change hit us, and our clothing pooled around us as we became smaller and covered with fur.

"Miss Clare, Doreen, you stay between Caleb and me," Jessie arrived quickly. "We'll protect you as well as we can."

We squeaked our thanks and moved behind Jessie as our Krelk overlords arrived to take us to the cage fight of the century.

Rajeon

"Normally, I'd remove the otters because they have a separate value, but I won't this time. I think having a noticeable weakness or two will make things interesting to our bettors," Je'Dik's grin was sharp. Since he always wore those confounded goggles, nobody could see whether that grin reached his eyes.

He'd come himself to see what our company looked like before sending us into the fight. A few highly-placed Krelk were with him; they wore the skins of rare animals, decorated with plenty of platinum and gold.

Fuckers.

"The capture tunnels are in place," one of his subordinates arrived to inform Je'Dik of our means of arrival. He wasn't taking chances with any of us; some of us could attempt an escape, in his estimation. He wanted all of us there, whole and healthy for the fight, there was no doubt of that.

How he'd managed to put who knew how many capture spheres together to form a tunnel between us and the large one where the fight would take place no longer concerned me.

Je'Dik was wealthier and more devious than most everyone knew. "Walk single file through here," Je'Dik pointed toward the north side of our sphere. "It is now connected to the battlefield. Anyone refusing to move along in an orderly fashion will be shot by my associates, with a ranos pistol."

Nyarr and Le took first and second position. The alligator brothers came next, followed by the boar brothers, then Monty the bear and Clyde, who'd become a huge draught horse. Jessie came next, with Clare and Doreen following him, and Caleb coming behind Doreen. They intended to keep our otters safe as long as they could.

Then the werewolves came, Ishaan first in line, followed by Chuck and Will. Ishaan snarled at Je'Dik as he passed the bastard. He wanted retribution for Sanjay.

I did, too.

The other vamps came next. Loor and I would be the last two in line. I nodded to Loor, who preceded me, and I took the last spot. I didn't bother to look at Je'Dik as I passed; he and his entourage were no doubt counting the money this would bring them when all was said and done.

"Any last words?" Je'Dik called out to me in Alliance common after I passed into the tunnel.

"Fuck you," I replied in English before stalking after Loor. Je'Dik's laugh followed me into the tunnel.

The moon was high overhead as we walked into the largest capture sphere I could ever imagine. Across the field stood the Northern gang of vampires. This far away, I couldn't make out their features in my current shape.

There were more than thirty of them; I could tell that much.

Thirty-seven, Nyarr sent an exact count.

A few saplings and several taller trees littered the landscape of our battleground, but none were close enough or substantial enough to provide good cover or protection. They could get in the way of a few fights, but that remained to be seen.

Walking forward, I brushed close to one of the taller trees on my way to join the others. When a low hanging branch became a hand to grip my arm, I stopped dead in my tracks.

How many? I gripped my medallion.

All of them, came the reply.

Clare

Rajeon stopped for a moment next to one of the trees scattered throughout the battleground. Its leaves hid him in shadow for a moment from the bright moon hanging overhead.

When he walked forward again, a deep frown marred his face. Was he only now realizing that we faced nearly forty vampires and most of us would die within seconds?

It's too late for blame, Clare, Mom sent to me. I turned toward her; a front paw was pressed against her medallion, which had shrunk to fit her size and to hide in her fur. *But it's not too late for forgiveness,* she added.

I considered that for a moment. If Rajeon died, did I want my last words to him be *fuck you?*

Raising a paw, I touched my medallion. *I loved you, Rajeon. I guess I still do. If I don't see you after—then all is forgiven.*

Baby, keep your head up. Right now, we're still alive, and as long as I live, I won't ever stop loving you.

Yeah. I couldn't go on, I was starting to choke up.

"Stay low," Jessie whispered as an amplifier blared overhead. The first words I didn't know—they had to be in Krelk or something else I didn't understand. Then, the announcement came in English.

"Welcome, all, to the biggest cage fight, ever," Je'Dik's voice boomed around us. "Tonight, we have thirty-seven vampires facing a variety of shapeshifters, vampires and a few exotics. As you know, exotics have the ability to turn battles in their favor, so if you haven't placed your bets, you still have a few moments to do so. Hurry, the flag to begin the fight will rise soon."

See the flag over the VIP seats? Nyarr sent to all of us. We turned our heads. The large, red flag rested atop the cloth overhang. Its pole extended roughly ten feet above that. *When the flag is raised to its highest position,* Nyarr continued, *a gong will sound and the battle will begin.*

Why won't he say what the exotics are? I sent to Le.

Because he doesn't know exactly what we are. He may have a good guess on me, but no solid proof.

Is that good or bad?

Could be either, we'll see soon enough. She was still in human shape; she wasn't tied to a moon-change as I was. *Plus, he's milking them for bets,* Le said. *Some will bet on us, others against us. They'll appreciate the surprises, I suppose.*

Would she become the jaguar? I was afraid to ask. It was a cinch nobody would bet on the otters. We were toast and we knew it.

We have teeth and claws, Mom reminded me. *We go down fighting.*

Understood. I didn't add that I hoped biting vampires was similar to biting fish.

Clare, Doreen, stay close to a tree, Rajeon sent to us.

Which tree?

Any tree. It doesn't matter.

I guess we'll stay close to this tree, Mom turned her head to a cottonwood nearby; cottonwoods grew fast and this one had shot up in the formerly bare field during the Krelk takeover. Mom and I scooted toward the tree; Jessie and Caleb moved with us, already in protective mode. Maybe Rajeon told them to go to the tree with us; I couldn't tell.

Good choice, Rajeon's voice whispered in my mind. *Now, we wait for the flag and the gong.*

I didn't reply, although the whole thing sounded purely medieval to me.

"Sam, Freddie, get your brothers close to trees, Rajeon says it's safer," I heard Jessie whisper as the alligator and boar brothers searched for a good position.

The flag's rising, Ishaan informed us. *Get ready.*

Mom and I looked at one another. In this shape, I had to forcefully bring her human face to mind and commit it to memory. This could be the last time we saw one another, and I had to remember.

The gong sounded and thirty-seven vampires raced toward us, as fast as they could run.

Rajeon

Ishaan didn't wait; he loped toward the lead vampire and they crashed together near the center of the field, both going down in a snarling tangle of teeth and limbs. The crowd of Krelk, lining the outside of the sphere and in the higher seats, roared with delight.

Our other werewolves did the same, attacking the nearest vampires quickly. That left thirty-three still coming after us. Le changed, then, and her larger-than-life jaguar removed two vampire heads with a quick sweep of claws.

That's when the crowd went crazy, and the roar was deafening.

Almost time, a voice whispered in my ear. Our three other vampires joined the fight, selecting their adversaries carefully and engaging. There were now eight separate fights going on in center field, and that's when Nyarr and Loor stepped forward, raising their arms.

A thick mist began to rise from the ground, filling the sphere until the crowd could no longer see.

The vampires attacking us would rely on their sense of smell, except that Nyarr had already taken this into account and infused the mist with the scent of roses.

Time, whispered the voice.

Every tree inside the sphere began to grow swiftly, until they reached gigantic proportions, filling the empty space to capacity with limbs, roots and leaves. Not far away, I heard the shriek of a dying vampire.

As was expected. Now, I waited to see what Je'Dik intended to do next.

CHAPTER 16

*C*lare

Mom and I had been lifted up by the tree itself as it grew, leaving Jessie and Caleb free to protect themselves. Outside, I could hear the dissatisfied roar of the crowd; every tree inside the sphere was now huge and their leaves and limbs, amid dissipating mists, now concealed the fight from spectators.

I figured Je'Dik was furious, and I had no idea what he'd do next. The announcements in Krelk began as Jessie and Caleb dispatched two enemy vamps beneath the cottonwood's branches; I jerked when they screamed and turned to ash in front of my eyes.

I couldn't see anyone else from our side; the trees and leaves were too large and too thick. The air from the mist that had come from Nyarr and Loor still bore the heavy scent of roses, meaning nobody's nose would work sorting out friend from foe. We had to rely on sight, and as it was night and the sphere was still filled with a low, ground-hugging mist, that wasn't the most reliable method, either.

The shriek of vamps continued, however, as the announcements began in English. "This will only be a momentary setback, I assure you," Je'Dik sounded angry and conciliatory at the same time. "I'm sending micro-cameras and other troops in to clear the sphere, so your entertainment will resume."

The enemy is dispatched, Ishaan informed us. *The trees helped.*

Did Nyarr and Loor do this? Why hadn't they done it to begin with, so we could escape before things came to this?

Rajeon said our medallions wouldn't reach outside the sphere. Maybe their power wouldn't either, but it worked inside this sphere. Were they waiting for this? Planning it and keeping it from us?

Probably. The reason came to me, then; we had to act normal, and that would have been a stretch for most of us.

What was the plan, now? Would we get out of this, or would Je'Dik continue to send in troops until we were dead?

Krelk coming in, Rajeon sent. *They'll have laser pistols at first—a ranos weapon could break through the sphere. Everybody, get close to a tree and stand as still as you can. Pass the message to anyone who can't hear me right now.*

Leaves rustled around Mom and me, then, and the tree grew a protective lattice that surrounded our bodies.

I'd seen that once before, when Rajeon—*the trees were pod'l-morphs.* Could they do what Rajeon did? Could they all turn to diamond thorns and kill Krelk?

Everything was as still as death after Rajeon warned us again not to move. Krelk stepped quietly among the trees, rifles at the ready as they searched for us.

Why couldn't they see us? Was it something the warlocks were doing?

A Krelk moved beneath our cottonwood, walking right past Jessie and Caleb, who weren't even breathing, I think.

The tree grew an extra limb; it followed the Krelk. I was afraid to move my head to watch. Moments later, there was a sound that was quickly cut off and a diamond-studded limb withdrew where I could see it.

One down. Who knew how many more to go?

Rajeon

Half his Krelk are dead, I sent. *Je'Dik is sending in the next wave.*

Who or what? Le asked.

Ra'Ak and kapiri, I replied. *Get everybody ready; this could go south in a hurry.*

The leaves of my cottonwood hung near the entrance of the sphere; I'd chosen that space quickly, when the battle began.

It gave me a clear view of Je'Dik and his furious responses to the clouding of his cage fight. If his audience weren't asking for their money back already, they would soon. Desperate, he'd called for the Ra'Ak and kapiri who served him.

Ra'Ak were powerful enough to blow the sphere apart if they became angry. Once that happened, Je'Dik would have no control over them. I'd be forced to move fast if the sphere were destroyed. Even then, the entire operation hung on a split-second chance, and nobody knew whether it would bear fruit.

How many Ra'Ak? Nyarr asked.

Sixteen, I replied, *and twelve kapiri right behind them.*

Damn.

Agreed. Don't do anything stupid.

I was about to tell you the same thing. Why didn't we ask for a High Demon? he lamented.

Too late, now. At least a few of us can fight those things, but the second they learn this isn't going to be a picnic for them, well, you know what could happen.

I do, and when those Ra'Ak start dusting inside this sphere, it could be worse. That could kill some of ours, and you know it.

Yeah. I know it. Here they come; Je'Dik's sealing the entrance.

Clare

Ra'Ak are coming in—sixteen of them, Le warned. *Twelve kapiri are with them. Remember the Ra'Ak dust when they die, so be prepared.*

Is Sam okay? Mom asked.

Sam is fine for now. Stay alert; things could turn nasty with this bunch.

I shuddered; I recalled how far we'd moved away from the battle Le fought with a single Ra'Ak, and that thing had blasted outward with such force it still could have injured us.

We didn't have the luxury of that much room inside the sphere. If a Ra'Ak died, we could all become targets. If they lived, it would be exactly the same. Most of us didn't have Le's capabilities.

Well, he advertised the cage fight of the century, Loor said. *I guess he's going to get it. Doesn't matter that we've already won, by his definition. He's not satisfied and he'll make us pay.*

We knew that going in, Rajeon told him. *Steady, I'm about to take on the first one.*

Rajeon

For a pod'l-morph to kill a Ra'Ak, we had to employ the element of surprise. They could fold space and would do so inside the sphere if they felt threatened. Nyarr had already warned Le not to make an official challenge to any Ra'Ak.

There were reasons for that, and I'm sure we'd understand better when this was over. For now, I had to work silently so as not to forewarn the last Ra'Ak who entered the sphere.

Moments passed as the lead Ra'Ak disappeared among leaves and giant trunks of trees, searching for the rest of us. The kapiri wove between Ra'Ak and avoided the foliage as well as they could.

Whether Nyarr's and Loor's concealment spells would work with the Ra'Ak remained to be seen. They'd hidden everyone from the Krelk well enough, but the Krelk weren't as powerful or crafty as the Ra'Ak.

Je'Dik on the other hand, was only half Krelk. The other half of his DNA ensured he was as cunning as any opponent.

He'd kept the Ra'Ak in reserve, just for this purpose. He likely didn't care that we'd killed his Krelk soldiers—he only cared that he and his audience couldn't see it. Nyarr and Loor had destroyed the micro-cameras, and that prevented him from knowing exactly what he faced.

Pulling in Ra'Ak, however, evened those odds a great deal. From the outside, the sphere no doubt looked like an over-filled terrarium, where the plants had grown past all expectations and blocked the view.

If the Ra'Ak carried cameras with them somehow, then the audience would again have a live feed.

I understood that was true the moment Le attacked one of the monsters who'd found her, and the crowd roared its approval. Time to take my monster down and see what happened afterward.

Clare

The trees drew back to allow Le room to fight the Ra'Ak; I could hear the monster's roar and Le's yowl in reply as they went at each other.

Another thing happened, too; there was shifting in the lower limbs and a widening of the larger of those. I learned why not long afterward; Freddie, Sam and their brothers, and surprisingly, Clyde and the werewolves, too, were walking high paths created by the pod'l-morphs.

Mom and I were released by our branches and urged to travel with the others; I had no idea where they were sending us, but it was away from the ongoing battle between Le and the Ra'Ak.

Far to the side, near the entrance, I heard it; another Ra'Ak had been killed and his dusting hit the sides of the sphere like huge rocks thrown against thick glass. Other Ra'Ak roared in response, and I could hear a rushing sound as they disappeared from one place and reappeared in another.

Still, the sounds of Le's battle reached us, while the trees urged us down the widening path of limbs to escape the danger it presented.

Clare, Rajeon's voice whispered in my mind as a separate limb aligned with the one I walked with the others. *Come with me, darlin'.* Rajeon had become a tree, too. Hesitating for only a moment, I cautiously stepped onto his limb, which grew to hold me like a cradle.

We have them out of the way of danger, a new voice informed us. *Go.*

I barely had time to squeak as Rajeon's limb covered me even more as the roars and explosions of the Ra'Ak and their dusting came. Like twenty cannons going off in succession, each one made me cringe farther into the protective nest that Rajeon created.

The last explosion, however, was massive, and the ground shivered beneath us as we were momentarily deafened by the noise. Immediately after came the stench of fried electronics, or something like it, followed by angry shouts of the Krelk crowd.

They've blown out the capture sphere, Rajeon shouted. *Move!*

Rajeon

Krelk were running—those who hadn't been knocked down by the force of the capture sphere's destruction.

I and my fellow pod'l-morphs were already employing roots turned to diamond and other hard substances to grind those Krelk to dust.

More than anything, though, I searched the running crowd for Je'Dik. If we failed here, he'd escape and set up elsewhere, and we'd be in the same circumstances again.

Find Je'Dik, I heard Nyarr's shout. He was riding a fellow pod'l-morph like a sea captain in a storm, holding onto the mast of a giant limb and searching for our quarry.

Behind him, Le ran, the pod'l-morphs around her creating an opening to allow her giant jaguar to pass, until she aligned herself with Nyarr and paced him in his makeshift crow's nest.

Clare, after we began to move, raised her head over the protective wall I'd built around her, although I doubted she'd be able to see anything between my limbs and thorn-studded diamond leaves as we followed the fleeing crowd.

I was close enough now to shoot limbs and tendrils into that mass of Krelk, flinging them aside in my search for Je'Dik. Nowhere did I see him—he was slightly smaller than the others because of his mixed parentage, and the goggles he wore made him a standout anywhere.

I can't find him, Le reported.

Nor I, Loor responded.

I haven't seen anything of him, I admitted.

Rajeon, Clare shouted in my mind, *he's crawling up your trunk, like he knows who you are.*

Get back, I shouted at the others. I had no idea what Je'Dik thought he was doing, but I didn't want to take chances. Clare was with me, and I sure as hell didn't want him coming after her.

And that's when I felt it—he'd stabbed me, somehow. I barely had time to consider how impossible that was before I froze in place, unable to move. Everything went dark.

Rajeon! Clare's cry was the last thing I heard.

Clare

He's hurt Rajeon, I shouted to anyone who could hear. Pod'l-morphs came to help, but Je'Dik carried a dagger with him; one that he used to stab anyone who came close. Even through diamond thorns, the dagger was effective.

Whatever it was, it looked as if it were designed to kill pod'l-morphs. After striking three who thought to intervene, the others pulled back. A terrible, purple glow began to form around Je'Dik, then, as he continued to climb Rajeon's frozen limbs.

Was he coming for me? How did he know I was here?

He's looking for Rajeon's brain, Nyarr said. I had the idea he was answering someone else's question, but I heard his reply, as did everyone else. *I can't get a spell to stick*, Nyarr added—*Je'Dik's got some kind of shield up that prevents it.*

Why is he looking for Rajeon's brain? I sent to Nyarr.

To kill him. Right now, Rajeon's paralyzed, like they all were in the long sleep. If Je'Dik finds where Rajeon's brain is, he can kill him with the dagger he holds.

Wh-where is his brain? I watched in horror as Je'Dik continued his swift climb up Rajeon's branches.

I'd imagine he'd keep you close to it, Le answered. *It makes it easier for him to ensure your safety—until now.*

Je'Dik's almost here, I breathed, terrified.

Stand your ground, Mom told me. *Teeth and claws, remember?*

I love you, Rajeon, I told him, though he couldn't hear me. *I'll stand my ground and we'll go down together.*

Hunkering down, I waited for Je'Dik to reach us—Rajeon and me. *Teeth and claws* echoed in my brain. Teeth and claws—those were any otter's strengths, and their weapons.

Je'Dik's goggled head poked above my hiding place, and he grinned. "An otter?" his translator sounded. "Well, you'll have to move," he began, raising the dagger he carried.

I didn't wait. Leaping forward, I bit his nose and clawed his face, making him shriek in pain. Finer scales covered his face, very much like those of a fish.

I knew how to deal with fish.

He dropped the dagger and screamed again as I bit so hard his nose detached from his face. Spitting that foul piece of him out, I clawed his face again, until my claws caught in his goggles and wrenched them off. For the barest of moments, and forever, I stared into Je'Dik's angry, pain-filled gaze.

And then the world stopped.

Everything stopped.

Streaks of light began to whirl counter-clockwise around us; terror-filled shouts sounded below and around us. I had no idea what any of it meant, as my eyes were still locked with Je'Dik's.

Until a final darkness came, and I knew no more.

Rajeon

I woke in a place I knew, solely by the scent and the taste of the soil between my roots. As the clouds cleared from my mind, I recalled I'd wakened like this once before.

I was on Avendor, my roots buried in the life-giving soil of SouthStar's groves. Who knew how long I'd been asleep?

"Only a hundred years, this time, but I suspect you didn't get the same dose of the paralytic."

I knew that voice. Opening the mental eyes of my tree form, I looked down upon Zaria, and then I remembered.

Je'Dik.

Clare.

"Je'Dik's dead, thanks to Clare. Change and talk to me, Rajeon."

It took several moments for me to recall how to do so. Eventually, I stood before Zaria, dressed as I'd been on my last assignment. I was afraid to ask about Clare. Afraid I'd hear that she was gone, and out of my reach forever. I shivered in the warm air and studied my boots for a moment.

"I'll take you to the big house," Zaria sighed and shook her head at me. "We have a lot to discuss, and you should probably eat something while we do that."

Her black hair shone in Avendor's sunlight, her bright blue eyes studied me, searching, no doubt, for how I felt—how much my mission had cost me physically and emotionally.

"I still have my medallion," I said, reaching up to touch the spot where it rested beneath my shirt.

"Yes. I hope it helped in some small way. I had to turn off the protective part of it to lure Je'Dik in," she sighed. "I'm sorry about that."

"If Je'Dik's dead, then it was worth a hundred-year sleep." My words were croaked—I hadn't spoken for a century and it was revealed in my voice.

"Come on, let's go." She folded us to the big house, where the owner of SouthStar's gishi groves lived.

A plate of food was set in front of me, along with a cup of coffee and a generous glass of orange juice. I drank that first, then lifted my fork and listened while Zaria told me of the last few minutes of my mission.

Fairlawn Point, Missouri
   Clare

I woke that morning, feeling disoriented in the extreme. It was one of those times when at first, you have no idea where or when you are, until eventually the world rights itself and you remember.

My cell phone alarm went off seconds later, pulling me from my warm bed. Yawning, I considered how nice it would be to have someone make coffee for me every morning—or even some mornings, while I got ready for work.

On the drive to the hotel, I thought about my life and how it had become such a boring routine that it frightened me at times. Mom always said I could quit and work the farm with her, but I wasn't sure that was the life I wanted, either.

Something felt off, too. Like there was a hole growing inside me, and I had nothing with which to fill it.

Or the understanding of what could possibly fill it.

"The kids in three-fourteen dropped all their bath towels in the hot tub and clogged up the returns. I've shut it down to get the towels out, and now we're getting complaints about the hot tub not working," Freda, the night assistant manager, informed me as I walked into my office.

Lifting the phone from its cradle, I told housekeeping to take fresh towels to three-fourteen, then called Kenneth, our maintenance man, to see what the prognosis was for the hot tub.

"I got this," I turned to Freda. "Go home."

"Gladly. Every day, it's the same thing, just different people," she muttered, pulling her purse out of a file drawer and moving toward the door.

"Yeah." Normally, I wouldn't have agreed with her, but somehow, today had dawned differently. I couldn't put a finger on how that was, because it was a typical, spring day in Missouri.

"Oh, somebody left a business card for you, and a note," Freda said. "It's in your middle desk drawer."

"Is it a complaint?" I asked.

"No."

"Then I'll get to it later."

"See you in twelve hours," Freda said and left me alone in my office.

"Hot tub is functioning again," Kenneth informed me over the intercom. "Want me to put up a sign?"

"We already have a sign up that all children have to be supervised in the pool and hot tub area," I said, pinching the bridge of my nose. "What else should we add to that?"

"Just say no to delinquency?" Kenneth suggested.

"Right. The company will certainly approve that," I said dryly. "Thanks for the quick turnaround, Ken. As always."

"Welcome," Kenneth said and ended our communication. Sighing, I opened the middle drawer of my desk and lifted a cream-colored envelope from it. My name was spelled out on the front in a hand I didn't recognize, so Freda or another staff member hadn't written it.

Curious, I lifted the flap—it was nice stationery and something we didn't provide at the hotel. The business card had *Formidable Security* written in a bold font across the glossy, black card. The name *Randl Gage* was written in a smaller font on the lower left, with a phone number listed on the lower right.

Opening the folded note, I read what Mr. Gage had written.

Clare, I'm recruiting in the area for the next two days. This is an exclusive opportunity, and one I think you'll enjoy. If interested, call the number on my card, or meet me for lunch at noon tomorrow at Lena's Diner in Fairlawn Point. This will mean a raise for you if you decide to join my company, and you will also have the opportunity for extensive travel if you'd like.

Randl.

I blinked—travel sounded nice, actually. I wondered if I'd be dealing with towels dumped in hot tubs by unsupervised children, before realizing that I probably wouldn't. A raise? That also sounded nice, but what would I be doing?

Lena's Diner was my favorite breakfast and lunch spot in Fairlawn Point, and I had the day off tomorrow. Lena's was a public place; what could it hurt to meet with someone who had such a nice business card?

Shoving the note and card in my purse, I set about my normal duties during the day, punctuated by the usual *we're out of shampoo* or *we need directions to a good restaurant*. All the while, too, I felt the gnawing emptiness inside that no food could fill. When Freda showed up for the night shift, I was more than ready to go home.

"See you day after tomorrow," Freda called out as I grabbed my purse and almost ran for the door.

"Yeah," I told her and headed for my car.

"Can you come over this morning and help plant tomatoes?" Mom asked when I answered the phone early the following morning.

"I can, but I need to leave by eleven to clean up; I have a lunch meeting."

"You have a lunch meeting?"

"Yeah. Somebody is headhunting in the area, so I'm gonna listen to the spiel and see if it's anything I want."

"You mean they're hiring managers and employees away from other businesses?"

"That's right."

"I thought you liked managing the hotel."

"Until towels got thrown in the hot tub yesterday."

"Well, that might do it," Mom surmised. "I always thought you were wasting your talents there, but what do I know? What is this company that's headhunting?"

"It's a security company, or so the card says. I'm getting a free lunch out of it, so I can listen and eat."

"Sounds good. Maybe I'll come into town with you and get some shopping done. I can grab a burger somewhere and meet you at the hardware store. I need a few things."

"All right. I'll drive us in."

SouthStar Groves, Avendor

Rajeon

"How many?" I stared blankly at Zaria. She'd just given me information that almost stopped my heart.

"Je'Dik has eleven brothers, and now that he's dead, you know they'll come out of the woodwork like cockroaches."

"They're all like him? Half Krelk and half devil?"

"Looks that way. All created at the same time, and all given similar orders by their sire."

"You have names?"

"Not yet. I'm sure we'll get them when they poke their ugly heads up from the slime where they're hiding. Je'Dik only knew of them; he didn't know them personally. It's safer for them this way."

"Because you couldn't see that in them, if you did get to look past their goggles, huh?"

"That's likely. And it also tells me exactly who perpetrated this monstrosity on us."

"Yeah." I pinched the bridge of my nose at the news. I understood clearly who that was—the same one who'd put me and the rest of my species to sleep for eons, to serve a selfish purpose that he'd created.

"We recovered Je'Dik's dagger, but there are probably eleven more just like it, with his brothers."

"Evil bastards," I grunted.

"Exactly. Now, I'd like you to rest for a few weeks, and then report to Sirena for duty—unless you're not up to it."

"Hell, I'll go tomorrow," I growled. "It'll take my mind off—other things."

"Then rest there. I won't allow you to go out again until I'm sure you're ready. By the way, your performance on this last mission was exemplary. I think we may be able to reward you with a few extra talents, because of that."

"What kind of talents?"

"Mindspeech. Folding space. That sort of thing. You'll receive them when you're ready for the next mission."

"I really need something to keep me busy during the down time," I pleaded.

"All right, you can help train a few recruits."

"Better than nothing," I agreed.

"Good. I'll take you to Sirena tomorrow morning. Be ready after breakfast."

"Yes, ma'am."

Zaria folded away, leaving me to contemplate my future. She hadn't said anything about Clare after mentioning her name once. That spoke volumes. Clare had perished bringing about Je'Dik's demise, and Earth had traveled back to its intended timeline, without a Krelk invasion.

Once Zaria could see through Clare's eyes just how Je'Dik had interfered and when, she could change it and send Earth spinning in the right direction.

For some.

Not for all.

"I put clothing and such in your guest suite, along with a bag to carry it." Bill, who often cooked for the big house, wandered into the kitchen where I sat, mourning something that had clearly been out of my reach the whole time.

"Take what you want with you," Bill said. "Want more coffee or juice?"

"I'll take juice," I said. "I've only had water for the last hundred years."

"I hear that," Bill agreed and went to pour another glass of juice.

Clare

Mom and I stopped setting out tomato plants around eleven; I took a quick shower at her house and changed into an outfit I'd brought that was suitable for an interview. She dressed in jeans and grabbed her reusable grocery bags to toss in my back seat.

Town wasn't far away; we arrived in less than fifteen minutes. I found a parking place close to Lena's. Mom headed for Shelley's burger place; I walked toward Lena's. Pulling the door open, I took a deep breath and stepped inside.

"Hey, Clare," Sunni, a waitress who'd worked at Lena's for nearly a quarter-century, greeted me. "Your party is at the last table by the window." She pointed to the left.

"Thanks, Sunni."

"Oh, no problem." She leaned in to whisper, "He's blind."

A quick, indrawn breath was my only reaction as I stared at her. Nodding, I turned left to meet Randl Gage, who appeared to be staring out the window.

"Mr. Gage?" I asked as I reached the table. I wasn't sure what the protocol was, but I could see his eyes were as pale as the fur on an arctic fox.

"Clare, so pleased to meet you," he smiled and stood, extending his hand.

How had he known where to put his hand? ran through my mind as I reached out to shake.

"I don't always need normal sight," he chuckled, as if he'd read my mind. "Sit down. We'll order lunch, then discuss business."

Doreen

A new sign hung in the hardware store window as I reached out to open the door. Aaron, the store owner, was supporting Dan Felton over John Gibson for Sheriff of Fairlawn Point. For once, Aaron was choosing the better candidate over an old friendship, and I agreed with him.

"Doreen, what can we help you with today?" Aaron looked up from filling slots of a display with seed packets.

"I need to get a new trowel; the handle cracked on my old one and it's pinching my hand," I told him. "If you have organic fertilizer, I need some of that, too. Clare will be here after a bit, and we can load it into her trunk."

"How many bags, Ms. Coquina?" Sanjay walked from the back of the store to ask.

"Eight," I told him. I knew he was werewolf, just as he knew I was a shapeshifting otter. There were a few others in town, plus a vampire or two, but we only saw the vamps at night.

Aaron didn't have a clue that we were anything except human, and we intended it to stay that way.

"I'll take them to the dock; tell Clare to back up and I'll load," Sanjay said.

"She's having lunch with somebody who wants to hire her," I said. "She'll call when she's done."

I heard the bell tinkle over the door and turned to see if I knew them. Most people in Fairlawn Point knew one another.

"Sam, I haven't seen you in a while," Aaron greeted the man I didn't recognize.

"Came up to see if you had anybody in the area who knows how to grow organic," Sam said. "I heard there are a few farms in the area, and I figured you'd know them. We want to go organic, and we're willing to pay somebody to get us on board."

"Doreen, here, knows just about all there is to know," Aaron pointed toward me. Sam grinned and walked toward me, holding out his hand. "Sam Haliday," he introduced himself.

"Doreen Coquina," I said and shook his hand. I got his scent—he was a shifter, too. He drew in a breath; he was discovering the same thing about me.

"Doreen, can I buy you a cup of coffee?" he asked. "I'd like to talk about how to get this thing started. We have folks asking for organic produce, and we've never done that before."

"I'd be happy to help," I shrugged. "Aaron, can you hold my stuff until Clare gets here? I'll take Sam down to Lena's."

lare

"You'll be coordinating schedules and filling slots with the necessary employees. At times, you'll travel with them, unless that makes you uncomfortable," Randl told me. We'd only made small talk while eating. Then, when we'd finished our meal, we got down to business, just as he'd said.

"I can create schedules easily; it's something I do now at the hotel," I said. "I wouldn't mind travel, actually."

"I heard the same thing from your staff; that you don't stop or rest until every shift is covered, and you'll pitch in to help, no matter what the job, if there's nobody else. I know you're down an assistant manager, and you've been covering half that shift yourself, to make sure the hotel runs smoothly. That's the kind of person I'm looking for."

"You talked to my staff?" I squeaked. He grinned. "One of my employees stayed at your hotel last week. She gathered information, after seeing that the hotel ran like a well-oiled machine."

"Well, this certainly sounds interesting," I said. "If you can promise that we won't be digging towels out of the return on the hot tub, I think I'd be even more interested."

He laughed, and that's what I'd hoped for. "It starts out at one-fifty per year, with bonuses and such. At times, the work we do can be dangerous, but you've told me already you were in the military. I hope that doesn't frighten you away from the job."

"How dangerous?"

"That depends on how much danger you want to expose yourself to. We run security on ships, Clare. You can stay in one place and coordinate who to send where, or you can travel on one of the ships with our crew. Occasionally we run into pirates, but we have ways of dealing with them."

"Wow. Really? And one-fifty? As in," I blinked at him.

"One hundred-fifty-thousand, to start. If you join a crew aboard ship, that's even more. You'll go through a training period first, of course, but one-fifty is your base pay."

"I won't lie, I looked you up online last night after I got home," I told him. "Everything looks good and your company has a stellar rating. How soon would the job start?" He appeared to be amused at my choice of words for a moment.

"The standard two weeks, once you give notice," he smiled. "The training will be elsewhere, of course, and we'll provide transportation and uniforms."

"How often will I be home?" I asked.

"You'll have three weeks' vacation every year, unless there's an emergency of some sort. We'll provide transportation to and from, as part of your benefits."

"I have no idea why you're not swamped by resumes," I said.

"Clare, working for my company is by invitation only. Unsolicited resumes are returned unopened. I know you're thinking that this is too good to be true," he went on. "I assure you the hours can be long and the work often difficult. It can be extremely rewarding, however."

"Can I give you an answer tomorrow?"

"Of course. I'll be leaving after tomorrow, though. Think it over carefully, Clare. I would love to add you to my roster."

He rose from his seat and shook my hand again. "I'll take care of the check on the way out." Unerringly, he lifted the paper check off the table as if he could see it clearly, then walked toward the register.

I watched as he even moved aside to allow someone to pass him between tables. My mind went briefly to a superhero who was blind and still managed to fight off aggressors. I wondered if Randl Gage was something like that.

That's when Mom walked into Lena's.

With a man.

"I'm taking the job," I told Mom as Sanjay loaded organic fertilizer into the trunk of my car. "I'll call tomorrow morning, then turn in my notice afterward."

"You get three weeks' vacation?" Mom asked for the third time. "That's better than anything you've ever had before."

"Looks that way. Are you really going to Sam's farm, to show him how to grow organic vegetables?"

"Aaron says Sam is an old friend, who buys from his store down south. They just don't have anybody down there with the right skill set to teach organic farming."

"He's a gator shifter," Sanjay mumbled, hefting the last bag of fertilizer into the trunk and shutting it. "I've scented them before."

"An alligator?" I turned to Mom. "Cool."

"Formidable Security, Le speaking," the voice informed me.

"Uh, hi," I said, feeling suddenly awkward. "My name is Clare Coquina. I told Mr. Gage I'd call today and let him know about the job. If it's still available, I'd like to take it."

"It's yours," Le's voice sounded warm—and happy. "We'll come pick you up at Lena's, if that's all right, in two weeks. Pack a bag with two weeks' clothing. You'll have access to a laundry during training."

"All right," I said. "Can you tell me who'll pick me up?"

"I'll come for you," she said. "It won't be a problem."

"Then I'll be waiting," I told her. "Thank you."

"It'll be a pleasure working with you, Clare."

Mom and Sam came to see me off; I hadn't seen Mom smile so much in a long time, and I'd never seen her smile at a man like that. *Ever.*

At least I wouldn't worry about her so much, if Sam were around. We'd had dinner with him three times since he and Mom started working together, and already he was protective of her, but not overly so.

"Who's coming to get you?" Mom asked as we sat at a table in Lena's, having coffee.

"She said her name was Le, with only one e. She called me last night to confirm."

"I hope you like this new job, and if you don't, anybody will hire you when you come back," Mom said.

"Corporate said they'd have a place for me if I changed my mind," I nodded, toying with the small container of sugar and sweeteners on the table.

"They're not stupid," Mom said. "They should have offered a raise."

"They did. It wasn't near what I'll be earning at Formidable."

"Clare?" A woman with Asian ancestry walked up to our table. Her long, dark hair hung in a braid down her back, and she moved like a dancer, or an elite athlete. "I'm Le," she smiled and held out her hand.

"Clare," I stood and shook with her. "Le, this is my mother and her friend, Sam."

"Doreen," Le shook with Mom. "Sam," she turned to him. "It's a pleasure to see you."

"Would you like coffee?" Mom asked.

"Oh, no, thank you. We're on a tight schedule, today, I'm afraid."

"Mom?" I turned to her. The reality of my leaving was now setting in.

"Give me a hug and stay in touch, baby girl," Mom pulled me into a firm embrace.

"Good luck, Clare," Sam said when Mom let me go. "Let us know if you need anything."

"I will," I brushed moisture away from my cheeks. "I'm ready," I told Le. "My case is up by the register. Sunni's watching it for me."

"Then we'll go," Le smiled at Mom and Sam. "You'll have regular communication, I promise. Just in case, here's my card with my personal number," Le handed a business card to Mom.

"Thank you." Mom's smile was a bit watery.

"Let's go," Le said. I followed her to the register, retrieved my case and we went out the door.

"Just down this way," Le pointed to the right. I assumed her car was parked there somewhere.

We'd gone perhaps fifty feet before we were flung into the universe, and I barely recalled any of our journey, it was so short.

Rajeon

"How many trainees?" I asked.

"Five, for now," Travis said. I sat in his office, drinking a cup of Falchani black tea with him. Some didn't like the taste. Others didn't like that it kept them awake too long. I enjoyed the taste of it. Had I not been in my current funk, I'd have asked for a second cup.

"They're here," Cle-Anne folded into Travis' office.

Travis, who'd been leaning back in his chair, his feet atop his desk, dropped his boots on the floor with a thump. "Hey, Dusty," he greeted Le.

"Dusty?" I frowned at Travis before turning to Le.

"He and Trent called me Cleanie when I was little, because my name looked like *clean* when it was written in English. That is, until Dad threatened to beat it out of them. They started calling me Dusty after that, as an inside joke. Dad was about to threaten them again when I said I liked it. They're the only ones who use it, though," she made a face at Travis.

"I can't help it if everybody else is afraid of Caylon," Travis huffed.

"Like you're not?" This was shaping up to be a family fight, sure enough.

"Don't we have trainees?" I interrupted. "We need to do orientation and give them their schedules."

"Oh, right," Travis waved a hand. "This isn't over, *Dusty*," he grinned maliciously at Le.

"Not by a long shot, dragon-boy."

Clare

I recognized two fellow trainees immediately. "Ishaan? Jessie?" I whispered as I entered the meeting room. Ishaan and Jessie sat next to each other at a wide table, waiting for our instructor to arrive.

"Clare?" Ishaan and Jessie rose from their seats, astonished that I'd been hired, just as they'd been.

"I had no idea they'd hired others from Fairlawn Point," I said, walking toward them on legs that felt numb. I hugged both of them before taking a seat next to Jessie.

"That one is a friend, Caleb," Jessie pointed to the dark-skinned man sitting opposite him, "And that's Clyde," he introduced the other man. "They're from West Helena, Arkansas."

"That's where Sam's from," I said.

"I worked for Sam, until Randl came looking to hire me," Clyde admitted. "Didn't want to leave, but Randl thought it was important."

"Same here," Caleb agreed. "When I heard Jessie was taking the job, well, I was on board, too."

"Ishaan?" I turned to him.

"I, ah, had a special invite," he hedged. "From a friend."

"Welcome, everyone," Randl appeared from nothing at the head of the table. I jumped in alarm at his sudden presence. The only one who didn't immediately react was Ishaan, and I wondered why that was.

"Your instructor will be here shortly, to give you information about your training schedule, and what we actually do," Randl said. "Now, the biggest announcement I have to make is this; you five have been brought back in time, by nearly half a century. Your work will take place in the future. I know that it doesn't make much sense to you now, but you'll hear all about it from your instructors. If any of you have a change of heart after hearing those things, you only have to say the word and you'll be transported to the Earth of your natural timeline immediately. Any questions?" Randl looked around the room.

"We're not on Earth now?" I asked.

"We're on a world known as Sirena," Randl replied. "But I'll let your Chief Instructor give you the particulars. Here he is, now. Everyone, this is Rajeon Dare."

Someone walked into the meeting room. He was followed by Le and another man, but his head swiveled so quickly in my direction it was frightening.

"Clare?" He spoke my name in the barest of whispers, and memories slammed into me like a train going full speed, nearly sending me to my knees. It took forever and no time at all before I was in his arms and he was kissing me like there was no tomorrow.

As there wouldn't have been, had I refused the job.

I wept as he kissed me, too, but they were tears of joy.

How had I forgotten him? How?

"Darlin', I thought you were dead," Rajeon held me away from him for a moment, to take in my face—and my tears. Emotion filled his words; he could barely contain his joy.

"Rajeon, I didn't remember you. At all," fresh tears fell.

"Baby, that's how things happen on a successful mission," he said, pulling me against him again. It didn't take a genius to determine that we were now the only ones in the room.

"The planet settles into the groove it's supposed to be in, without the Krelk invasion, or whatever else it is that threw things off. You did it, Clare. You made that happen, did you know that?" He was now kissing my hair and rocking me gently in his arms.

"But," I said against his shoulder.

You allowed me to see Je'Dik's eyes, another voice informed me—a female voice that wasn't Le's. *I was powerless to do anything about your situation,* she went on, *until I learned how and when he'd interfered, sending Earth on a collision course with the Krelk. You chose to fight and ended up saving Earth.*

Who are you? I didn't think she'd hear me without my medallion, but she did.

Zaria, she breathed her name in my mind. *Welcome to the Formidables, Clare. I've placed your medallion on the table. Wear it always. You deserve it.*

"Welcome to the Formidables, darlin'," Rajeon held me away again and echoed Zaria's words. "Your medallion is there on the table." He let me go so I could pick it up.

Before, it had a smooth surface on both sides. Now, it bore engraving.

It was in English.

Trust your heart if the seas catch fire, was written on one side.

Live by love though the stars walk backward, was inscribed on the other. It was a quote by e.e. cummings, and it fit beautifully.

"The stars did walk backward," Rajeon whispered as I hung the medallion around my neck. "For both of us."

The End